A Moment to Dance

Jennifer Faye

This is a work of fiction. All characters and events portrayed in this book are fictional and a product of the author's imagination. Any similarities to real people, living or dead, is purely coincidental and unintentional.

Published by Lazy Dazy Press

Thanks & much appreciation to:

Content Editor: Tessa Shapcott

Copy Editor: Joyce Lamb

Whistlestop Romance series:

Book 1: A Moment to Love

Book 2: A Moment to Dance

Book 3: A Moment on the Lips

Book 4: A Moment to Cherish

Book 5: A Moment at Christmas

Contents

About This Book

A teacher, a cowboy firefighter, his young nephew and a sweet puppy...

Teacher Ella Morgan is moving to Whistle Stop for a chance to start over. She's inherited a mountain cabin—in dire need of renovation—as well as a sizable tax bill. Her teaching job isn't going to cover the accumulated debt. She needs cash, and soon.

Firefighter Tony Granger has returned to his hometown in order to take over the family ranch and be the guardian of his orphaned nephew. But being a single parent isn't coming easy, and he's worried he won't succeed with his plan to adopt the boy, especially if Johnny's grades don't improve. He needs a break, and fast.

When Ella finds out Tony doesn't have a partner for the Dancing with the Firefighters' benefit contest—which is offering a large cash prize—and he asks her to tutor Johnny, it looks like their problems might be solved. But when a rescued puppy leads them into danger, they find their greatest strengths.

Chapter One

A new town.

A clean slate.

And a chance to begin again.

Ella Morgan stepped out of her car onto the quiet street of Whistle Stop, New Mexico. The April sunshine rained down on her as she lifted her smiling face to bask in its warmth. After the whirlwind of settling into the cabin she'd recently inherited and learning the ropes to her new teaching position at the local school, she was plain worn out. All she wanted to do was grab a few items for dinner at Marty's Market and head home.

She stepped onto the curb to put money in the parking meter when a young boy in a white T-shirt and denim shorts darted in front of her, causing her to teeter to a halt. Ella shook her head in disbelief before dropping a quarter in the meter.

A gentle breeze tickled across her skin, carrying with it the aroma of grilled burgers. She sucked in a deep breath, and her stomach rumbled. She glanced up the street at the white block building with the red and white awning—Benny's Burger Joint. She sighed, remembering how her grandparents had treated her to one of Benny's huge green-chile cheeseburgers smothered in melted Monterey Jack cheese while on summer vacation. That was back in the good days—back before it all went so wrong.

She swallowed her craving and started toward the little market, anxious to put some distance between herself and the diner. No sense daydreaming about a dinner she couldn't afford. At this point, she had to keep track of every penny—

A swift movement caught her attention. The same young boy dodged between two parked cars. He stepped into the street and came to a stop. What in the world was he doing? Juggling something in his hands? A small animal?

The hum of an approaching vehicle had her peering down the road. A red pickup at the other end of the block barreled toward them, going far too fast.

Her heart clenched.

"Hey! Move!" she screamed, waving her arms in the air.

The child didn't budge.

Had he heard her? Did he have any idea of the danger he was in?

An angry horn blast sent adrenaline surging through her body. With her long skirt hiked up, she raced the short distance to the boy.

The squeal of tires sounded as she lunged forward. Her fingers clenched in the boy's shirt. With every ounce of strength, she yanked. The force threw them both back between the two parked cars.

The jolt of the child's body bumping into her and the unevenness of the pavement caused her to stumble. Her free hand flailed through the air. With a thud, her backside landed hard on the asphalt. Her back teeth rattled together. The boy, with his heavy backpack, landed on her legs. In a fraction of a second, the tractor-trailer rumbled past. A gust of warm air rushed over her as pain ricocheted from her hip down her leg. Thank God, they were safe.

The child yanked forward, struggling to free himself from her hold. He didn't appear to be more than nine years old. And lucky for her, he was skinny.

"Let. Me. Go. You're ruining my shirt."

Not realizing she still had her fingers clenched on the back of his shirt, she loosened her grip while still keeping an eye on him. This child was too young to be left to his own defenses, as was evidenced by the near-miss with the truck.

"Where are...your...parents?" She struggled to get the words out between ragged breaths.

The boy pulled away from her. "I don't have any."

"What's your name?"

He backed away from her toward the sidewalk while still cupping something in his hands. "I'm not telling you. You're a stranger."

Not only had she risked her own neck and most likely ruined her favorite skirt to save him, but now he refused to be cooperative. She frowned at him. If he wouldn't give her a straight answer, surely one of the town's residents would stroll by and let her know where he belonged.

In answer to her thoughts, she heard a vehicle slow to a stop. A door opened, followed by rushed footsteps. Good. Someone was here to help sort things out.

"What's going on?" a deep male voice bellowed.

If the man's thunderous tone was meant to gain attention, it did the job. The boy rushed over to the man, obviously familiar with him. Ella straightened and dusted herself off. She frowned when she detected a long rip in her skirt. She might be able to mend it, but it'd never be the same.

With a resigned sigh, she turned her attention to the man. She had to crane her neck to see the man's face. My, he was tall, probably six-four, if not more. Her line of vision drifted down to his navy T-shirt, which was pulled snug over his broad chest. Her gaze lingered, taking in the white insignia of the Whistle Stop Volunteer Firefighters in the upper left corner with Station House 87 printed below it. She wondered if he was in fact a fireman. By the looks of his hefty biceps, he certainly was strong enough.

"I'm waiting for an answer," the man's voice boomed.

When she found him staring at her instead of the child, she was startled. Her gaze moved to the boy. The kid shot her a smug now-you're-in-trouble look.

The scowling man shoved his deep brown Stetson higher, revealing a hint of dark hair. His tanned face was obscured by a bit of scruff, but it was his eyes that did it for her. Their chocolate shade with gold flecks drew her in with their intensity. He wasn't bad-looking—a shame he was so abrasive.

"She grabbed me." The boy pointed an accusing finger at her.

The man crossed his arms and glared at her. "You better tell me why you had your hands on him before I call the sheriff."

The once-deserted sidewalk now had a few people passing by. Ella glanced over her shoulder to find pedestrians pausing to stare in their direction. She wrung her hands together and turned away. Heat flared in her chest and rose to her cheeks.

Just what she needed—a scene sure to be followed by gossip. She'd hoped to leave that all behind in Albuquerque. For the first time, she wanted to fit in, feel accepted. And if the cowboy kept shouting, he'd ruin her fresh start in Whistle Stop.

She lowered her voice to a hushed tone. "Must you raise your voice? People are going to think I've done something wrong."

His unwavering gaze held a clear sign of wariness. "Haven't you?"

She glowered back at the infuriating man. "No. I haven't. You're making a scene for nothing."

He glanced around, noticing the people gawking. A forced smile pulled at his lips. "It's okay," he said to the people. "Just a little misunderstanding."

Once the people moved on, he turned back to her and crossed his muscled arms. "You still have some explaining to do."

Irritation swirled in her chest. How dare this man stare at her as if she'd committed a crime? She'd just saved the boy's life. And worse, she could still feel people staring at the back of her head. So much for her desire to keep a low profile.

She bit back her indignation and strained to keep her tone neutral. "The boy ran into the street and was about to get hit by a truck when I yanked him out of the way."

"I was okay. I'm not a little kid anymore." The child pulled his shoulders back as his chin jutted out. "She's the one who made me fall."

The man's eyes opened wide before he gave the boy a quick once-over. "Johnny, are you okay?" The child nodded. "Good. Now explain what you're doing here. You're supposed to be waiting for me at the community center."

"I waited, but you forgot me. Again."

The muscles in the man's neck flexed. He cleared his throat. "Some things came up at the ranch. I had to deal with them before I could leave."

"Uh-uh. You forgot me."

"I did not." The man's voice rose again. He waved a finger at the little boy. "You should have waited. I'm only five minutes late."

"Nuh-uh. More than that."

The man glanced at his watch. "Er...ten minutes late."

This was getting them nowhere. Ella stepped between the aggravated adult and the wide-eyed child, hoping to defuse the situation. "Perhaps the boy was confused about what to do."

Johnny glanced at her, his eyes alight with surprise that she'd come to his defense. Still, she agreed with the man. The child was far too young to be running around town—even this small town—by himself. She sensed a deep-rooted problem between father and son, but since this wasn't a school issue and Johnny wasn't her student, she must tread lightly.

The man shot her a cold, hard glare that caused the breath to catch in her throat.

"Thank you for saving him, but I'll handle things from here." The man turned to the boy. "None of this excuses you from running off. And what's that you're holding?"

"A puppy." The little boy held out his cupped hands. "Something's wrong with him."

What in the world? An ugly yellowish slime and black grease covered the poor creature cradled in the boy's palms. Worse yet, the wee thing wasn't moving.

The man knelt down to inspect the ball of filthy fur. Ella stepped closer, her heart thumping hard. She pressed a hand to her chest. Had the animal died?

Please say it isn't so.

"It hasn't moved since she knocked me over." The child glared at her before turning to the man.

Had she done something to injure the puppy? Her body tensed as she replayed the events in her mind. If she had, it'd been inadvertent. And the memory of that red semi with its shiny chrome bearing down on the boy confirmed that she'd done what was necessary.

The giant of a man moved with slow, steady movements as he took hold of the animal. His long, lean fingers slid across the soiled fur, pausing over the tiny rib cage. "He's still breathing, but he doesn't look good."

The concern reflected in the man's eyes touched something deep down in Ella, making her re-evaluate her opinion of him. No man who cared for a helpless animal could be all bad. Perhaps there was more to this man than his loud, gruff exterior.

"May I see the puppy?" She hoped the man had missed something.

He held out his hands. The small puppy looked to be some sort of miniature schnauzer-poodle mix. She visually examined the animal's matted fur, noticing the outline of his ribs. She was hesitant to touch him for fear of making things worse. "What in the world happened to him?"

Johnny shrugged.

She'd always had a soft spot in her heart for animals, though she'd never been allowed to own one as a child. Some day she planned to adopt a puppy, once her life was settled.

Johnny stood next to her, tears tracking down his pale cheeks. Her heart ached for the little boy. She blinked back the moisture gathering in her own eyes. How could someone be so depraved as to try to drown a helpless puppy in...what was that? Motor oil? The thought sickened her.

Johnny's backpack slipped from his shoulder, landing on the ground with a thud. He scrubbed his eyes with his grungy hands. Ella blinked repeatedly, trying to keep her own emotions in check. She couldn't make this moment any worse for the child. Her gaze collided with the worried look in the man's eyes.

She had to do something, anything but stand there. She reached into her purse and withdrew some tissues. Ignoring the foul stench, she wiped the slime from the dog's tiny muzzle, then his eyes, followed by the rest of his face. The dog didn't resist, as though understanding her intent was to help him. Or maybe he was too far gone to care.

"This little guy needs a vet," she said, realizing she was stating the obvious. It was just that she didn't want the man to give up on the puppy.

"There's none in town, but tomorrow there's one stopping by my ranch to check on a couple of horses. I could ask him to have a look...if he lives that long."

In response, the puppy moved his head and eked out a whimper. Ella glanced up to find a smile tugging at the corners of the man's mouth. Her heart leaped with joy. This little puppy was a fighter. There was no other way to explain him living through such misery in his short life.

"He's gonna live." Johnny smiled through his tears.

Ella noticed how the child's happiness reflected on the man, easing the stress lines on his face. The man was actually pretty good-looking when he wasn't scowling at her. She couldn't resist smiling herself. It just seemed like the right thing to do at the moment.

"Don't get too excited," the man warned. "We don't know what might be wrong with him."

"Where exactly did you find him?" she asked the boy.

He pointed to Pete's Gas and Lube.

There wasn't a person in sight. The bay doors were shut, with a closed sign on the office door. None of this made any sense. Who would do such a despicable act?

"Pete's out of town," the man supplied. "On a fishing trip, I think."

She frowned. "I wonder how the puppy ended up in this condition."

"I was walking home and heard something." Johnny stroked the puppy, oblivious to the animal's desperate need for a bath. "I found the puppy in some icky oil."

Her heart sank, thinking of someone trying to drown a puppy. How could anyone be so evil?

Uncomfortable with this line of thought, she rubbed her hands together. Her fingertips slipped beneath her long sleeves and massaged the uneven scar tissue. When she realized her actions, she yanked the cuffs down over her wrists as far as they would go.

"Thank you for saving Johnny." The man's gaze met hers, making her heart stutter.

"You're welcome." She forced the words out between dry lips.

"As for you, little man, you aren't off the hook. We need to talk more about how you were supposed to wait for me."

"Your dad is right," she added. "It's dangerous wandering around town by yourself."

The man's brows scrunched into a dark line, but before he could say anything, Johnny spoke up. "He's not my dad. He's my uncle. My parents died."

So Johnny wasn't lying earlier. Sympathy welled up in her for this little boy who'd lost his parents and for the uncle who was obviously struggling to fill the role of guardian.

"Thanks again," the man said. "I should get these two home."

After a brief wave good-bye, she turned to gather her stuff from the ground. As she did, her gaze landed on Johnny's backpack. She hesitated, not eager to once again deal with the giant of a man.

His booming voice had already created a scene. She glanced around, relieved to find the few people who'd stopped to gawk had now moved on. The last thing she wanted was to be the focus of more raised eyebrows or pointed stares.

After all, the whole reason she'd moved here was to get away from the gossip.

Not create more.

This just wasn't his day.

Tony Granger sighed. He had to do better, for Johnny's sake. Something like this could never happen again. As hard as he tried, he just couldn't get this parenting stuff down pat. Did all parents find it this hard? Or was he the only one to find this role to be the ultimate challenge?

"Let's go home, Uncle Tony. We gotta take care of the puppy." Johnny started for the truck parked on the other side of the street.

"Stop!" Tony grabbed the boy's arm, halting him from running into the street. Had the boy learned nothing from his near-death experience moments ago? "You can't just run into the road. Haven't you learned that by now?"

"But we gotta hurry." Johnny's voice rang out with rising panic. "If anything happens to him—"

"Slow down." Tony worked to keep his tone light. He knew the boy was still upset over the puppy. "Little man, I'll do what I can to help him, but without a vet in town, I'll have to wing it."

Johnny's eyes shimmered with unshed tears. "You can do it. You run a ranch. You know all about animals."

Tony wished he felt as certain as Johnny. He didn't say anything as he patted his nephew's shoulder.

With Johnny's adoption proceedings on the horizon, Tony knew he needed to do better with his parenting skills. And with Johnny's grades taking a nose dive and Tony failing at every turn to spark the boy's interest in schoolwork, Tony had launched a search for a qualified tutor. But even that tactic had not been successful. Either the teachers he approached were already booked, or their schedules simply didn't accommodate after-school tutoring.

Tony's gut churned. It was imperative he impress upon the court investigator and the judge just how much he and Johnny belonged together. He'd do anything for the boy—if only he knew what to try next.

Of course, the surprise visit this afternoon from the court investigator hadn't helped things. The woman overseeing the pending adoption had hammered him for spending too much time isolated out on the range as well as not focusing enough of his attention on Johnny. That had actually been the high point of the meeting. By the time the woman left, Tony was hopelessly distracted and behind with his work, which had caused him to be late picking up Johnny.

Tony's jaw clenched. It wouldn't happen again.

Once Johnny was situated in the pickup with his seat belt secured, Tony cautiously laid the puppy on the boy's lap. "Be gentle with him."

"I will." Johnny say up straighter. "I'll take real good care of Patch."

"Patch?"

"Yeah. His fur is different colors."

Tony swiped his palm over his jeans, trying to remove the grime and gook the puppy had left behind. "Don't go naming him. If he lives, we can't keep him."

"But—"

"We'll talk later." Tony closed the truck door.

After Johnny had lost his mother and father not quite a year ago, the last thing his nephew needed was to get attached to a puppy they couldn't keep. He didn't want to be the bad guy, but as soon as they were certain the puppy would be fine, he'd have to find it a good home.

Tony crossed in front of the pickup where his gaze settled on the woman who'd saved his nephew's life. From a distance, her petite body, light blond hair, and delicate features held an eerie similarity to those of Jessie, his ex-fiancée. He'd made a point of trying not to think of her during the past few months.

Once upon a time, he'd based his whole world around Jessie. But after she'd found out he'd assumed responsibility for his orphaned nephew without discussing it with her, she'd packed her bags—not that talking to her would have changed the outcome. Jessie wasn't ready to settle down with a family. She claimed she was too young, at twenty-five, to be saddled with someone else's kid.

Someone else's kid.

After all these months, her words still stung. How could she think that? Johnny wasn't just anyone's kid.

Damn. These memories weren't welcome.

He had more important things to concern himself with, like making sure Johnny never ran off on his own again. Yet, there were moments when Tony caught himself wondering… If things had been different… If he'd handled everything better… If Jessie had been more patient… Then he wouldn't be juggling the ranch on his own while trying to be a single parent, a position that made him feel inept, even after eleven months of on-the-job training.

"You forgot this," the woman called, holding out the familiar backpack.

Tony shook his head in disbelief as he strode across the street. Yet one more mistake he'd made today. "Thanks. You saved me another trip into town."

"Is the puppy okay alone with Johnny?"

"The boy is good with all sorts of creatures. He'll yell if there are any problems."

Tony reached for the backpack, unable to look away from this intriguing woman. "I guess we should introduce ourselves. I'm Tony Granger."

He extended his hand to her and noticed the slight hesitation before she slipped her slender fingers into his grasp. Her gaze met his, and their stares locked. He found himself entranced by her vivid blue eyes.

"Ella Morgan."

"I haven't seen you around before. Are you new to town?"

"Uh, yes." She pulled back her hand, and he reluctantly let go. "I took a position at Whistle Stop Elementary School, teaching fourth grade. It's only a temporary position until the end of the school year, but I'm hoping to get hired permanently."

He eyed the long-sleeved cotton blouse, which emphasized her narrow waist—exactly the right size to wrap his hands around and pull her close. The way her figure-hugging denim skirt brushed against her calves left him musing over thoughts of her shapely legs.

He halted his meandering thoughts. What was he doing fantasizing about her? A woman was a complication he didn't need at this juncture in his life. He didn't even know her. He should turn and walk away. But his boots remained rooted to the spot on the sidewalk.

After all, he owed her an apology. "I'm sorry. I didn't mean to be rude when we met. You have to understand, when you see some stranger holding your nephew, you act first and think later."

"Apology accepted."

His voice deepened when he admitted, "I don't know what got into Johnny to just take off on his own. He knows better—"

"Like the way you know better than to forget to pick him up?" She eyed him like he'd just been caught cheating on a test.

She saw right through him, knew he was a phony, a fake. His lips pressed firmly together. This past year had been nothing but starts and stumbles. If this stranger saw his sham, he inwardly cringed to think what the trained court investigator must have observed.

He might be able to run a successful ranch, but he didn't have the first clue how to be a parent—even though he had every intention of doing his best for Johnny. But like his father had taught him, the best of intentions were a waste of time without any follow-through. Tony would follow through one way or another. He wouldn't give up.

"I was on my way, but then...ah, never mind." He wasn't about to mention the court-appointed investigator. "I should go."

She lifted a brow. "Kids must be a priority."

"He is." Tony clenched the strap of the backpack, and he strode away.

He wasn't going to waste his time making excuses. This woman had obviously made her mind up about him. And none of it was good.

Chapter Two

This talk would require taking the long way home.

Tony turned on the left turn signal. He wanted Johnny's full attention without the distraction of the television or video games. Tony needed to talk to the boy about his dangerous escapade, but he was uncertain how to verbalize his concern.

Being a single parent wasn't easy for him, especially when he sympathized with Johnny for losing not one but both parents. Perhaps he did overcompensate at times by letting Johnny get away with more than he should, but there was no way today's stunt could be swept aside. He just had to find the right words to make Johnny understand how close he'd come to—

Tony couldn't finish the horrific thought. No matter what Ella Morgan thought of his parenting skills, or the lack thereof, he was grateful she'd been there for Johnny.

Before Tony could figure out where to start, Johnny blurted out, "The lady—she was kinda nice, huh? Pretty, too."

Tony glanced over, catching the dreamy look in the boy's eyes. "Yeah, sure, kid. She seemed nice enough. But I got the impression you didn't like her much."

Johnny shrugged. “That was before she helped Patch.”

The boy’s referral to the puppy by name had Tony gripping the steering wheel tighter. He’d have to deal with the puppy situation next. “I’m grateful Miss Morgan was there to help you. Do you know how dangerous it is running into the street?”

“But I had to get Patch some help.”

He was concerned about the puppy, too, but the utmost thought on his mind was dealing with Johnny’s risky actions. He struggled to find the right words. “When you knew I was running late, why didn’t you call home?”

His nephew shrugged. “I figured you were busy. And...”

“And what?”

“I didn’t want to get you in trouble. Someone might tell the judge, and he’d take me away.” The last words were barely above a whisper.

Tony’s thoughts slipped back to Ella. She’d been quick to point out his screw-up with Johnny, as if he hadn’t already realized his mistake. Worse yet, it’d take only one comment from her about his irresponsibility to set tongues a-wagging in this tight-knit community. Would she do such a thing? Would she relay the tale and unintentionally threaten his chances to finalize Johnny’s adoption?

Pain started to pulse in his temples. He couldn’t let that happen. Johnny deserved to grow up on the ranch where his father devoted his entire life. In fact, both Tony and his brother had had good childhoods with great parents...that is, until Tony started spreading his wings and thinking there had to be more to this world—something better than cowboying.

He'd been wrong. The fresh air, the wide-open land, and the animals grounded him. And that's what he wanted for Johnny.

Tony made a mental note to speak to Ella about not mentioning their run-in to anyone. He couldn't take any chances. Nothing could go wrong with this adoption.

"No one will take you away." Tony clamped a hand over the boy's shoulder and gave him a reassuring squeeze. "You, me, and Grandma, we're family. We'll stick together no matter what. Now stop worrying."

He was doing enough of that for both of them.

Tony took a moment to gather his thoughts and concentrate on traffic. He still had to drive home the fact that Johnny needed to think before he acted. The boy was bright, sometimes too bright for his own good. And he was impetuous. A stern reminder of the rules should do the trick.

Confident this would be easily dealt with, Tony said, "In the future, I want you to wait for me to pick you up. No more wandering off."

"But—"

"No buts. Understood?"

"I guess," the boy mumbled.

"No guessing either. Do you understand me?"

Johnny nodded. "Yes, sir."

Tony merged the pickup onto the one-way road encircling the town square. A dust cloud enveloped the truck, and he slowed the vehicle to a crawl. The gusting wind pushed sand and dirt onward. A large tumbleweed skidded directly in their path, forcing him to jam the brakes in front of the Poppin' Fresh Bakery.

With the road clear, he continued on. His glance skimmed the town's stucco storefronts. Nearly half of their showroom windows were empty. The shops had closed due to the declining economy. Some businesses had endured the tough times, but not many. Once, the town square had been the meeting spot for folks to share a bit of their day. Now the square was run-down, and barely a soul bothered with it.

Although, if his mother and her friends had their way, new life would be breathed into the center of town. The revitalization project was kicking off with a benefit dance competition. He'd never seen Whistle Stop so excited about an event.

His gaze came to rest on a couple of young women, Penny and Mimi, stepping out of the Beautiful U Salon. They flashed him huge smiles and waved. He hesitantly returned their gestures. Both of them had been encouraged to ask him for a date. He'd declined both of their offers. He hated how Mrs. Sanchez, the town gossip and his mother's closest friend, had labeled him as Whistle Stop's most eligible bachelor.

It didn't matter how many dates his mother and Mrs. Sanchez tried to set him up on, he planned to keep turning them down. The last thing he had time for was a relationship when he was having serious difficulties learning how to be a parent. And after waiting a year to get this close to finalizing the adoption, he wouldn't take the chance of a new romance delaying the proceedings if the court decided to check out a new woman in his life.

When they exited the other side of the square, Johnny returned to talking about Miss Morgan. "Do you know her? I seen her at the school before."

"It's *I saw her*. And you saw her because she's teaching the fourth grade." The new teacher might be the answer to helping his nephew's sinking grades. He wondered how she'd do as a tutor. Would she be kind and patient? Or expectant and rushed? As quickly as the thought occurred to him, he dismissed it. He refused to ask the buttinsky for help.

"She sure is pretty," Johnny said.

Tony shook his head. He couldn't blame the kid for having a small crush on her. If she hadn't needled him with that disapproving look, he might have been willing to give her a second, or third, glance.

Although she did need to let down her long, blond hair that she'd had pinned up and undo a button or two of her blouse. The provocative image quickened his pulse. As his mind's eye recalled her long sleeves and denim skirt that brushed her ankles, he wondered what she'd been thinking when she'd dressed for the warm day.

"Well?" Johnny asked, jarring Tony from his wandering thoughts. "Can we keep Patch?"

The abrupt change in the conversation left Tony struggling with how to deal with disappointing his nephew. "Grandma's allergic to dogs, and he might trigger one of her asthma attacks. We don't want that to happen, right?"

"No." The boy wiggled in his seat and tapped his foot repeatedly against the dash. "How 'bout he lives with the ranch dogs?"

Tony reached over and stilled the boy's leg. "The pup's much too small to become a working dog." He paused, trying to think of a way to explain so he would understand. "Have you watched *The Wizard of Oz*?" When Johnny nodded, Tony continued, "Remember Toto? How he could fit in the basket on Dorothy's bike? Well, when this dog grows up, he'll be about that size. Much too small to run around the barn where he might get hurt. He'd be much happier living in a house and curling up on someone's lap."

Someone like Ella, who'd insisted on helping the puppy. The memory of her triumphant smile when the pup perked up created a funny sensation within his chest.

"That's not fair." The glumness in Johnny's voice chewed at Tony.

Every boy deserved a dog, and someday he'd make sure his nephew got one. "I know. I'm sorry. Sometimes life isn't fair."

A couple of minutes later, Johnny asked, "Can we bat the ball around after dinner?"

Tony breathed a sigh of relief, thankful Johnny had dropped the subject of keeping the dog. He knew it wouldn't be their last conversation on the subject, not until he found the pup a good home, but he'd gladly take this small reprieve.

"Can we, huh?" Johnny prompted.

Tony took his responsibilities seriously, including baseball practice. Yet, his thoughts strayed to the mountain of dirty laundry peeking up over the edge of the hamper. He'd put off the task far too long, and he wasn't about to let his mother do it, no matter how many times she offered. She did enough as it was. More often than not, he found himself pulled in more than one direction at the same time, and she stepped in to help. But her health wasn't the best, so he tried to limit the pressure on her.

"Sorry, little man. We've got the laundry to start and your homework to go over. How about Sunday afternoon?"

"But—"

"Johnny." Tony's voice came out sterner than he'd intended, but it certainly seemed to gain the boy's attention.

"I guess."

No matter what Ella thought, he was doing his best. The real question was, would his best be enough for the court investigator—and, more important, would he do right by Johnny?

Ella strode up the sidewalk toward the market. A few people here and there gave her a puzzled glance, as though wondering about the scene she'd had with Tony. Let them wonder. She pulled her shoulders back and lifted her chin slightly. She hadn't done anything to be ashamed of, and she didn't owe anyone an explanation.

She turned a small plastic cartridge over with her fingers. She'd found the thing on the ground next to her after Johnny had pulled away. She suspected it might have been jostled from the boy's pocket. She'd check with him at school on Monday.

Her thoughts turned to her immediate problem—coming up with money to repair the neglected cabin she'd inherited from her grandmother. The place held so many happy childhood memories—emotions she longed to recapture. First, she needed to come up with the cash for the back taxes and a new roof before the monsoon season arrived with its torrential rains and flash flooding. She didn't want her cozy home turned into a life-size fish bowl.

Sure, her new job at the elementary school provided enough for her to get by on, but it was only a temporary position. The principal was just now taking résumés for the opening in the fall term. She hoped that her foot in the door would give her an edge over the other applicants.

But in the meantime, there was no way she'd be able to stretch her meager paycheck to cover the pending expenses. She'd applied for a home improvement loan after she'd decided she wanted to move here, but the bank claimed she was already overextended with education loans and a couple of maxed-out credit cards. Now she needed to find another source of funding and quickly.

As she neared the market, she took in the various sales and public activities taped to the plate-glass windows. One particular poster caught her attention. She paused to read, *Dancing With the Firefighters Competition—limited entries*, scrolled out in bright red marker. Not giving it much thought, she started to turn away when the words *CASH PRIZE* jumped out at her.

Should she enter? Maybe she'd dismissed the idea too soon. After all, she had been president of her swing dance club in college. They'd had a professional instructor sponsor their group as well as show up each week to teach them the proper steps. Oh, how she'd enjoyed the whole experience.

Ella carefully read the colorful sign again. Anticipation started to thrum in her veins, and she longed to kick up her heels. Until recently, she'd devoted herself to caring for her sickly grandmother and then settling her estate. What would it hurt to have a little fun and hopefully win enough to pay the taxes and help with the new roof?

But the entry fee wasn't cheap. The thought dampened her enthusiasm. And if she lost, she'd be even more in a bind. Was this gamble worth taking?

She worried her bottom lip. Maybe she should learn a little more about the contest. She reached for her cell phone and dialed the number. A busy signal greeted her. With a sigh, she disconnected the call. She'd call again as soon as she got home.

After purchasing a few essentials, including creamy chicken-flavored ramen noodles, a couple of cans of tuna and, most important, some ground coffee, she headed home. Twenty minutes later, she unlocked the cabin, rushed inside, and kicked off her pumps before dropping onto the couch. The more she thought about it, the more excited she got about the contest. She was going to do it. She was going to dance her way into the winner's circle. She smiled, excited about the possibilities.

Although she still had a problem. She didn't have a partner nor anyone to ask. The thought niggled at her, but with her mind made up to do this, she wasn't going to let minor problems deter her. First, she had to get her hands on some tickets, and then she'd worry about finding a partner.

Before she had time to change her mind, she grabbed the phone and dialed the number from the sign. On the third ring, a female voice answered.

"Hi," Ella said. "I'm calling about buying tickets for the dance contest."

"Sorry, we're sold out."

Those four little words snuffed out her glimmer of hope. "Oh, no!"

"However, if you'd like to watch the competition, we still have tickets available for the dinner and show.

We're raising money to fix up the town square and reopen the train depot. How many dinner tickets will you need?"

"But I really need to win the grand prize." Ella bemoaned the fact more to herself than to the woman on the other end of the phone.

"You and half the county." The woman's light tone carried with it a smile. Instantly, Ella liked her. "You know what? Let me take your name and number in case a contest ticket becomes available."

Ella shrugged. What could it hurt? "My name's Ella Morgan."

"Oh my goodness! I was going to call you this evening and thank you."

"Thank me? For what?"

The woman chuckled. "I'm sorry, dear. I didn't mean to confuse you. I'm Carlota Granger, Johnny's grandmother."

A moment of clarity struck her. This woman was Tony's mother. Though she'd met the man only that afternoon, thoughts of him littered her mind.

"My grandson's tendency to act first and think later is an inherited trait. I pray he never does something so dangerous again. Thank you for watching out for him. I don't know what I'd have done if anything had happened to him..." Her voice crackled with raw emotion.

"I'm glad I was there to help out."

The woman sniffed as though fighting off tears. "We both are."

"By the way, I found something I believe belongs to Johnny. An electronic game card of some sort."

"Oh, yes, he'll be missing that." There was a pause before the woman spoke again. "I'd really like a chance to thank you in person. Would you like to stop by tomorrow, say, around eleven, for coffee?"

Perhaps pleading her case in person would sway the woman to help her with the dance contest. After all, someone might still need a partner. And it wasn't like she had any other pressing plans for the weekend. "Sure, I'd like that. And I'll bring the cartridge with me."

While Carlota gave her directions to the ranch, Tony's image came to mind. Would he be there? It was quite obvious that he was a busy man. She felt confident that the chance of running into him again was slim.

It wasn't that he was hard on the eyes—far from it. The problem was that he seemed like a naturally loud man, not a good person to be around when you wanted to fade into the background. If he ever found out about her past... She inwardly cringed, thinking of him mentioning her secret in public with his booming voice. Then everyone would know. The raised eyebrows and whispers would start again.

Not that any of that would happen. She intended to take a wide berth around him, and she hoped he would do the same. They obviously wouldn't get along, but that didn't mean she couldn't be friendly with his mother. One thing had absolutely nothing to do with the other.

Chapter Three

Beneath a clear blue sky, Ella drove under a black wrought-iron sign that read Circle G Ranch. She turned onto a bumpy dirt lane and soon approached the sprawling ranch house. She pulled to a stop. Small boulders and cacti skirted a sweeping veranda. The place was charming and had a welcoming appeal.

With it being Saturday, she once again wondered if she might run into the cowboy...and Johnny. Maybe she should have arranged to meet the woman in town at the Green Chile Cantina or the Poppin' Fresh Bakery. Ella scanned the area, finding no one out and about. She was getting worked up about nothing.

Again, Tony's handsome face came to mind. She assured herself that her only interest in seeing him was to learn how the puppy made out. Because no matter how good-looking Tony was, they weren't compatible. And even if they were, she wasn't interested in starting a relationship—with anyone.

She stepped out into the bright sunshine. Wide-open fields with desert grass swaying in the breeze stretched out in all directions with a few horses racing over the countryside. The vastness of the land gave the illusion that the world was truly flat. After living within the constraints of the city for so long, she was surprised to find herself drawn to the openness. A smile tugged at her lips before she turned away and started up the path to the house.

Seconds after she knocked, Mrs. Granger greeted her with a broad smile that plumped up her rosy cheeks. "Hello, Ella. Right on time. Come in."

The woman's dark hair and brown eyes resembled Tony's, but her short stance was the complete opposite of her six-foot-plus son. "I just made a fresh pot of coffee. Would you care to join me for a cup?"

"I'd love some."

Ella stepped inside and immediately noticed the Southwest décor with various types of artwork in shades of tan, black, and turquoise. But beyond the niceties, the place had an easygoing, homey atmosphere, something her grandmother's prim and proper home had lacked.

"Your home is lovely, Mrs. Granger."

"Thank you. Please, call me Carlota."

Ella followed the kind woman into the kitchen. The sun shone through the numerous windows surrounded by frilly turquoise curtains and bounced off the light oak cabinets. The whole room was bright and cheerful, just like Carlota.

Ella's imagination ran wild with images of Tony as a young boy snatching cookies from this very counter and then racing out the back door to play in the enormous backyard. Her early years were spent in a cramped mobile home, unlike this spacious ranch house, with her mother and little brother. Ella's smile wobbled as she recalled her mother and brother. In the absence of a father, they'd still managed a happy life in their humble home—until that one fateful night.

The brutal images washed over her. Ella stared blindly out the window as her fingertips slipped beneath her sleeve and massaged her scarred arm. She'd been only twelve when she'd awakened on the couch to find an ugly orange inferno engulfing the rear of the trailer where her mother and little brother slept. A wall of smoke had rolled over her, sucking the oxygen from her lungs. After failing to reach her family, a neighbor found her on the floor, choking. The man had carried her outside to the arms of an arriving firefighter. Though her throat burned, she'd begged the fireman to help her family, but he'd been unable to do that as raging flames shot up into the dark sky. It was too late. Her family was gone.

Ella blinked repeatedly. She hadn't delved into those horrific memories in a very long time. She'd worked so hard to move on. And now wasn't the time to get caught up in the past. Determined to maintain her composure, she shoved the memories to the back of her mind. No one in Whistle Stop knew her past. None of them looked at her differently, like her grandmother's neighbors had. People's memories were quite long. But while she was in Whistle Stop, she didn't have to worry about what people were thinking.

"Go ahead and have a seat." Carlota's words cut through Ella's harried thoughts. "I just need to grab my medicine, and then I'll be right with you."

Ella took a seat at the large wooden kitchen table. When she glanced toward the sink, she noticed Carlota sorting through a bunch of prescription bottles on the little wood ledges on either side of the window. Ella couldn't help but wonder if the woman's health was the reason Tony had stepped up to be Johnny's guardian. The thought of Tony riding to his family's rescue earned her respect, even if he was struggling with the enormity of the responsibility. But what exactly had happened to both of the boy's parents?

None of which was any of her business, she reminded herself.

Carlota turned to her. "Now let me get you that coffee."

"Can I help you?"

"Thanks. But I've got it." Carlota poured them each a cup of hot brew. She moved toward the table with a slight limp. "Do you take sugar or milk?"

"Both, if you don't mind."

"I don't mind at all."

Before she forgot, Ella fished the game cartridge from her purse. When Carlota joined her at the table, she held it out to her. "This is what I found on the road."

The woman accepted the black plastic card. "My grandson has a fascination with those electronic games. I'm so glad you found it. They certainly aren't cheap."

"Not a problem." Ella bit down on her bottom lip as she sought a way to lead into her other reason for this visit.

Carlota gave her a hesitant look. "You look like a woman with something on her mind. I know we've only met, but sometimes it's easier talking to a stranger. So spit it out."

Carlota's openness and easy manner had a way of easing Ella's anxiety. She hadn't discussed her financial difficulties with anyone but the attorney who settled her grandmother's estate. There was an easiness in Carlota's gaze. It would feel so good to open up and talk to someone about her troubles.

But Ella needed to plead her case carefully, making sure the woman understood how important entering the competition was to her. "I don't know many people in town, and I was hoping you could connect me with someone who would be willing to sell me their tickets for the dance contest."

Carlota added some milk to her cup and gave it a stir. "If you don't mind me asking, why is this contest so important to you?"

It was too late to back out now, so Ella kept going. "I just moved to Whistle Stop. I've inherited a small cabin on Roca Mountain from my grandparents."

Carlota's face lit up. "What were your grandparents' names?"

"Ron and Margaret Morgan."

A light of recognition shone in Carlota's eyes. "Well, this is a small world. Your grandparents used to be bridge partners with me and my husband."

"I...I didn't know that."

Carlota added a dash of sugar to her cup and gave the coffee another stir. "Years ago, your grandparents would vacation in a cabin on Roca Mountain, and we spent many summer evenings together. I read about your grandmother's death in the paper. I'm so sorry for your loss."

Ella carefully considered her next words. She'd had a tenuous relationship with her grandmother during the best of times. *Time to change the subject*.

"My grandfather said this town is full of the friendliest people. He always enjoyed his visits here."

"I hope you've had a chance to meet some of the townsfolk." Carlota's expression was one of maternal concern.

"Actually, I did make a friend at the elementary school where I teach. Her name's Melissa. She's the receptionist."

"Oh. I've known Melissa her whole life. In fact, she graduated high school with Tony. She's a sweet girl. Have you gotten to know anyone else? Let's see. Who would be about your age? There's Ana at the Green Chile Cantina and Piper at the Poppin' Fresh Bakery."

"I've been too busy looking for a second job to socialize. My job at the school is only temporary."

"I was a teacher there until a few years ago when I had to retire early for health reasons. It's a great place to work. Are you planning to apply for the permanent position for the fall term?"

Ella nodded. "I have to go through the interview process again."

Carlota smiled. "I still have friends there. I'll put in a good word for you, if you'd like."

"I would. Very much. I had to sell everything in Albuquerque in order to cover my grandmother's bills. All I have left is the cabin." She pressed her lips together, shocked all of that had come gushing out.

"Oh, you poor dear. That must have been so rough on you. At least you were able to keep the cabin your grandfather built with his own hands. He was so proud of the place."

The weight of responsibility resting on Ella's shoulders increased as the mention of her beloved grandfather awakened feelings of loss. He had been the peacemaker. The glue that held the family together. After his death in her early teens, things became strained with her grandmother, who would never let Ella forget that she'd lived while her mother and brother hadn't.

"This cabin, is it where you live now?"

Ella nodded. "I moved in a little more than a week ago, and I did my best to clean the place, but there's a ton of repairs to be done. Things I can't even begin to do myself. After those high winds the other night, there's hints of daylight visible in the roof. And I...I don't have anywhere else to go." She couldn't bring herself to admit just how bad things were with the back taxes hanging over her head.

"Oh my. So that's why you're anxious to enter the contest?"

"Yes. Do you know if anyone still needs a dance partner?"

"I really want to help you, but once people found out the details of the dance competition and the prize money, we sold out in a couple of days." Carlota eyed her carefully. "Although my son has a couple of tickets. Perhaps Tony needs—"

"I need what?" Tony stepped inside the back door. When his gaze zeroed in on Ella, his eyes widened before a frown settled over his tanned face.

His mother turned. "Ella, you've already met my son, Tony."

Ella gave him a stilted smile. "Hello again."

He didn't move from the doorway. "Howdy."

The drawl of his deep voice made her insides quiver with excitement. When his brows lifted as though to question why she was staring at him, she lowered her gaze to her cup. But curiosity got the best of her. She glanced up to see if he looked half as good as she remembered.

While mother and son exchanged pleasantries, Ella took in his faded jeans and flat abs. She swallowed hard, telling herself she should look away. Against her better judgment, she continued her perusal of his broad chest and shoulders before settling on the solemn expression on his handsome face. Her empty stomach fluttered with a nervous energy.

He didn't budge. Instead, he crossed his arms and leaned against the doorjamb. His poker face masked any hint of his thoughts. Had he known she was going to be here? She doubted it. If he had, she wondered if he would have shown up. She highly doubted it. They'd gotten off to a very rocky start.

Tony's gaze met hers. "I wasn't expecting to see you again so soon."

"Your mother invited me." He surely didn't think she'd come to see him, did he? Well, he was partly right. Now that she knew he had tickets to the dance competition, he was exactly who she needed to talk to. Not letting the chance to get a ticket slip through her fingers, she sent him a smile. "I'd like to discuss something with you before I leave."

He frowned. "Does this have something to do with yesterday? I told you, I'll handle things with Johnny. I'd appreciate it if you wouldn't mention the incident to anyone. This town thrives on gossip."

Ella's mouth gaped. This was the same man who'd made a scene, accusing her of mistreating his nephew for anyone in Whistle Stop to hear, and now he wanted a favor from her? He was worried people might find out? She had a feeling he was a bit late worrying about keeping the incident hush-hush after he'd practically shouted at her in town.

"Of course she won't say anything," Carlota said, filling the awkward silence. "How is the puppy?"

Tony continued to hold Ella's gaze, as though waiting for her to confirm his mother's assumption, but she wasn't feeling so generous at this particular moment.

"Tony," his mother prompted, "we're waiting to hear about the puppy."

"After a couple of baths, we finally got the little fella cleaned up. He's out in the tack room until we find him a home, but he doesn't have much of an appetite. The vet says nothing more can be done. All we can do now is wait."

"I hope he feels better soon," Carlota said, vocalizing Ella's thoughts.

"We're all hoping the same thing, especially Johnny." Tony rubbed the back of his neck. "I wish he wasn't so attached to the pup."

Ella caught Carlota's gaze shifting from her to her son and back again. Intrigue twinkled in the woman's eyes. Surely Carlota wasn't thinking that she and her son might hit it off, because that was never ever going to happen. Wasn't their incompatibility obvious?

"Before I forget, I have something you're gonna want to see." Carlota slowly rose to her feet. She winced as if her joints were bothering her.

"Don't get up," Tony said. "Show me later."

"Nonsense." The woman lumbered over to the counter and picked up a legal-sized envelope. "I found this on the floor in Johnny's room. It must have fallen out of his backpack. Thought it might be important."

"Thanks." Tony glanced at the envelope, but he didn't bother opening it. He stuffed the thing in his pocket. "I didn't know we were having company."

Carlota filled him a mug of coffee and handed it to him. "Here. Take this and go sit down." She spoke in a don't-give-me-any-back-talk voice. "Our guest is going to think I haven't taught you any manners."

Ella couldn't help but notice his reluctant obedience as he moved toward the table. How could a guy who respected his mother be all bad? Perhaps she should give him a second chance.

Tony took the seat across from her. Instead of looking at him, she added yet another spoonful of sugar to her already sweetened brew and made a point of stirring thoroughly.

Seconds of strained silence ticked by before Carlota joined them at the table and jump-started the conversation with glowing compliments about the improvements Tony had made to the ranch. Ella noticed how he stiffened when his mother sang his praises. He definitely didn't come across as vain, even though he sounded quite accomplished at keeping the ranch afloat.

"He's even a member of the volunteer fire department. They're sponsoring the dance competition. It made for a great title. I mean, who could resist Dancing with the Firefighters? Some of the proceeds will go toward revitalizing the town square and the train depot, but I already told you that." His mother snapped her fingers. "Darn memory keeps failing me today. What are you guys planning to do with the fire department's portion of the proceeds?"

Tony leaned back in the chair, crossing his arms. "I'm sure Ella isn't interested in the new equipment needed at the fire station."

"Don't mind him." Carlota waved her hand as though to shush her son. "Besides being a worthy fundraiser, the dance will be the biggest social event to hit the county in years. We're fashioning it after that dancing show on television."

"The contest was all my mother's idea," Tony chimed in, the pride evident in his voice. "She's gone above and beyond the call of duty to not only help the fire station, but also to find a way for the entire community to pull together to help the town. She's even lined up a panel of three qualified judges to entertain the audience with their commentary." Carlota's face beamed as her son continued to brag about her accomplishments. "And if that isn't enough, she somehow finagled a car dealership into sponsoring the whole event. There's even going to be a dinner for the audience before the show, and the audience gets to take part in the contest by voting for their favorite couple."

"That's so impressive." Ella turned to Carlota, truly awed by her organizational skills. "You've done an amazing job."

The woman waved her hand in a nervous gesture. "I can't take the credit. An entire committee worked hard to pull this event together. I only did my part. Everyone in Whistle Stop is excited about revitalizing the town and attracting new business. The first step is fixing up the town square. And what better way to raise money than by having some fun? Even Tony bought a couple of tickets."

His brows scrunched together. "You mean the ones you forced on me."

Tony certainly had Ella's full attention now. He held two tickets he apparently didn't even want. The paramount question was, would he give them to her? They certainly weren't on the best of terms, but if he didn't want them, someone should put them to good use.

Ella swirled the spoon around her cup before taking a sip. The liquid rolled over her tongue. Definitely too much sugar. She nearly choked on the syrupy coffee. With great effort, she swallowed.

The brew hit her stomach, making her feel nauseated. Or was that Tony? He wasn't going to make this easy on her. Not at all. How exactly should she ask for his tickets?

"Ella's interested in entering the contest," Carlota uttered before Ella could muster up the courage. "Since you haven't found a partner yet, maybe you two could team up."

He shook his head. "I don't think so."

Oh, no. He wasn't going to dismiss the idea that easily. He had absolutely no clue at the depth of her desperation. At this point, she had no backup plan, nowhere to go. She needed to retain ownership of the cabin and make it livable again.

Before she could formulate a rebuttal, Carlota continued, "You just got done telling me this morning that the court investigator complained about you spending too much time overseeing this ranch. If you participate in the contest, you'll not only be helping the community, but you'll also be participating in the same fundraiser as Johnny. Remember, he's singing in the opening performance. You'll be teaching him social responsibility."

Tony crossed his arms. "When you came up with this idea, I told you I didn't want to be involved. That hasn't changed."

Carlota turned back to Ella. "What my son keeps forgetting is that he's the fire chief. He has an obligation to participate in the Dancing with the Firefighters Contest."

"And what you insist on forgetting is that I don't dance." Tony's tone was firm.

"You can learn. And besides, consider how you'll be helping Whistle Stop by aiding one of its teachers. You know how hard it is to attract teachers to these remote desert towns. And if the board hires her on permanently, she'll eventually be Johnny's teacher. So you'll be helping everyone by dancing with her."

Wait. This wasn't exactly what Ella had in mind.

She eyed Tony's towering height and broad chest. The thought of him holding her close revolved in her mind at a dizzying pace. He was certainly attractive enough, but she had no intention of being swept across the dance floor in his very capable arms.

Her fingers tugged at her long-sleeved T-shirt. She wasn't about to give this macho man an opportunity to stumble across her ugly secret, and then have to stare into his milk-chocolate eyes that would be filled with either pity, or worse, revulsion. Been there, done that. The last man she'd felt secure enough to share her physical imperfections with had been repulsed to the point of walking out on her. She wasn't dancing with Tony. No way. Never. There had to be someone else she could dance with.

"Ella, why don't you stay for lunch?" Carlota turned to her. "I'm going to grill some burgers. With this being a working ranch, we eat what we raise."

"I'd love to try one." Anything would be a welcome change after a steady diet of ramen noodles. More important, she wasn't about to give up on the contest. Tony didn't want to dance with her or anyone, so maybe she could talk him into giving her both of his tickets. Surely finding another dance partner couldn't be too terribly hard.

"Good. I'll fire up the grill." Carlota started for the back door when the phone rang. She frowned and hesitated, as though contemplating whether to answer it. "I'll take this in the other room. If it's about the fundraiser, it could take a while. Why don't you two get to know each other better while I'm gone?" Her eyes twinkled with mischief as she smiled at both of them before withdrawing to the other room.

Tony moved to the tiled counter and placed his cup in the sink. "If I didn't know better, I'd say she had that phone call planned so she could leave us alone together."

"She wouldn't do something like that, would she?"

Tony faced her. "I learned long ago to never underestimate my mother." He chuckled. "Since I haven't bothered to find a partner for the contest, she's made a point to parade almost every single female in the county past me. I'm guessing you are her last-ditch effort."

His words stung. Ella attempted to shrug it off, but she couldn't let it slide. "I've never been considered a last-ditch effort by anyone, least of all a total stranger—"

His eyes widened. "Whoa there. Slow down. I didn't mean it the way you took it. I'm sure you'd make someone else a great partner."

Just not him.

If only she could get her hands on his tickets, she'd be better off finding someone else to dance with. An out-of-towner—someone she'd never see again—would be more desirable. Someone incapable of stirring up such an influx of emotions.

She'd learned a long time ago to hide her imperfections from the world behind a veil of cloth, no matter how high the mercury rose. Her mind spiraled back in time. She recalled being a little girl and fighting her way toward the back bedroom to try to save her mother and brother. The fire had engulfed the mobile home quickly. When part of the ceiling fell, it hit her outstretched arms. Later, in school, numerous kids had made pointed comments about her ugly scars and avoided her because she was different. She'd learned quickly to keep her scars a secret.

"You're wrong about your mother." Ella wanted to make sure to drive home this one point. "She invited me here so I could return something of Johnny's. I doubt she'd try to fix you up with me, especially since she doesn't even know me."

"Yes, she would. She loves playing matchmaker, but I refuse to play along."

"You don't have to worry about me. I'm not interested in a relationship." When his eyes filled with skepticism, she added, "Not with you or anyone else. I already have enough to deal with."

"That's good to know. I've got to go." He pushed the back door open and walked away.

He didn't have to sound so pleased about her lack of interest in him. Ella pursed her lips as she glowered at his retreating figure.

She had moved to this out-of-the-way town with every intention of leading a quiet life. Here, no one knew her or her past. She was just Ella Morgan, schoolteacher. And it'd stay that way, provided she got her hands on the money to save her home from ruin—

The contest prize!

She'd been so distracted, she'd nearly forgotten about the tickets.

She couldn't let Tony walk away.

"Hey, wait." She tore off after him.

Chapter Four

TALK ABOUT A NARROW escape.

Tony turned the corner of the house and stopped. But now he had another problem to deal with. He yanked the ominous envelope from his back pocket. This wasn't his first correspondence from the school. A band of stress tightened around his chest as he scanned the brief, hand-scrawled note. Johnny's grades showed no improvement.

The paper crinkled in Tony's fist as his back teeth ground together. None of the study guides or flash cards had helped. A drastic step was needed to snap Johnny out of this downward spiral.

"Tony! Wait."

He lifted his head just as Ella bounded around the corner of the house. She barreled straight into him. The force of the collision caused her to stumble backward. He instinctively reached out. His hands gripped her waist, pulling her to him. She stared up at him with the most entrancing blue eyes. His gaze slipped down past her pert, little nose to her lush, pink lips.

She pulled free of his hold. "Sorry."

He continued to stare into her mesmerizing eyes. Their color was unique. They were as light as the summer sky, and yet there was a depth to them, as though they'd witnessed much—perhaps too much.

He tugged at the neckline of his T-shirt. Boy, the sun was unusually hot today. Then he noticed the long shadow the house cast over them. Not even the gentle breeze did a thing to cool him down. Was he the only one who was hot and bothered?

"Uh...no problem." He cleared his throat and shuffled his feet. What had he been thinking to let himself get lost in her eyes? "I've got to get back to work."

"Wait. This won't take long."

"What won't?" Surely she didn't intend to push the subject of them hooking up for the contest. That wasn't going to happen. Especially not with a woman who eroded his common sense with just one look and had him wondering about the shadows lurking in her eyes.

Ella tilted up her chin. "How much do you want?"

"For what?"

"Your tickets to the dance contest."

He crossed his arms. "Why should I do you a favor? You won't even promise to keep yesterday's episode between us."

"I won't lie to people, but I promise not to bring up the subject." She sighed. "Besides, with your loud mouth, half of Whistle Stop must have heard you yesterday, and by today the other half has heard the gossip."

"They won't know the details. They won't know how I screwed up. Not unless you tell them."

"If I give you my word I won't go around talking about you, will you sell me your tickets?"

Was she blackmailing him? Nah. A woman who refused to lie wouldn't sink low enough for blackmail. He gave her a long, hard look. He wouldn't consider himself an expert at reading women, but he'd swear that look in her eyes was one of desperation. What had put it there? Was she in some sort of trouble?

"Why should I sell them to you?"

"Because you aren't going to use them."

"Says who? You heard my mother. I need to get more involved with the community."

Ella's cute, little mouth pressed into a firm line, as though she was trying to figure out her next move. He could easily imagine her as a child, stubborn and determined.

"Are you serious?" she asked. "You're really going to participate?"

"Maybe." He sure didn't want to, but he had to do whatever it took to impress the court.

He glanced back down at the teacher's note crumpled in his hand. Maybe he was looking at this situation all wrong. Now would be the ideal time for him to swing a deal to get Ella to help Johnny with his studies. He'd certainly failed. And his mother hadn't fared any better. Perhaps a certified teacher might have some proven techniques to get through to his nephew.

Tony hesitated. She wasn't much more than a stranger to him. His gut told him she was a good person, but what did his gut know? A little more than a year ago, he thought he and Jessie would be an old married couple by now, with a baby on the way. He couldn't have been more wrong.

Instead, Jessie had skipped out on him when he'd needed her the most, and in place of having his own baby, he now had his brother's child to raise.

Damn. These memories weren't welcome.

"Name your price for the other ticket." Ella's voice drew his attention back to the present.

The suggestion of them partnering for the dance came across as a terrible idea. Letting her get closer to him would just give her another chance to observe his parenting skills. If she didn't approve of what she saw, what would she do?

Then again, what choice did he have but to trust her? His back was against the wall. He either found a way to turn around Johnny's grades, or risk losing him.

The school would have already done a background check on Ella before hiring her. And she'd won Johnny over when she'd helped with the puppy. So what was he waiting for?

Tony swallowed hard. "I want you to tutor my nephew after school."

She shook her head. "I meant a dollar figure."

"I don't want cash. Johnny must pull up his grades. I can't afford for the court investigator to give the judge an unfavorable report."

"Why me?"

"He gets frustrated when I show him how to get the answers, and my mother is too much of a pushover to make him listen. I looked into hiring a teacher in the area, but they're in short supply. The ones I talked to have families of their own and can't spare the time."

"I don't think so. We didn't get off to a good start."

Tony kicked at a stone. The woman was as frustrating as she was beautiful. "How long are you going to hold that against me?"

"Not you. Johnny." She craned her neck to look up at him. "He wasn't happy when I stretched his T-shirt trying to pull him out of the roadway."

"Oh, don't worry about that." The tension in Tony's shoulders eased. "You totally won him over when you helped with the puppy. He even thinks you're pretty." Now why in the world did he go and add that? But as a splash of pink tinged her cheeks, his only thought was of how cute she looked. His nephew certainly had good taste.

"I don't know." She clenched her hands and glanced away.

"I'll do whatever it takes to make this work."

"So you're offering to be my dance partner if I tutor your nephew?"

Dancing was the absolute last thing he wanted to do. "Yes, I'll be your partner. Do we have a deal?"

"The thing is, I must win. I need the money to pay the back taxes on the cabin and repair the hole in the roof before the wind and rain destroy it."

So that *had* been desperation he'd seen in her eyes. He now realized why she was so eager to get his extra ticket. The thought of her in a run-down shack gave him pause. She wasn't exaggerating about her need to win. He wasn't Fred Astaire, but he'd give it his best attempt. They both had a lot riding on the outcome of this contest. She needed the money, and he needed Johnny to improve his grades so his adoption wasn't held up, or worse, denied.

Tony lowered his arms, hitching his thumbs in the corners of his jean pockets. "I understand. I'll do my best to see that we win. So is it a deal?"

"Slow down. Can you dance?" Her gaze searched his.

"A...a little."

The sunlight made her flaxen hair shimmer. "Not good enough. I need someone with experience if winning is to be an option."

This opportunity was slipping through his fingers. He had to find a way to make it work. Johnny was counting on him. "You're new to town. Where else are you going to get a dance partner on such short notice?"

"Good point. But if you aren't any good, it'd be a waste of time."

Tony paused, considering the problem. And then it dawned on him. If he was going to help his nephew and score points with the court, he'd have to pull out all of the stops—no matter how uncomfortable it made him. "What if I spring for dance lessons?"

Her eyes rounded. He'd finally succeeded in leaving her speechless. It took some of the sting off the thought of wasting his time learning to dance. He sure hoped he was a quick learner.

She studied him with those very astute blue eyes. "Are you that worried about Johnny?"

Tony shifted his weight from one foot to the other. He really didn't want to go into details of just how bad things were, but if he wanted to get help for his nephew, he had to suck it up and lay it all out on the table. He'd do anything for Johnny, from dance lessons to groveling.

"Yes, I'm worried." He cleared his throat. "I'm afraid they'll hold him back a year. But most of all, I'm worried they'll take him away from the only family he has left. So will you please accept my proposal?"

"Uncle Tony! Uncle Tony!"

They both turned to find Johnny running toward them, his arms pumping and his little legs pounding the ground. *What the...?*

"What are you doing here?" Tony approached his nephew. His gut churned with unease. "You're supposed to be at Melissa's place, working on your science project with Bobby."

The boy sniffled, wiping his tears with his arm. "I was worried about Patch. He didn't eat this morning."

"Calm down, little man. Maybe he just wasn't hungry."

"Uh-uh." Johnny shook his head. "Something's wrong with him. I don't want him to die, too."

Sympathy washed over Tony as he crouched down to talk to the boy. "Does Bobby's mother know you're here?"

Johnny nodded. "She brought me home so I could check on Patch."

"She did? But I was going to pick you up later."

"Bobby's mom said she didn't mind. She wanted to talk to Grandma about the dance contest."

The dance seemed to be the only thing on people's minds anymore. His mother had certainly thought up a very popular fundraiser. He was proud of her, but he wished he could have been left out of the entire affair.

Tony escorted his nephew to a bench on the patio. He glanced up, catching Ella's concerned gaze. He turned back to Johnny and put his arm over the boy's slim shoulders. "I know you're worried about the puppy, but I want you to listen to me. This morning the vet said we can only do so much for him. The rest is up to the little guy." They talked for a minute before Tony got to his feet. "I'll be back. I'm going to go thank Melissa for bringing you home. I'm sure Miss Morgan won't mind keeping you company."

Johnny's wary gaze moved to Ella. "I don't need her to watch me. I'm not a baby."

"No one called you a baby. Now sit and don't move."

Talk about bad timing.

Tony had just been starting to let down his guard and let her in. And though Ella knew better, she'd liked it—she liked him. The burly giant had a heart of gold. And he loved his nephew. That was abundantly clear.

Ella moved to the bench and gazed down at Johnny. "Mind if I join you?"

The boy shrugged and scooted to the far end of the bench. For a long time, neither spoke. Ella, having lost her own mother at about his age, felt an immediate bond with the boy. She wanted to reach out to him and let him know he wasn't alone, that she understood his deep, agonizing grief. The words teetered on the tip of her tongue, but she hesitated. Experience told her those words coming from a stranger wouldn't be of any comfort.

"Uncle Tony just has to make Patch better."

She had to strain to hear Johnny's mumbled words. "I hope he can. Patch is very lucky you found him. You saved his life."

Johnny looked up at her. "You helped."

She smiled, feeling the beginning of a friendship firming up. In truth, she hadn't done much, but her chest warmed at the boy's insistence that she'd assisted in some small way. "I'm glad I was there at the right time."

A couple of minutes later, Tony exited the ranch house and approached them.

"Can we go take care of Patch now?" Johnny sent his uncle an expectant look. "You have to get him to eat."

Tony's shoulders slumped. "Johnny, you must realize that even if he recovers, it doesn't change the fact we can't keep him."

"Just don't let him die." Johnny's voice cracked with raw emotion.

"Did you try canned puppy food?" Ella piped in, grasping for anything that might help. "I bet that's pretty appetizing and easy to digest."

"I picked some up when I ran errands in town this morning," Tony said. "Wait here. I'll run and grab it from the truck." In no time at all, he returned with a small paper bag in hand. "Okay, let's go."

Johnny rushed to his uncle's side, but then he paused and turned to Ellie. "Do you want to come see Patch?"

She worried her bottom lip, holding back her response. The truth was she couldn't wait to see the little guy, but she didn't want to overstep. She shot Tony a questioning glance over Johnny's head. He nodded his agreement to the idea.

She turned a smile to Johnny. "I'd love to."

"Great." Johnny reached for her hand. "Come on."

Hand-in-hand, all three set off for the barn. She hesitantly sent a glance over the boy's head to his uncle, the gentle giant. For just a moment, she imagined this was what it must be like to have a family of her own. A smile tugged at her lips.

As though he sensed her staring at him, Tony turned to her. His gaze caught hers, sending her heart racing. This wasn't good. He couldn't think she was interested—because she wasn't. She glanced away. They were dance partners. That was all.

Before long, Johnny's fingers slipped from hers. He raced across the pasture. Her hand hung limp at her side. She missed the connection, the sense of being wanted.

The silence hung heavy between her and Tony. She knew they'd have to forge some sort of friendship if they were to be successful at dancing together. She took it upon herself to ask questions about the ranch.

"It's impressive. Is it all yours?"

He nodded. "As far as the eye can see."

He'd never be accused of being long-winded, that's for sure. She struggled for another question. "So, one day all of this will be Johnny's?"

"That's the plan. If that's what he wants."

Tony sure wasn't making her attempt at conversation easy for her. Slowly, his answers grew longer until, finally, he launched into a full-fledged explanation about the details of the sprawling ranch and what it was like to tend to a herd of bison.

They paused by the wooden fence surrounding the paddock. She glanced over at him to find him staring at her. When his gaze dipped to her lips, the breath hitched in her throat. The tip of her tongue moistened her lips. What was she doing? Encouraging him?

She was playing with fire, but she couldn't help herself. The need to feel his touch thrummed in her veins. She'd been so alone, so isolated, for so long—

He cleared his throat and glanced away. "The land a mile or so up the road is where I plan to build my ranch house."

"This is an idyllic location with the backdrop of the mountain range in the distance." She tried to sound casual, even though her heart was pounding. "I don't know if I'd rather have the kitchen window face the mountain so I could watch the splash of colors as the sun sets while I did the dinner dishes or if the picture window in the living room should face it."

"Definitely something to consider."

"Perhaps the living room should face the pasture so you can admire the horses. I can't imagine ever getting tired of them." She caught herself rambling about things that were none of her concern. Heat flared in her cheeks. "Not that I have any say in the matter."

"I'll keep your observations in mind."

Anxious to put some distance between them, she turned to the barn. "Thanks for telling me about the place, but Johnny probably thinks we forgot about him."

As if on cue, Johnny came running out of the barn. "Uncle Tony, come quick! The puppy made a *big* mess. Boy, does it stink." The boy scrunched up his nose and waved his hand. "Gross!"

Tony groaned and rolled his eyes. "I'm coming."

"A parent's work is never done." Ella broke out in laughter at his pained expression.

She hung back as Tony strode ahead to deal with the aforementioned mess. The interior of the barn appeared to be well-kept and orderly. The scent of fresh hay and wood tickled her nose. The stalls were empty, but each was clean and marked with the horse's name painted in green on a large wooden horseshoe.

A yip from the pup broke the silence. Thank goodness the puppy was hanging in there. Ella rushed to the far end of the barn and paused at the doorway.

"Looks like he passed more of the motor oil." Tony got to his feet and disposed of a handful of paper towels. "Hopefully, that's the last of it. I'm not a vet or anything, but with the way the little guy is running around, I think it is a positive sign."

While Tony washed up, the puppy bathed Johnny in kisses. Ella quietly watched the scene as a smile tugged at her lips. Johnny's face glowed with happiness. Her heart melted into a puddle. She couldn't remember ever seeing such a sweet sight.

"He's better!" Johnny turned to his uncle. "Can't we keep him? Please?"

Tony moved to Ella's side. "I'm afraid not. I put up some flyers around town. If we can't find him a good home locally, I'll have to put an ad in the surrounding city papers."

Sympathy for the puppy and the boy welled up inside of her. She wanted to beg Tony to change his mind, but it wasn't her place to interfere. She was certain Tony had his reasons.

"What if no one wants him?" Johnny's chin hung low.

"Surely someone will want this sweet pup." She longed to alleviate some of Johnny's concern. "Maybe it'll be someone you know."

"All of our friends either already have a dog or don't want one," Tony said. "How about you? Would you like a puppy?"

Her gaze moved to the little ball of fluff. The idea of having the puppy fill the silence of the cabin totally appealed to her. She hadn't even held the puppy, and already her heart was pitter-pattering with love for him.

"You can't." Johnny clutched the puppy close to his chest. "I'll never see Patch again."

"Actually, I don't live far from here," she said, still toying with the idea. "Do you know where Roca Mountain is?"

A light of recognition lit up the boy's brown eyes, the mirror image of his uncle's. "One of Uncle Tony's ranch hands lives there. But you still can't have Patch. He's mine."

Tony knelt down and opened a can of meat, dumping the contents into the dog dish before sliding it in front of Patch. The little guy sniffed it. All three of them held a collective breath as they waited and watched. The puppy hesitated, staring at the food. Seconds dragged into minutes. When at last Patch licked at the food, they all sighed.

"He's gonna live!" The smile returned to Johnny's face.

"Yeah, I reckon he is." Tony smiled, softening the worry lines etched in his face.

A zap of attraction quickened her pulse. When the puppy finished eating, Tony bent over and scooped him up. Determined to ignore it, Ella moved off to the side. She needed distance between her and this man who filled her with a nervous energy.

Still, she couldn't help turning back and catching sight of that strong cowboy wearing a dopey grin as he pet the puppy. The sight tugged at her heartstrings. She should turn away or head home, but her feet wouldn't move.

"Please. Can't we keep him?" Johnny pressed his hands together as he sent his uncle a pleading stare. "He'll be good. I promise."

"It doesn't matter how many times you ask, the answer's still going to be no." Tony handed the puppy to Johnny. "I'm sorry."

Ella couldn't tear her gaze from the strong man patting the boy's shoulder in an attempt to comfort him. The love between them was blatantly obvious.

They chatted softly, as though they were, in fact, father and son. She found herself wondering how she'd react if she were in the same situation with her own child. A deep emptiness consumed her.

Tony straightened and turned to her. "Do you want to hold the little guy?"

She smiled and nodded.

The boy frowned and backed up.

Tony's brows drew together. "Johnny, let Miss Morgan hold him."

The child's bottom lip stuck out. "Fine. But she can't take him home."

"I won't. I'll stand right here."

Johnny eyed her up, as though deciding if he could trust her. At last, he handed over the puppy. "Be careful. He's little."

"I will." Boy, Tony had his work cut out for him when he attempted to separate these two. She didn't envy him.

Ella rested the fuzzy guy against her shoulder and nuzzled him. She couldn't remove the silly grin from her face. The pup's wet tongue ran over her cheek, causing joyful laughter to fill her throat. His short tail swished vigorously, and he gave a couple of excited barks. Now she totally understood how Johnny had become so attached so quickly.

"Isn't Patch awesome?" Johnny asked.

"Definitely." The puppy rewarded her with another sloppy kiss.

Tony crossed his arms and leaned against the doorjamb. "Seems as though he's got you wrapped around his little paw."

She couldn't argue. She adored Patch, even though his multicolored coat was uneven, as though matted fur had been trimmed in order to run a brush over him. Big, sad eyes stared up at her, tugging at her heartstrings. He was such a mangy mess that he was actually cute.

She reluctantly returned the furry guy to Johnny. "He's a"—she'd started to say cutie, but in his current state, that wasn't the right word—"sweetheart. Thank you for allowing me to hold him."

Her immediate instinct was to adopt the puppy, but one look at the love reflected in Johnny's eyes as he gazed at Patch told her it'd be the wrong thing to do. She doubted Johnny would forgive her for taking the puppy. Her chances of successfully tutoring him would be zilch. Surely Tony would relent and let the boy keep the puppy. She hoped.

Johnny sat down to play with Patch while Tony escorted her back to the house. They walked in silence. Intensely aware of the man next to her, she forced her gaze to remain focused directly forward.

"Do you want the dog?" Tony's question jolted her from her thoughts.

She stopped outside the kitchen door. "Now isn't the right time for me..." She raised her head, and their gazes locked. "Although I think we'd be happy together."

His lips lifted at the corners. "We would, huh?"

Heat rose in her cheeks. "I...I was referring to the puppy."

"Of course you were." Though his smile faded, amusement glimmered in his eyes.

His teasing had her tightening her hands until her nails bit into her palms. She forced her fingers to relax. Did he know she found him attractive? Would that cause him to rethink their arrangement for the contest?

"So will you take Patch?"

Her chest ached, knowing what her answer must be. She had to be responsible here and do what was best for everyone instead of following her heart.

"Won't you change your mind and find a way for Johnny to keep him? They've obviously bonded."

Tony raked his fingers through his hair. "It won't work. Not now." His gaze searched hers. "You seemed to bond with the puppy."

"He's adorable, but I don't think me adopting Patch would be a good idea."

"You never know. He might end up being your good luck charm. Just promise me you'll think about it."

She nodded and started into the house. Why did she feel as though she was continually getting in deeper with this guy? Still, she wanted to save the puppy from being just another cute face stuck in a small cage with no family to love him.

"Wait," Tony called out.

She hesitated before turning back. He jogged to her side. He stood so close to her that the gentle breeze carried with it the soft scent of his spicy aftershave. He certainly didn't have that rank odor of a man who'd worked out on the range all day. Not even close. His aftershave mingled nicely with his natural manly scent, creating quite an intoxicating combination. It teased her senses and awakened long-ignored desires.

At that particular moment, the only thing Ella could think about was leaning into him. His arms would slip around her waist while her hands slid up over his muscled chest to his broad shoulders.

Caught up in her fantasy, her gaze zeroed in on his lips. If she leaned a little closer—

"You still owe me an answer about tutoring." His voice jolted her from her fantasy. When she didn't immediately respond, he added, "Don't forget, I'm springing for dance lessons, too."

Ella's mind swirled with conflicting thoughts. Agreeing to spend more time with him—time in his arms—was dangerous. But very tempting. However, she was already having very vivid daydreams about him, and that spelled trouble.

She had to keep her mind on the competition. And at this point, Tony was the only available ticket in town. She smothered a groan.

The lessons he proposed would be the key to taking home the cash prize. Winning the competition would no longer be just a fantasy but a serious possibility. "You're really serious about the lessons?"

He nodded. "Do we have a deal?"

Chapter Five

HAD SHE DONE THE right thing?

After a delicious lunch with the Granger family, Ella drove home, all the while rolling around the events of the day in her mind. Memories of Tony's lopsided grin and the twinkle in his eyes throughout lunch kept coming to the forefront. There was definitely a lot more to him than the intimidating, protective side she'd witnessed at their first meeting. And this other side of him appealed to her in a way that no other man had. She groaned. Why was she letting him get to her?

He was just a cowboy. Nothing special.

Except he was tall, muscled, and had a sweet side that was utterly irresistible.

All of this had her wondering if she'd given him the right answer. Her stomach quivered as she recalled how Tony's eyes had gleamed for the briefest second when she'd told him that she'd tutor his nephew...as long as he gave his best effort to help her win the dance contest.

However important the prize money was to her, there was something more important—Johnny. The little boy had been the ultimate deciding factor. How could she live with herself if she didn't help the troubled boy? Maybe in some small way this was her chance to pay penance for the wrong she'd done years ago.

Ella pulled into her rutted driveway on Roca Mountain and climbed out. She paused, taking a moment to appreciate the tranquil sound of birds singing as a gentle breeze rustled through the trees. She inhaled a breath of fresh mountain air mingled with the slightest scent of pine and smiled. Even though the outside was overgrown with brush and dead vegetation, she could still envision the beauty lurking in the shadows.

The thought of turning her back on this place and letting Mother Nature have her way with it saddened her... No, she wouldn't let that happen. At last, she felt at home. For years, she'd moved through her grandmother's house like a visitor, afraid to break one of Gran's many rules. But here on Roca Mountain, Ella could unwind and be herself without all of the stress.

When someone called her name, she turned, finding Tracey Romero, her childhood friend, strolling down the road. They'd spent a number of their summers together, hiking all over this area, collecting pinõn nuts and using their imaginations to make up games. Ella hadn't realized how moving here would truly feel like coming home.

The young woman waved with one hand while the other rested protectively over her belly, rounded with her first child. A longing for her own family swept over Ella with such unexpected force that it stole her breath. There was no point hungering for something she'd never have. She didn't deserve a family, not after what she'd done. She swallowed her yearning and ignored the empty spot in her heart.

Ella moved to the end of the drive to meet her friend, whose long, dark hair was pulled back in a ponytail and whose cheeks were a dusty pink. "Nice day for a walk."

"The doc told me I had to slow down. No jogging until the little one makes its big appearance. But Doc Willard agreed to one leisurely stroll a day." She gently patted her midsection. "So how's the new job?"

Ella grinned like an overgrown kid. "I like it. A lot. In fact, I like the whole town."

"Now all you have to do is fix up this place. I wish I could give you a hand, but after the scare with this little guy or girl, I don't want to overdo it."

"Don't worry. I have everything under control. I even have a plan to raise the money to pay for a new roof." Tony's image flashed in her mind. She couldn't wait to find out what it'd be like to be in his arms—on the dance floor, of course.

"What's your plan?"

"I'm entering the dance contest."

Tracey's dark brows lifted. "Really? Rumor has it all of the tickets sold out a long time ago. How'd you land some?"

Heat swirled in Ella's chest and climbed up her neck, setting her cheeks ablaze. "Tony Granger had an extra one."

She realized her mistake in mentioning Tony's name when her friend's eyes lit up. The last thing she wanted to do was stand here and discuss the man who could irritate her one moment and, in the very next instant, make her pulse spike.

"So you snagged Tony for a partner." Tracey grinned. "You'll be the envy of every single woman in the county. They've all been trying to hook up with the most eligible bachelor in Whistle Stop. Who wouldn't? He's sooo hot. You'll have to give me all of the juicy details."

"Tracey!"

"What? Are you going to stand there and try to tell me you aren't anxious to be held in the arms of that hunk? I mean, have you checked him out?"

She certainly had checked him out. How could she not? The thought of running her hands across Tony's firm chest and over his broad shoulders caused a tightening in her abdomen. The idea of being held so close to him revolved in her mind at a dizzying pace. She'd let desperation cloud her judgment. She'd been crazy to agree to this arrangement. But what was done couldn't be—shouldn't be—undone.

Ella swallowed. "You're married and pregnant. You aren't supposed to notice those things."

Her friend groaned. "Boy, you have a lot to learn. A ring on your left hand doesn't mean you automatically become blind."

Ella opened her mouth to mount a defense, but unable to find an escape from the hole she'd dug for herself, she pressed her lips together. No way was she digging herself in any deeper.

"If I wasn't married," Tracey continued, "I might have thrown my hat in the ring to date him."

"We aren't dating. We have an arrangement."

Tracey laughed. "Is that what people are calling it these days?"

"I'm serious. I'm tutoring his nephew in exchange for him being my dance partner and providing us with lessons."

Tracey's amusement faded. "I should have known he'd turn it into something boring."

"What's that supposed to mean?"

Tracey paused as though deciding whether to repeat what she knew.

"Don't just leave me hanging. What do you know?"

"It's nothing—"

"It's something. Now spill it, or I'm letting your husband know about how you used to skinny-dip—"

"I was just a kid. And...and I didn't know there were boys around." Color filled Tracey's cheeks. "It was only once. And you dared me."

Ella sent her an expectant look. She wouldn't really tell on her, but if the threat got Tracey to spill what she knew about Tony, it was worth it.

"Okay, it's just that ever since Tony moved back to town, he's been a hermit. He's polite with all the ladies, but he never takes any of them up on their offers for dinner. I wouldn't be surprised if he hasn't taken some sort of oath to remain a bachelor—especially after what happened to him."

Ella should let the whole subject drop right here. Tony's past was none of her business—absolutely none. But no matter what she told herself, curiosity clawed at her.

What could have turned him into a confirmed bachelor? The ideas started dropping in her mind like a row of dominos. Cheated on? Jilted at the altar? Or was he harboring some deep, dark secret of his own? Did they at last have something in common?

"What happened?" Ella blurted out.

"I'm a little surprised you don't know."

"Why would I know? It isn't like we're close or anything."

Tracey sent her a knowing look. "Not yet. Give it time."

"Quit being ridiculous and just tell me what you know."

"Not quite a year ago, his older brother and his wife were on their way home from visiting him in Santa Fe when a drunk driver hit them head on and killed them instantly." Her voice dropped to a whisper. "The gossip mill says Tony's girlfriend dumped him when he decided to move home to oversee the family's ranch and assume responsibility for his nephew. He's never once complained or cried into his beer. At least not as far as I've heard."

A deep sadness came over Ella as her thoughts turned to Johnny, who was much too young to lose both of his parents to such a preventable accident. Thankfully, Tony had been there to step in and take care of his family.

She'd have to be careful, or soon she'd end up liking him for all of his fine qualities. His dreamy smile could easily be her final undoing. But that couldn't happen. She couldn't put herself in the position of forming an intimate relationship with him. He'd expect her to open up about herself—about her past. And that was something she refused to do.

At not quite seven thirty Monday morning, Tony trudged across the dry, uneven field with his cell phone pressed to his ear. "Do you really think that's our best option?"

"Yes, I do," Josie, the local dance instructor, said. "Shall I go ahead and pencil you in for the lessons?"

If this was what it took for Ella to fix her home and for Johnny to gain a qualified tutor, Tony didn't see that he had any choice. "Go ahead. If Ella has any problems with the time or whatever, I'll give you a call."

He slipped the phone into his pocket as a yawn escaped. He gave his head a firm shake as he stepped up to the back door of his mother's house, eager for another cup of coffee. After a night of tossing and turning, trying to decide if he made the right decision by hiring Ella to tutor Johnny, he'd barely gotten a wink of sleep. By the time he'd rolled out of bed long before the sunrise, he'd resigned himself to the inevitable.

Once inside the door, he slipped off his cowboy boots. What he really needed now was some of his mother's extra-strong brew. That'd keep him on his toes. He looked up, and his gaze collided with the woman who'd filled his thoughts the night before. He blinked, but she was still there, sitting at the kitchen table with his mother.

"Howdy," he said, trying to remember if they'd had plans to meet. "Are you here to see me?"

She smiled. "Actually, I stopped by on my way to work to give your mother these Mexican wedding cookies to thank her for lunch the other day. Would you like one?"

"Maybe later." His tone lowered in disappointment. "Don't let me interrupt. I just came to get some coffee. I'll be out of here in a jiff."

Another yawn threatened to escape, but he smothered it. He didn't need his mother inquiring about his exhaustion, especially not in front of Ella, who looked as fresh as one of the daffodils in his mother's kitchen window.

"I'm afraid the pot's empty," his mother said. "I didn't realize you'd be in for your break this early. I'll get another pot started."

"No, stay there." He waved her off. "I've got it."

What was the real reason for Ella's presence? Was it as innocent as she claimed? She was just being friendly with his mother?

Not one of his girlfriends had been close to his mother. In fact, his mother outright disliked Jessie, saying she was nothing but trouble. Not that Ella would ever be his girlfriend. It's just now that they were involved...er, um, dance partners, he felt uncomfortable with his mother and Ella getting too chummy.

Still, his mother certainly treated Ella differently than she had Jessie—he retrieved the coffee from the cabinet—but that didn't mean he should act any different toward Ella. They weren't even friends. Were they? He filled the filter with scoop after scoop of the potent coffee until he realized he'd put in too much and had to remove some.

Looking back on his relationship with Jessie, he realized that they'd dived in far too quickly. She didn't like being tied down to anything—even him. When he had talked about the future, she'd always changed the subject. Sure, they'd had an apartment, but even that had been a month-to-month obligation. Ella wasn't so different in that respect. With no family in Whistle Stop and her home in dismal condition, how long would it be until she moved on?

He turned on the faucet and filled the pot with cold water. As he went through the motions, he continued to compile reasons why getting any more involved with the pretty teacher was out of the question.

His interaction with Johnny had taught him the value of setting down roots. They were the lifelines that held a person steady when the winds of loss or disappoint threatened to flatten you. They held you firm and steady through the good and the bad. Ella didn't have those roots that bind...

"Tony, did you hear Ella?" his mother asked, breaking into his thoughts.

"Sorry, I was thinking about work." He refused to share his thoughts with anyone.

"She wants to know if you'll be calling about the dance lessons this week."

He flicked the On switch on the coffeemaker. "I talked to Josie this morning."

"You called already?" Ella uttered. And then, as though she realized she'd vocalized her astonishment, her cheeks grew rosy.

"Yes, I did. She said that with the contest, her schedule is filling fast."

Ella's face creased with concern. "Is she able to squeeze us in?"

He nodded. "We talked it over, and knowing how important winning is to you, I went ahead and scheduled us for three lessons."

"So that's what? One per week?"

He chuckled. "No, we decided if you and I are to be competitive, we'll need at least three dance lessons per week."

"What?" Her eyes opened wide. "Do you really think we need all of those lessons?"

Hadn't she been the one who was all gung ho about making sure he could dance so they'd win? Why was she suddenly being so hesitant?

"You do want to make sure we'll win, right?"

"Oh, yes. Definitely." Her gaze lowered. "It's just that I...I didn't think you'd be so dedicated."

"Tony takes all of his obligations seriously." Carlota reached for a cookie. "If he says he'll do something, you can count on him."

He frowned at his mother, hating when she bragged about him. "The lessons are Mondays, Wednesdays, and Fridays at five-thirty. If that doesn't work for you, I can try to work out something else."

"That'll be fine. If it's okay with you, I'll talk to Johnny's teacher and see where he is with his classes. I was hoping to tutor him on Mondays, Wednesdays, and Fridays after school. We can adjust the time if needed, you know, because of the dance lessons."

Tony gave her a pointed look. "Are you sure you're up for doing both on the same days?"

She took a moment to consider it. "Actually, it should work out perfectly. This way I won't have to wait around after school for the lessons."

Tony nodded. A calmness settled over him, as if everything was going to work out for all of them. "Then I'll see you later. Our first lesson is today at five-thirty sharp."

Chapter Six

THIS WAS ALL GOING to work out.

It had to.

Tony eased his pickup around the corner and past the front of the library. He immediately noticed Ella standing in the shade just outside the door. He supposed he could have pulled into the no-parking zone, but he drove past the small stucco building with a sign—Whistle Stop Public Library—in the middle of the small well-kept yard. He wanted to park and walk Johnny to his first lesson. It had nothing to do with seeing Ella again. He assured himself that it was the action of a good parent—something he longed to be.

"This is stupid," Johnny complained for the umpteenth time. "I don't need a tutor."

After running out of platitudes and encouraging speeches, Tony decided it was time for brutal honesty. "If you don't do this, they'll most likely keep you in third grade next year while your friends move on to fourth grade. You wouldn't like that, would you?"

The boy's head lowered as he shook it. Satisfied Johnny understood how important these lessons were to him, Tony didn't bring up how Johnny's declining grades could also severely impact the possibility of

Tony adopting him. The boy was already dealing with enough. He didn't need to feel insecure about his home, too.

"Come on." Tony reached for the door handle. "Let's not keep Miss Morgan waiting any longer."

Without a word, Johnny climbed out of the truck, slammed the door closed, and headed for the sidewalk. Tony took a moment to gather the study materials that he'd been using to help Johnny, not that he'd had much success. Still, he wanted Ella to know that he'd really tried to be there for his nephew, like he imagined a real dad would be. He didn't want her assuming he was too busy to be bothered. He'd made the time. He just didn't know how to reach his nephew.

With the texts and study guides tucked under his arm, he rushed to the sidewalk only to find Johnny already talking to Ella. From this distance, Tony couldn't hear what was being said, but he watched as her pink lips lifted into a smile that lit up her eyes. A ball of jealousy pinged in his chest. He found himself longing to be the person to put her at ease instead of making her stiff and nervous, like she'd been in his mother's kitchen.

When he joined them, he found Johnny withdrawing into the shell that he wore like armor. Tony had been hoping Ella could charm the boy into accepting that these lessons were important. As it was, Tony expected another visit from the court investigator any day now, and when the woman showed up, he wanted to reassure her that he had adequately handled Johnny's declining grades.

"Hello, Miss Morgan." Tony chose to use her formal name, not only for Johnny's sake but also because it felt good to put a little distance between them with their dance lesson less than a couple of hours away.

"Hi." She flashed him the remnants of the smile she'd shared with Johnny. Her gaze slid to the stack of books he carried. "Are you returning all of those to the library?"

Tony cleared his throat and held out the books to her. "Actually, they are for you. They're the books I borrowed from the school and some workbooks I bought to help Johnny. I marked where we left off."

Her pencil-thin brows rose as she reached out to take them. Their fingers brushed, sending a tingly sensation up his arm. Boy, if this was the way his body reacted every time they touched, he'd never make it through their dance lesson.

Get a grip. She's just Johnny's tutor. She's not right for a one-night-stand. Definitely not.

And he couldn't—wouldn't—start something more.

"These will be a great help. Thank you." Turning to Johnny, she said, "Shall we go inside? I have a spot reserved where you and I can go over the material your uncle gave me."

Johnny shrugged. "I guess."

He wasn't exuberant, Tony mused, but then again the boy hadn't outright refused Ella's offer. That was a start. Johnny might keep a tough shell around himself most times, but Tony knew firsthand how sweet his nephew could be, if given the chance. Now if only Ella had the patience to get past the boy's defenses.

Ella and Johnny had started into the building when Tony called out, "His grandmother will pick him up at a quarter after five so you'll have plenty of time to get to the dance lesson."

Ella's face creased with worry lines before she nodded. So he wasn't the only one having reservations about their lesson. Was she worried about his capabilities? Or was her concern far more personal?

Less than five minutes in Tony's presence, and he'd totally unnerved her.

Ella mentally chastised herself. She had to do better—for all of their sakes.

She turned her full attention to Johnny as he sat at one of the library's large tables, looking utterly bored. "From the size of this stack of books, it looks like you and your uncle have been working hard."

The boy shrugged his thin shoulders. She needed the boy to interact with her if they were going to make any progress. Tony might think the distance between her and Johnny was beneficial to this venture, but she disagreed. She needed Johnny to relax so he could absorb the information they were about to cover.

"I hear you're having most of your problems in math. Is that right?" she asked, still trying to break the ice.

Again, the boy's shoulders rose and fell. "Why do you care?" Johnny mumbled, then his face pinched with anger. "You want to take away my puppy."

She wished Tony had never considered her giving the puppy a home. "Johnny, I do care about you. As for the puppy, I didn't say I would take him."

The boy slanted her a suspicious look. "But Uncle Tony said he thought you'd change your mind."

"He did?" This was news to her.

The boy nodded.

"Well, he's mistaken."

Johnny's eyebrows lifted as his skeptical gaze met hers. "Really?"

She nodded. Not letting the dialogue lapse, she said, "I hear you're very smart. Your mom must have been so proud of your good grades."

Johnny's face filled with a startled expression. "You knew her?"

"No. But from what I've heard, she loved you very much, and she wanted you to do well in school." Ella didn't know this for a fact, but she couldn't imagine a mother who wouldn't want the best for their child. "Don't you think?"

He gave her a small smile before nodding.

Happiness welled up in Ella that he'd finally smiled, which was a good sign that he would eventually open up to her. "How about we start with math?"

Ella grabbed the workbook Tony had given her and flipped through it. She noticed the strong, sure writing, obviously Tony's, and some shaky numbers, which must be Johnny's. What bothered her was that most of the writing was Tony's. Instead of making Johnny work his way through the problems himself, it appeared that Tony had intervened far too often. He was obviously full of good intentions, but not good at sitting back and letting the boy use what he'd learned.

"My mom used to help me with math. Every night. Then she'd give me Oreos and milk before I went to bed... I...I miss her..."

The little boy's whispered confession tore at Ella's heart. No child should lose a parent. "I'm so sorry that she's not here. But I'm sure she's watching over you and wanting you to do well in school. You wouldn't want to let her down, would you?"

He shook his dark head.

The remainder of the session flew by. In fact, it went so well that they ran a little late. After Johnny's grandmother picked him up, Ella grabbed her belongings and rushed for the door. She hated to be late for anything, but second thoughts about agreeing to be Tony's partner had slowed her pace.

By the time she stepped foot on the asphalt of the small parking lot, she was leaning toward calling Tony and telling him that she just wasn't up for dancing that night. After all, the kids had kept her on her toes all day. And then there had been her somewhat stressful session with Johnny. Who would blame her for taking the rest of the evening off?

Yet as she searched her purse for her phone, her fingers brushed against the latest estimate she'd received for a new roof. She pulled out the yellow sheet of paper and unfolded it. The price included the cost of new windows, which she hadn't realized were in dire need of replacement. Her chest tightened as she thought about the rate at which the repairs were accumulating. And these were just the ones she knew about. How many more would be uncovered?

She couldn't back out of the dance lessons, no matter how tempting the notion. The prize money was her only hope to pay the taxes and repair the cabin.

Once behind the steering wheel, she reached forward to start the engine and noticed her wrists. Blotchy skin sneaked out from beneath the long sleeves of her blouse. The sight of the web-like scars made her inwardly cringe.

She reached inside her purse and pulled out a tube of makeup. With a twist, she removed the cap and gingerly applied a dab of concealer to each wrist where the marks were obvious. She didn't stop until she had significantly camouflaged the scar tissue. Satisfied that she'd done her best, she put the car in gear.

When she turned the corner near the dance studio, she spotted Tony already waiting. He was propped against the tailgate of his pickup. His black T-shirt hugged his muscular chest and broad shoulders. The temperature inside her car rose dramatically, and her mouth grew dry.

This is a very bad idea. But it's too late to back out now.

Where is she?

Tony checked his wristwatch for the fifth time. Maybe Ella had changed her mind. He grabbed his cell phone. No missed calls. And no new messages. The hum of an approaching vehicle caused him to glance up. Spotting Ella in the driver's seat, he drew an easy breath. He slipped the phone back into his pocket. When her car slipped into a spot across the street, he strode over.

He opened her door for her. "You showed up."

She shot him a guilty look. "Sorry I'm late. Johnny and I were on a roll."

"Seems I'm not the only one who loses track of time. So it went well?" he asked as they made their way to the sidewalk.

She stopped and turned to him, lifting her dimpled chin to look up at him. "It took a bit for him to relax and realize I wasn't the enemy."

"Why would he think you're the enemy?"

She pressed a hand to her hip. "It would appear you told him that I'm taking his puppy."

"I did not. I—" Tony stopped his defense as a memory came to him. He shook his head, realizing where Johnny might have gotten that idea.

"What?" Ella sent him an expectant look.

"He must have overheard me talking with my mother."

"And you were telling her that I would change my mind about adopting the puppy?"

He shrugged, feeling like a student who'd been caught talking during a test. "I said I hoped you would change your mind."

"Okay."

"Okay?" He was confused. "Okay, what?"

"You explained. I understand. Let's move on."

So the little lady could be reasonable. He liked that about her. In fact, if he was honest with himself, there was a lot he liked about her. Beauty and spunk, quite an attractive combo.

"Come on." She started across the street. "I have a contest to win."

He rushed to catch up to her. "You mean *we* have a contest to win. But don't worry, with me having the prettiest partner, the judges will be so distracted we're bound to take first place."

She paused and glanced at him. Surprise danced in her eyes as color flared in her cheeks. He'd never met a woman who could blush so easily. How could someone as gorgeous as her be so unaccustomed to flattery?

She hurried past him and entered the modest brick building where the soft twang of guitar strings accompanied a soft male voice singing about heartache. Oh, this wasn't a good way to start their six-week affair—um, arrangement.

The tip of his cowboy boot struck the doorframe, and he lurched forward. Thankfully, he quickly regained his balance, and Ella didn't indicate that she'd noticed his klutziness. Why did this teacher with her long-sleeved blouses and skirts unnerve him? Even when she'd blushed at a casual compliment, it gave him a strange sensation in the pit of his stomach.

"Hello, Tony." Josie, the dance instructor, smiled at them. "I still can't believe you arranged for dance lessons, but I'm glad you're up to the challenge."

Not thrilled with the idea of making a fool of himself on the dance floor, but needing to follow through with this plan, Tony kept his reservations to himself. "I'll do what it takes."

"Great." Josie crossed the room and turned off the stereo. Her petite figure still looked as fine today as it had when she'd danced on Broadway. He remembered as a boy how proud the town had been when she'd made it big in New York. When she'd gotten older, she'd returned to her hometown a star and started this dance studio.

"I've had this long-standing dream of becoming the next Fred Astaire." He forced a laugh that sounded hollow even to his own ears.

"I don't know if we have that much time." Josie smiled, letting him know she was joking. "Want to introduce me to your friend?"

He glanced at Ella. Her spine was straight and her hands were clenched. She looked as uncomfortable as he felt. "This is Ella Morgan. She's new to town."

Josie smiled and extended her hand. "I hope you're enjoying Whistle Stop."

"Very much." The women shook hands before Ella moved to the side to place her purse on one of the folding chairs lining the wall.

"Let's get started." Josie moved to the center of the dance floor. "You'll need to master three dances for the competition, but we'll start with some basic footwork first. Have either of you taken formal lessons?"

Tony shook his head. When he glance at Ella, he caught a gleam of confidence in his partner's eyes.

"Nothing formal," Ella said, "but I was president of our swing-dance club back in college." She went on to explain about the dance instructor who'd sponsored the group.

As Ella talked about her experience, his lips lifted. Seemed he'd lucked out and landed himself a ringer. Maybe this arrangement wouldn't be as bad as he'd originally imagined. His smile quickly faded upon realizing Ella would expect him to learn some intricate steps and learn them fast.

Josie walked over to the iPhone docked with a speaker and turned on some country music. "We'll start with the two-step. Then the western swing, which is the two-step with turns. Are either of you familiar with these dances?"

They both shook their heads.

"Not a problem." Josie twirled a wooden rod between her fingers. "Let's get started. Face each other. Ella, place your right hand in Tony's left."

*Her hand in yours...your other hand goes lower on her waist...*the words buzzed through Tony's brain. He stared into the eyes of his dance partner, determination showing in the arch of Ella's brow and the serious line of her mouth. When he didn't move to take her hand, her expression became that of a question mark. "Tony?"

His chest tightened. Damn. He'd never taken part in any high school dances for a reason—lack of interest. As an adult, he'd made a point of avoiding the live bands on Friday nights at Cactus Mike's Saloon. He certainly didn't belong here in this dance studio. What kept him from turning and walking out the door was Johnny—his only reason for being here.

Ella shifted her weight while frustration knitted her brows. "Are we going to dance? Or stand here?"

Tony's palms began to sweat. Not wanting Ella to notice, he quickly swiped them over his jeans. Ella placed her cold fingers in his grasp. He had to fight off the urge to rub them until they warmed. She might put on a calm and collected front, but obviously he wasn't the only one experiencing a case of the jitters. Time to put his best foot forward, so to speak, and hope he didn't trip her in the process.

"Place your other hand on his back," their instructor called out.

Ella lightly touched him, sending a prickle of eagerness over his skin. He tamped down his fervor and fought back the urge to pull her closer.

"A little higher. That's good. Tony, you'll start by stepping forward with your left foot. Ella, you'll step back with your right."

A whiff of her citrus shampoo teased his senses. Yet, when Ella's petite form brushed against him, his whole body tensed, forcing him to stifle a frustrated moan. How in the world was he supposed to concentrate on where his feet went when his mind remained centered on the lovely woman in his arms?

"Not quite right. Go back to your original positions." As they attempted to repeat the steps, Josie said, "Slow, slow, quick, quick."

Ella moved without hesitation, while he struggled to focus on his footwork. With her so close, his body grew alert and eager for more. When she repeatedly bumped against him, his calm exterior almost cracked, and he nearly came undone.

On edge and unsure of himself, he stepped forward instead of back and tripped her. Ella lost her balance. He yanked her body to his to keep her from falling. Chest to chest, he held on to her longer than necessary. When she looked up at him, her questioning gaze held his. An overwhelming desire to taste her lips pulsed through him. Under the spell of her luminous eyes, his head lowered as if on command.

Ella braced her hands against his chest and pushed. The sudden movement broke the spell. With his senses jolted back into control, he released her.

"I'm sorry," he mumbled, shocked he'd almost kissed her, and in front of Josie, too. What had he been thinking? Obviously, he hadn't been.

"It's okay," Ella said, but he couldn't tell if she was talking about his dancing flub or his lapse in judgment when he'd almost sampled her berry-red lips.

He rubbed the back of his neck. "This isn't working. I'm nothing but a total klutz."

Ella's mouth pressed into a firm line, giving her the look of a teacher who was about to lecture her student. "You aren't thinking about giving up and breaking our deal, are you?"

His jaw tightened. That's exactly what he wanted to do. How could this virtual stranger read him so clearly? He sure wasn't comfortable with her reading his thoughts. Up until now, quitting was never part of his vocabulary, but he didn't know if he was strong enough to resist his mounting attraction to her. Still, he had to try to do his best.

"Of course not," he said, wanting to prove he wasn't so predictable. "Let's try this again."

Josie paused the music. "You'd be surprised how many people watch dancing on TV and think it's so easy. They don't have a clue how much work goes into the choreography and the rehearsals. Now, are you two ready to try again?"

They gave the dance steps another whirl. When he stepped on Ella's toes once more, she didn't complain. He didn't know if he'd have as much patience as she had.

Josie shook her head. "Where's the chemistry? The excitement? You two should glide together and enjoy yourselves."

Tony wanted to groan, but instead he maintained his silence. There was lots of chemistry going on—any more and they'd combust and light up the evening sky. But he had no intention of pursuing this reaction between them—yeah, right. He wasn't a good liar, even to himself. He was all too eager to pursue Miss Morgan, on and off the dance floor.

"Okay, let's start from the beginning," Josie said.

Tony's arms fell to his sides as he put a safe distance between Ella and himself. What had gotten into him? His life was complicated enough with the pending adoption. So why did he find himself drawn to her?

Until this fleeting physical desire faded, he'd have to be very careful around her. He didn't want to give her the wrong impression—that he was interested in her.

Even if his circumstances were different, attempting anything serious would be a waste of time. Nothing lasted forever.

Romantic love amounted to a bunch of sentimental words found on the inside of a greeting card. He wasn't about to get caught up in that delusion ever again.

Chapter Seven

THE SUN SLOWLY MELTED into the horizon, splashing the sky with a brilliant array of pinks and purples as Ella stepped onto the sidewalk. Her mind reeled with the ramifications of enjoying herself a little too much during the dance lesson.

Remembering the way Tony had gazed into her eyes and then at her lips made her heart race. Her palms grew moist as she recalled the intense moment. If she hadn't pushed away, would this confirmed bachelor have laid a soul-stirring kiss on her?

She chanced a glance at him as they strolled across the street. His head was lowered as he escorted her to her car. What was going through his mind? Was he recalling what had almost happened between them? Did he want to finish what they'd started earlier?

She gave herself a mental jerk. She was letting her imagination get the best of her. He wasn't interested in her. And that was fine. In fact, it was for the best. They'd already worked past their awkwardness on the dance floor. She needed to make sure it stayed that way.

"We weren't so bad near the end," Tony said, interrupting her thoughts. "Now if I could just stay off your toes."

"Don't worry. We'll figure it out."

They stopped next to her car, and at last his gaze met hers. "Thank you for putting up with my screw-ups and for convincing me not to give up when I got frustrated."

She'd encouraged him to push through the mistakes for his sake as much as her own. They both had a lot riding on this contest. In the future, she'd have to watch herself around him and not get distracted by the way his presence made her heart tap-dance in her chest.

"How'd it go with Johnny?" Tony opened her car door for her. "You know, after you got past the issue with the puppy?"

She considered her reply carefully, not wanting to get his hopes too high and yet not wanting him to think she wasn't the right person for the job, because she truly believed she could help Johnny. "For today being only our first session, I'd say things went pretty well. It's a step-by-step process that can't be rushed. He did show me some of what you went over with him. He seemed to have retained most of it."

"That's a good start." He hesitated. "Isn't it?"

"Yes. But we still have a lot of material to cover. Don't expect miracles right away."

"I won't. Thank you for agreeing to help." He sent her a smile.

Ella forced herself to remain casual, even though his smile made her insides quiver like gelatin. She wasn't sure what he was most pleased about, the fact Johnny grudgingly worked with her or that Johnny remembered some of what Tony had taught him.

"How's Patch?" she asked, trying to keep things light.

"Ornery. I'm still hoping to find him a good home, but time's running out. Johnny is getting more attached to him every day. And I can't afford to have the boy's heart broken again. I'll give it a couple more days to see if I get any local inquiries. By the end of the week, I'll have no choice but to advertise in the surrounding cities."

The thought saddened her. "But then Johnny will never see him again."

Tony's cell phone buzzed, followed by the loud shrill of the fire whistle. He cursed under his breath. "I'm sorry. I've got to go."

"Something wrong?"

"I'm a volunteer firefighter, and I need to respond to this call, but I'm supposed to pick up Johnny from rehearsal at the community center. His class is doing a special presentation before the dance contest. Normally, his grandmother would fill in, but she's conducting a meeting with one of the contest sponsors."

Ella felt for his predicament. Being a single parent could be a tough balancing act. "Can I help?"

He glanced at her. Anxiety creased his handsome face. "I don't want to bother you with this."

"I wouldn't have offered if it was a problem. I can pick Johnny up and wait with him until your mother returns."

"Okay. I'll call and let them know you're coming." He ran his finger over his phone and then, as though he'd just remembered that she was standing there, he glanced up. "Thank you. I'll pay you back."

So much for her decision to keep from getting more involved with this cowboy, but how could she turn and walk away, leaving him in the lurch when she had absolutely nothing waiting at home for her, other than more work?

"Be careful," she warned.

"I'll be fine." The alarm sounded again, spurring him into action. "Thanks. You're the best."

Minutes later, as she made her way toward the community center, the wail of sirens could be heard over her car engine. She glanced in her rearview mirror, catching sight of flashing red lights. A shiver of anxiety raced down her scarred arms as she pulled over, allowing the fire trucks to race past.

For the next hour, she distracted herself by listening to Johnny talk about his day while they fussed over the puppy, which grew cuter every time she saw him. When Carlota arrived home, Ella made a quick exit. As much as she wanted to stay, she couldn't let herself get too comfortable with them. This wasn't just any family—it was Tony's mother and nephew.

Ella headed straight home to a dark, quiet cabin. She ate a solitary meal of mac and cheese with a side of tuna. Nothing fancy, but it was a much-needed change from her recent diet of ramen noodles.

Tonight, the silence was deafening.

She turned on the radio. Usually that helped. But not tonight. She shouldn't have agreed to look after Johnny—it'd reminded her of what it was like to be part of a family. A sadness welled up in her at the thought of never having one of her own. But she didn't deserve one, not after causing the deaths of her mother and brother.

With a sigh and a shake of her head, she forced her attention on the unfinished class work. Hopefully, that would settle her uneasiness. If only she could concentrate...

A few hours later, she stretched her sore muscles. Perhaps sitting hunched over the kitchen counter to work hadn't been her wisest decision, but it could be added to the long list of other iffy decisions she'd made lately. Satisfied that she'd completed enough work for the night, she headed for bed. The morning would arrive much too soon.

The crisp mountain air sent her scrambling beneath the comforter. Exhaustion coursed through her muscles. Still, her mind wouldn't rest. She contemplated how the various sides of Tony's personality surprised her.

His stiffness and hesitation at the beginning of their dance lesson had eventually given way to him loosening up and laughing at his own mistakes. She liked a man who could laugh at himself. The more she got to know him, the more she liked him, which threatened to erode her resolve to keep him at arm's length.

What made her think Tony would be any different from the last man she'd let herself get close to?

Her ex, Randy, had been a gym teacher at the school where she'd been student teaching. Maybe she should have expected it, with him being into a healthy body image and weight lifting, but she'd been drawn in by his charm and their common love for educating children. Still, when he'd spied her imperfections, he'd withdrawn. The recollection of revulsion mingled with pity in his eyes still stung. She didn't want to ever go through that again.

Tugging her sleeves over her hands, she wrapped her arms around her extra pillow. A chilly breeze around the old windows sent her snuggling deeper beneath the comforter. She closed her eyes and forced them to stay closed. Finally, a restless sleep claimed her.

Wearing a sleeveless red and white evening gown, she smiled up at Tony. He held her securely in his arms as he guided her around the dance floor.

"You're so gorgeous," he said, his breath tickling the side of her neck.

They stopped dancing. Her gaze met his. Tony's line of vision drifted down to her mouth. Her heart thumped with excitement. Desire rushed through her veins. With his hands on her shoulders, he drew her closer. Her eyelids lowered as she leaned into him. His lips grazed h ers.

His hands slid down her arms, stopping when they reached the uneven scar tissue. He pulled back. His gaze lingered on her disfigurement. Disgust filled his eyes. Tears clogged her throat and blurred her vision.

"I have to go." He turned and strode off into the murky darkness.

She choked down her anguish. "Tony, wait! Come back!"

The sound of her own voice crying out in the night startled her. She shot up in bed. Her eyes blinked open, and she searched the shadows of the still-dark room. He was not here. She blinked. Through the fogginess of her mind, clarity descended upon her. She realized it had all been a horrible, dreadful nightmare. She took a calming breath and collapsed back against the pillows.

She glanced at her alarm clock, finding it was almost time for her to get up. She swung her legs out of bed. Her bare feet pressed to the wooden floor. The cold jarred her fully awake. At the bedroom doorway, the aroma of a fresh pot of coffee reached her. She didn't know how she'd ever survive without a programmable coffee maker.

She filled a mug full of the steamy brew. While she doctored it with milk and sweetener, her thoughts returned to Tony. Why was it impossible for her to keep her distance from him even in her sleep?

What she needed was a little company to keep her distracted. Instantly, the image of Patch came to mind. With an excited puppy to keep up with, she wouldn't have the time or energy to waste on dreaming about that sexy cowboy.

She slouched back on the couch and pulled the crazy quilt over her lap. She lifted the mug to her lips to savor her first sip of coffee. The dark-roast blend swirled through her mouth. Her eyes drifted closed as she moaned. There was nothing that could compare with the first sip.

When she opened them, her gaze landed on the mantel where a shabby, blue teddy bear sat next to her brother's baby picture. Bittersweet memories of her little brother dragging the bear through the yard filled her mind. Timmy would perch the stuffed animal on the back of his toy dump truck and drive it over the little dirt hills behind their trailer.

The recollection caused a knot of emotion to form in her throat. Timmy had always wanted a dog. He'd definitely approve of Patch. If only he would have lived...

Life fast-forwarded far too quickly.

Ella strode quickly through the small parking lot to the library Wednesday afternoon. Her feet barely touched the ground. A smile tugged at her lips. She'd just been notified that the next day she had an interview for a permanent teaching position at Whistle Stop Elementary.

She couldn't help but wonder if Carlota had put in a good word for her. Any help at this point would be so appreciated. Because every day that passed, she fell a little more in love—with the town. Though in her mind she saw Tony's handsome face. She gave herself a mental jerk. She really needed to focus on the possible and not the impossible.

And right now she had a very important task to focus on—Johnny's tutoring session. This would be their second meeting, and she hoped to make more progress in not only his studies but also in gaining his trust.

Afterward, it'd be time for her second dance lesson with his uncle. Her stomach filled with the sensation of a hundred fluttering butterflies. No. She wasn't going to worry about that now. She needed to give Johnny her full attention.

It didn't help that she was more nervous about this tutoring session with Johnny than she'd been for the first one. The more she got to know the boy, the more she wanted to help him. He'd already faced enough challenges in his young life. But another part of her wanted to ease the stress lines that marred Tony's face. If she could give Johnny the right guidance to turn his grades around, it'd certainly help all of the Grangers.

She'd just finished jotting a note in her day planner when Johnny walked in the door with his arms straining under a load of schoolbooks and his black backpack hanging from one shoulder.

"Wow. That's a huge stack of books." She jumped to her feet and moved to help him.

"Uncle Tony said to bring everything." Before she could reach for the books, the boy dropped his burden onto the wooden tabletop with a loud thump.

She glanced around, hoping to see Tony, but the doorway was empty. "Did you come by yourself?"

"Uncle Tony brought me."

"Where is he?"

"Gone. He had stuff to do."

Disappointment rained down on her, surprising her at how much she'd been anticipating their meeting. Definitely not a good sign.

"Why do you wanna help me? Is it 'cause Uncle Tony dumped me on you?"

Ella strained to keep the shock from her face. "He *didn't* dump you on me. He thought I could help you with your schoolwork." She pulled out a chair. "Come sit down."

Sadness pulled at the child's face as he sat down. "I don't think he likes having me around. He's always too busy or too tired to do much. Now he doesn't even want to study with me."

"Oh, Johnny, I can promise your uncle loves you very much. He asked me to help only because I'm a teacher and I might know of other ways to aid your education."

"My mom used to help me with my homework. Especially my math. She was really good."

"You must miss your parents a lot."

His head bobbed up and down. "They used to give me money for every A on my report card. Uncle Tony doesn't. I don't think he cares. I get in his way."

"That's not true. He loves you. I doubt your uncle knows about your parents' reward system, or he most likely would do the same. Your uncle still has things to learn, but he's trying. You could help him by telling him about what your parents used to do and what you'd like him to do, too."

Again Johnny shrugged. "Maybe."

"Let's see what we can accomplish before your uncle returns to pick you up."

Time passed quickly, and all too soon, Tony appeared at the doorway. While Johnny finished a math problem, she approached him.

"How's he doing?" Tony nodded to Johnny, his eyes filled with genuine concern.

"He's a very bright child, and I'm not saying that to be polite. I think part of the problem may be that he's bored."

Tony's shoulders straightened like a proud papa bear. "I've always thought he was bright. So what's up with the grades?"

She hesitated. She had to phrase this just right. She knew Tony didn't take well to criticism of his parenting skills.

"What is it?" His agitated voice boomed through the quiet library.

Johnny glanced up, as did the other library patrons.

"Shh...you'll get us in trouble," she reminded him.

He crossed his arms and frowned. "You still haven't said what you think the problem is with his learning."

"He's used to a different approach than you tried—the way his mother used to help him."

She quickly filled him in on what she'd learned from Johnny about his mother's tutoring techniques and her reward system.

Tony ran a hand over the back of his neck. "I had no idea."

"Try talking to him more. Get him to open up about his parents. It'd help both of you. You'd have a better idea about what he expects from you."

Tony took a step back. His eyes grew dark and unreadable. "I try my best."

She squeezed his arm. "I know you do."

"But it isn't enough. That's what you're thinking." He jerked away from her touch. "Johnny, we need to go. Now."

The boy slapped his schoolbook shut, grabbed his things, and headed for the door. "Bye, Miss Morgan."

"Bye, Johnny," she said as he rushed to follow his uncle. "Tony, will I see you at our lesson?"

There was a distinct hesitation, and then he nodded. "I have to drop Johnny off at home first. I might be a few minutes late."

"No problem."

He didn't say a word as he strode to the door.

He might show up at their dance lesson, but he wasn't happy about it. That much was abundantly clear.

Time had slowed to a crawl.

It was Friday afternoon, and school was out for the weekend. Ella should feel relaxed, but her nerves were taut. Her mind kept replaying the events of the prior evening.

She'd interviewed for the permanent teaching position at Whistle Stop Elementary beginning with the fall term. In the end, she thought she'd satisfactorily answered all of the school board's questions. The president said they'd notify her soon about their decision. Not wanting to jinx this prime opportunity, she decided not to mention the interview to anyone. If she landed this job, Whistle Stop would become her permanent home. Her home—she liked the sound of it.

There was a knock at her classroom door. Ella glanced up to find Melissa, the school's receptionist, who was quickly becoming a good friend. Dressed in navy slacks and a white blouse, she stepped inside the doorway. "How'd the day go?"

"It was fast."

"Aren't they all?" Melissa swiped her long brown ponytail over her shoulder. "The weekends are the worst. If you blink, they're over."

Her weekend would be anything but fast as she waited for the school board's decision. How long was "soon" anyhow?

Ella struggled to pay attention to what her friend was saying.

"What has you so quiet?" Melissa's eyes filled with worry.

"Nothing." Ella stacked a couple of workbooks she intended to take home in hopes of avoiding the loneliness that crept over her during the quiet evenings.

"I don't know you that well yet, but I know enough to sense when something's bothering you. Now out with it."

Ella knew that the interview had taken place only yesterday, but she was anxious for news. She thought it'd gone well, but she honestly didn't have a clue. And she had no idea how many applicants were vying for the position. She eyed up her friend, wanting to ask if she'd heard anything, but she didn't want to put Melissa in an awkward position.

"It's nothing." Ella was confronted with an I-don't-believe-you look. Maybe it would be good to talk to someone. "I'm just worried about the interview. I…I'm not sure how it went. I mean, I think it went well, but maybe I'm just seeing what I want to see—"

"Stop." Melissa waved her hands to get her attention. Then her friend sent her a reassuring smile, and her eyes twinkled as though she knew all of the answers. Melissa glanced over her shoulder at the open doorway, as though verifying they were indeed alone. "I really shouldn't say anything."

Anticipation sent Ella's stomach tumbling. "Say anything about what?" When Melissa pressed her lips into a firm line and shook her head, Ella prodded, "You can't just stop there. What do you know? Do you know who got the position?"

Please let it be me.

"Nothing has been decided yet." Melissa's voice lowered. "But I overheard them talking, and you've made the short list."

Ella squealed with joy.

"Shh…" Melissa glanced back at the door. "I don't want anyone to know I told you."

"Sorry." Ella gathered herself. "You don't know how much I've been hoping for this."

Melissa smiled. "I've got a pretty good idea."

"I just hope they decide soon. The anticipation is getting to me."

"I'm sure they will. Hang in there."

"Luckily, I have a number of distractions at the moment."

"That's right." Melissa's face lit up. "You have a lot going on. Seems you're putting down roots here in Whistle Stop. Have you considered adopting that puppy Tony has?"

The thought of the adorable furball tugged at Ella's heartstrings. And then it came to her what was missing at the cabin. She needed someone to share it with. There might be a lot of unknowns in her life, but she did know that giving a loving home to that sweet puppy was the right thing to do. Excitement fluttered in her chest.

She glanced at Melissa. "You know what? I'm going to adopt it. I'll tell Tony tonight at our dance lesson."

"Good. I'm so happy for you. I just know that things are going to work out for you." Melissa sent her a reassuring smile. "Speaking of your dance partner, has he stomped your toes lately?"

"Um...well, he's improving." Ella's face heated at the memory of being held so close to Tony.

"That good, huh?"

Her fear of losing her position at the school prompted her to ask, "Do you think people will take issue with me being so close to the parent of a potential student, you know, for the dance competition?"

Melissa's eyes grew round. "Is there something they should be concerned about?"

"No. Definitely not," Ella said a little too quickly. "I just want the permanent teaching job, and a small-town scandal could ruin that."

Her friend's expression grew serious. "I don't think so. As long as you don't give Johnny preferential treatment, and since he isn't in your class, you have nothing to worry about. If you and Tony were to get together, people would be happy—for both of you. In fact, his mother would probably throw a party. From what I hear, she's anxious for him to settle down."

"But we're not—together, that is. We're dance partners. That's all."

"Uh-huh. You keep telling yourself that. But I see how your face lights up when you talk about him."

Her face lit up? Ugh. It's a good thing she'd never tried her hand at poker. Sure, Tony was cute—er...drop-dead gorgeous was more like it. But she had restraint. She could resist his dimpled smile and dark eyes.

But for how long?

Chapter Eight

Tony had his hands full late Friday afternoon, not only filling in for a sick ranch hand, but also trying in vain to keep Johnny from getting more attached to the puppy. It was time the ad went in the Albuquerque and Las Cruces's papers. Hopefully there'd be a quick response. Putting it off was just going to make it worse for everyone. He'd take care of it first thing in the morning, before Johnny got out of bed.

And if that wasn't bad enough, he had to endure another dance lesson. Ella's comments about him not knowing his nephew well enough niggled at him. She didn't come straight out and blame him for the boy's dismal grades, but Tony knew it was his fault. He just didn't know how to do this parenting thing. For a man used to having the answers when it came to ranching or fighting fires, he found not knowing the correct course of action with Johnny quite unnerving.

Still, he'd given his word to see this contest through to the end, and that's what he'd do. He pulled up in front of the studio right on time. Ella stood on the sidewalk, waiting for him. He found himself staring at her, drawn in by her radiant smile and temporarily forgetting about his shortcomings as a parent.

Was it the anticipation of dancing with him that had her in such high spirits?

The thought drastically lightened his mood. He exited the truck, finding his steps lighter. She rushed forward. Her eyes twinkled. He fought the overwhelming urge to reach out and draw her near.

"Hi. I was waiting for you." A happy lilt filled her voice.

This time he was the one to smile. "Looking forward to our lesson?"

"No...I mean, uh, I have something to discuss with you."

Her words washed over him like a bucket of cold water. He should have known better than to let himself jump to conclusions. So if she wasn't looking forward to being held in his arms for the next hour, why did she look as excited as Johnny did on Christmas morning? Had she found herself another partner? His body tensed. Was she about to dump him for someone with more experience?

Frustrated with himself, he strode to the studio door and yanked it open. "Josie's waiting. We can talk later."

"Uh, sure." She entered the building, and he followed, determined to concentrate on the dance steps, and not on Ella.

Josie stood next to the speaker dock, waiting for them. "Right on time. Let's get started where we left off last time. We were about to try some salsa dancing."

Tony held back a groan. He'd gathered that the salsa was a sexy dance with lots of bumping and grinding. He glanced in Ella's direction. Her pastel skirt hugged her rounded hips—hips that would be rubbing up against him. His body thrummed with heated anticipation. He turned away, trying to think of anything but her shapely body.

"Tony, face Ella," Josie instructed.

He did as she instructed, but he made sure his gaze skimmed over the top of Ella's blond hair. One glance at her lush lips, and his good intentions would go up in flames.

"Now take Ella's right hand with your left."

He hesitated. A variety of conflicting emotions raged in his gut. He could do this. He had no choice. If he backed out of the dance contest, Ella might not continue to tutor Johnny, and if Johnny's grades didn't improve, then the court investigator would consider him an inadequate parent.

"Ella, place your left hand on Tony's shoulder."

She didn't move for a moment, but then she cautiously reached for him. Her touch was so light that he had to glance over to make sure her slender fingers rested against his shoulder.

"Ella, move your hand a little higher," Josie instructed, interrupting his wayward thoughts. "Good. Now, Tony, hold her other hand.

He glanced down at Ella's outstretched hand, noticing bandages on a couple of her fingers as well as a red angry blister on her palm. He gently wrapped his hand around hers, trying to avoid the irritation. He'd be willing to bet if he checked her other hand that it'd have similar abrasions. She must have started clearing the yard around the cabin. He wished that she'd get some help.

But he didn't have time to contemplate her plight any further as Josie continued with her instructions. "Both of you look into each other's eyes. Move closer together, you two. This is a romantic, sexy dance. Act like you're attracted to each other."

Tony didn't have to act. Ella was the first woman who'd tempted him to throw caution aside and enjoy himself without thoughts of the consequences.

Their bodies moved together as the Latin melody played in the background. He continued to hold her gaze, and he'd swear desire reflected in her eyes. He didn't know until that moment how much he wanted her to look at him that way. He longed to be responsible for this prim and proper teacher letting her hair down and getting a little rowdy. When she blinked and looked away, he strained to lasso his meandering imagination.

Stay focused.

Concentrate on the dance steps.

They tried the dance again, but he stepped forward instead of back and nearly tripped her. This wasn't working. He couldn't think when she was standing this close to him, with her fresh citrus scent teasing his nose, making him long to nuzzle up to her to get another whiff.

He released Ella and stepped back. "How about we go over the two-step again? I was just getting the moves down pat. One more try, and I should have it."

He failed to mention that the other dance allowed for some space between them—a chance for his brain to function. He'd speak to Josie later and request a less sensual dance be substituted for the salsa. He'd blame it on his lack of talent, not his growing desire for Ella.

When they finally called it quits, Ella led the way out the door. She paused on the sidewalk and turned to him. "We're getting a little better, don't you think?"

He knew most of the mistakes were his fault. "Yea. We're getting there. I should be going."

"I wanted to talk for a couple of minutes. I won't take much of your time."

He straightened to his full height, ready for the dreaded letdown. She'd found another dance partner. He was certain a lot of guys would jump at the idea of wrapping their arms around her delicate waist. He mentally kicked himself for not staying more focused during their lesson, for giving her yet one more reason to end their partnership.

"Listen, I'm sorry we didn't make more progress today," he said, trying to head off her rejection. "I had problems keeping my mind on the lesson. I've got a lot on my plate with Johnny and the puppy."

"That's what I want to discuss with you."

He paused and looked at her. She wasn't trying to let him down gently? The tight muscles in his neck loosened. "Did you find someone to take the puppy?"

"As a matter of fact, I did." She grinned up at him. "Me."

Suddenly, the idea of her taking the puppy didn't seem like the best option. Johnny was slowly opening up to Ella. In fact, the boy didn't even put up much of a fuss about their tutoring sessions anymore. If she were to take the puppy now, after Johnny had already formed an attachment, would the boy be willing to study with her? Tony seriously doubted it.

"Are you sure about this?" Tony asked, thinking of a way to talk her out of it. "You haven't had much time to think it over. Puppies are a big responsibility."

Her brows scrunched together. "Are you trying to talk me out of this?"

"No." Liar. The truth was, he'd much rather see the puppy go to her than a total stranger, but he couldn't help thinking how Johnny would take it. "I…I just don't want you to feel pressured to take the puppy."

"If you've changed your mind and decided to let Johnny keep Patch, just let me know. I'd be very happy for them both."

Tony shook his head. "As long as we're living with my mother, a dog isn't an option. She has asthma, and she's allergic to dogs."

"Oh, I didn't know."

"I'm planning to build a house, but I've had a lot on my hands lately."

"I understand. So you're okay with me taking the dog."

He hesitated. Either way, Johnny was going to take this hard. And Patch would be much better off with Ella. Reluctantly, Tony nodded. "But we should do it this evening. Every day that passes, Johnny gets more attached to the little guy. Last night, Johnny snuck the puppy into the house. He claimed the puppy was cold out in the barn. In the end, my mother had a scary asthma attack."

"Oh my. Is she okay?"

Tony nodded. "But I can't let that happen again." He really hated to separate the puppy and Johnny but he didn't know what else to do at this point. "You can follow me to the ranch."

Her eyes widened. "I don't know. I'm not ready to take him home today—"

"Don't worry. I've got everything you'll need for the night." Now that the decision had been made, he didn't want any delays.

"Oh. Okay. If you're sure you don't want to talk to Johnny first."

Nothing he said was going to make this any easier for the boy. Tony's gut knotted. "I'll take care of him."

The drive to the ranch took only a few minutes. They parked next to the barn, and Tony led her inside. Neither of them talked. He was thankful that Ella was respectful of just how hard this transition would be for Johnny.

The boy strolled out of the tack room, wearing a baseball uniform. He clutched the puppy to his chest. He glanced up, noticing her. "Hi, Miss Morgan. Did you come to see Patch?"

She nodded before turning a pleading look to Tony.

Guilt over separating the boy and his puppy ate at him. He swallowed the lump in his throat. "I have some good news," he said, trying to give this situation a positive spin. "Patch won't have to go to a stranger."

Johnny's eyes rounded with a gleam of excitement. "I can keep Patch?"

Not the reaction he'd been striving for. "No. But I found a local home for him."

His nephew's brow creased, and his bottom lip puckered. "You can't give him away. I love him."

"I know. I'm sorry." He approached the boy, but Johnny backed away. "I tried to tell you not to get too attached, but at least you'll know the puppy is safe with Ella...er, Miss Morgan."

Johnny glanced over Tony's shoulder at Ella. A tear tracked down the boy's face. "You can't have him! I won't let you!"

Tony wanted to do anything to make this moment easier for the boy. "Johnny—"

"No!" Johnny's eyes grew shiny. "I won't give him up!"

"How about if we set up a playdate?" Ella suggested.

Tony spun around. What was she saying? A clean cut would be best for the boy. Get it over with once and for all. “Don’t you think we should talk this over?”

“What do you say?” Ella looked directly at Johnny.

“I…I don’t know.” The boy nuzzled the squirming puppy.

Tony still didn’t like the idea of a playdate, but if it would make the transition easier for Johnny, who was he to complain? Tony grabbed a red leash and attached it to the dog’s collar. “Hand Patch over to Miss Morgan.”

Johnny’s red face turned up to him as a tear splashed on his cheek. “No. I’m not giving him up.”

Oh, crap. I’m handling this so badly. What do I do now?

As though sensing his complete loss at what to say or do next, Ella stepped up to the boy. “You can come see him any time.” The boy continued to tightly hold the squirming pup as Ella knelt down in front of him. “Isn’t it better that he goes with someone you know and like than to a stranger?”

Johnny shrugged. His gaze remained focused on the pup.

Then something crossed his mind that might persuade Johnny to give Ella the puppy. “And you don’t want Grandma to have another attack like last night, do you?”

Johnny glanced up at him and shook his head. Tony knew that last night’s episode had scared all of them. Not that this scene was any easier to deal with. Tears streamed down Johnny’s face and Tony hated what he had to do.

“I promise to love Patch just as much as you do,” Ella added.

Tony reached out, taking the puppy in his arms.

"I hate you!" Johnny ran out of the barn.

A fist in the kidney would've hurt less than Johnny's pain-filled words. Tony struggled to take in a breath. Johnny had never said those words to him before. They totally caught him off guard and left a painful bruise.

Tony ran a thumb over the puppy's side as he choked down his emotions. With the adoption hearing quickly approaching, things kept getting worse. This distance between him and Johnny was widening, and the only thing he knew to do was get rid of the source of the conflict. His gaze moved to the puppy. *Time to say good-bye*.

"Here." He held out the pooch. "I'll put his things in your car."

Before Tony could walk away, Ella spoke up. "Johnny didn't mean it. You know, about what he said before he left. He's just hurting and lashing out at the person closest to him. I could stay and talk to him if you think it'd help."

Why did she have to be so nice now? Couldn't she be that judgmental person he'd met last week? Where were the accusations that this was entirely his fault? If only she'd turn on him, he'd feel justified by what he had to say next.

"Maybe you should stay away for a while, until this blows over."

"But what about the tutoring?"

What about it? He ripped his hat from his head and raked his fingers through his hair. It didn't matter what he did now. He'd be doomed in Johnny's eyes.

"I don't know what we'll do about the tutoring sessions."

Ella's face noticeably paled. "You mean you might cancel them altogether?"

Chapter Nine

A week had passed, and Johnny still wasn't speaking to him. Tony had hoped that by now Johnny would have gotten past some of the anger, but so far they'd only progressed to nods and shrugs. Tony had apologized profusely. Still, Johnny said nothing.

Not that Tony let it deter him from escorting Johnny to his tutoring session. He realized the tutoring sessions were too important to be suspended. No matter what Johnny said—or, in this case, didn't say.

Why hadn't someone warned him that parenting was so difficult? The experience had given him a whole new respect for his own parents, who'd had to deal with the antics of two lively boys. How they'd managed was beyond his understanding.

Carlota agreed to pick up Johnny from the library so that Tony could get to the dance lesson on time. His friendship with Ella was a bit strained under the circumstances. He appreciated everything she'd done to help him out with the puppy, but he just couldn't forgive himself for making Johnny miserable.

Maybe if he concentrated real hard on the dance lesson, he'd be able to forget just for a little bit about the problems waiting for him at home. He hoped.

Josie moved toward the stereo system. "Let's get started. Take your positions for the two-step."

When Tony didn't move, Ella reached for his hand. Her skin felt smooth and soft, like satin. Her pale, slender fingers with pink nails curled around his hand, sending a jolt of awareness through him. His body longed to spend the next hour close to his exquisite dance partner. Yet, he tamped down his eagerness, knowing they had no future.

"What's the matter?" Ella asked, placing his hand on her waist. "Did you forget what we learned last time?"

Oh, he remembered their lesson. He remembered every agonizing moment of it. "Don't you worry about me. Just concern yourself with your own memory."

However, tonight, with Ella in his arms, he refused to get swept up in her floral scent. He refused to get distracted by the way her hips swayed. After all, he had a plan.

Concentrate on perfecting their routine. When the lesson was over, he could escape back to the peacefulness of the ranch before she could reestablish her spell over him. It would work if he stuck with the plan.

The music started to play in the background. Here they went.

"Okay. Left. Left." Josie clapped her hands in rhythm. "Right. Right."

When Ella leaned forward to glance down at their footwork, the scent of wildflowers caught his attention, and he found himself longing to pull her closer to breathe in more of the delicate perfume. His fingers itched to release her hair from its big, wooden barrette, to watch the blond curtain cascade down over her shoulders, to run the flaxen strands through his fingers.

No, he couldn't do this. He couldn't continue to torture himself with thoughts of a romance he refused to start. He couldn't put himself in the position of failing another person, like he did his whole family. He'd already made Johnny so unhappy with his parenting ineptitude.

Tony stopped dancing and stepped back.

Ella's eyes rounded with worry. "Did I step on your toes?"

"No, you didn't. I can't do this." He hoped she wouldn't ask questions he couldn't answer. "Josie, I'm sorry. I'll write you a check for the rest of the lessons."

"What are you talking about?" Ella gave him a puzzled stare.

"This whole thing is a mistake. No amount of practice is going to change the fact that I can't dance. I don't want to waste everyone's time."

Before Josie could speak, Ella grabbed his hand and headed for the door. "I want to talk to you outside." She turned to Josie. "We'll be right back."

Once they reached the sidewalk, she turned to him. "What was that all about?"

"Don't sound so upset. You were the one who didn't want us to be partners in the first place. You were right. I'm not a dancer. I'm a cowboy."

Ella frowned at him. "And that's it. You're just going to let everyone down."

"Don't worry. I'll explain it to my mother. I'll tell her that I have two left feet."

Ella crossed her arms as frown lines etched deeper into her fair complexion. "You can stop your pity party, or whatever has you acting like this. You're not walking out on me and these lessons." She poked a finger into his chest. "We both have obligations to fulfill, and you're not about to force me to let people down—people who are counting on me."

"Who's counting on you?"

"Your mother, for one. Johnny, for another. Did you see his math test this week?"

Tony nodded. "His grades are starting to come up."

"And I'm not about to quit on him. You made an agreement with me, and I expect you to hold up your end of it."

Her change of attitude surprised him. In any other situation, he might have taken her insistence on continuing their lessons as an admission of her interest in him, but he knew better. She was just doing what she had to do to help Johnny and to keep a roof over her head.

Tony shifted his weight from one foot to the other. "What if I could find you another partner?"

A light shone in her eyes. The idea appealed to her, and suddenly he hated the idea. But that made no sense. He didn't want to be here. He didn't want to dance. So then why did the thought of her in another man's arms dig at him?

"Chief Granger," Ella said, her tone firm, as though he were one of her students. Hands on hips, she frowned at him. "You have an important fundraiser to consider, and the whole town is counting on the fire department to help raise funds to rebuild this town. So suck it up and get your dancing feet back in there. We have a dance to practice, and we're wasting time out here."

He'd never seen her so bold. He now understood how she kept a bunch of rowdy kids under control. His resolve cracked beneath her determined stare. She was right. The town was counting on this contest being a success, including his mother.

"Yes, ma'am." He moved to the studio door and pulled it open. "After you."

Her renewed determination and professionalism drove Tony to try his best to catch on to the moves. By the end of the lesson, they'd perfected their execution of the Texas two-step. In fact, Josie clapped when they finished. And Tony found himself resisting the urge to grin. He didn't want either of the women to know how much this accomplishment meant to him. If only he had the same success while dealing with Johnny.

"That wasn't so bad, now was it?" Ella asked.

He shook his head. At last, he was making real progress. "In fact, it was pretty good."

"I agree." Her words said one thing, but her expression said the opposite.

"Then why are you frowning?"

"It's not the dance. I was thinking of Johnny and Patch. I feel so bad about separating them. He's still not speaking to me, which makes the tutoring sessions a real challenge." She eyed Tony as though wanting to say something more, but hesitated.

"Okay, out with it," he said. "What's going through that mind of yours?"

"Remember how I promised Johnny he could play with the puppy every now and then?" When Tony nodded, she continued, "Would you consider bringing Johnny to my cabin this weekend so he can see that Patch is safe and happy?"

"I don't know." Tony paused. "I'm not so sure letting Johnny see the puppy again so soon will help. It's likely to bum him out even more."

"I had the same concerns, but after seeing him at tutoring, something needs to lift his spirits. If you have another suggestion of how to ease his misery, I'd like to hear it."

He'd already racked his brain trying to find some way to make this situation better for Johnny, but he'd failed to come up with anything viable. Her suggestion actually had some merit. "When did you want to do this?"

"Does tomorrow at noon work for you?"

Instead of putting distance between them, they were continually being thrown together, it seemed. Still, he had Johnny to consider, and his happiness was more important than the conflict Tony had with Ella.

"It's a date." Talk about a poor choice of words.

He followed Ella outside, where they ran into Cord, a firefighter and lifelong friend of Tony's. Cord was accompanied by his girlfriend, Alexis. "Hey, Cord. This is the last place I expected to find you."

"And I've got you to blame." The man poked Tony's chest.

"Me?" Tony feigned innocence. "I don't recall asking you to dance."

"Humph. You set an example, and now all the women think their men should turn into Fred Astaire."

Tony chuckled. "It's for a good cause, right?"

Cord rolled his eyes, causing Tony to laugh harder.

"Okay, enough laughter at my expense." Cord eyed Ella. "So are you going to introduce us to your friend?"

"Oh, yes." He glanced at her. "This is Ella Morgan. She's teaching at the elementary school. Ella, these are my friends Alexis and Cord."

"Oh, that's right," Alexis said. "I heard through the gossip mill you were taking over the position at the school for Mrs. Vega." Alexis smiled and extended her hand. "I'm Alexis Greer. I'm also new in town."

"Good to meet you." Ella shook the woman's hand. "But I'm only going to be at the school until summer break. Well, that is, unless I get hired on permanently."

"I have a feeling you'll have a long future in Whistle Stop." Alexis's gaze swung over to Tony. "This place has a way of drawing people in and making them feel at home."

Cord cleared his throat. "Nice to meet you, but I wish it was under different circumstances." His brow furrowed as he glanced up at Josie's studio. "Lexi laid down the law and said this was our chance to learn to dance like those stars on television. She thinks it might come in handy if I can ever convince her to make me respectable and take a stroll down the aisle with me."

Alexis's mouth gaped open before she elbowed him. They all broke out in laughter. Tony envied their easy playfulness. Not that he needed anyone like Alexis. He was just fine on his own. All he needed was his horse and the wide-open landscape.

"Apparently, Alexis likes to take chances with her toes." Tony smiled, thinking they truly did make the perfect couple—if there was such a thing.

"I always live on the edge with this guy." Alexis stuck her hand through the crook of Cord's arm. "After all, I traded in my business suits for him, didn't I?"

Cord eyed them. "So I hear you two are the competition to beat."

"Who? Us?" Tony couldn't believe that anyone would consider them competition. He glanced over at Ella. She was good. He was the one holding her back. Guilt gnawed at him.

The four of them stood there, talking about the dance contest, for a couple of minutes. Both women were excited about it. And both men were dreading getting all dressed up and dancing in front of the town.

"Well"—Cord checked his watch—"time to live dangerously. You two have a good evening."

Once they said good-bye, Ella unlocked her car door. "I'll see you tomorrow."

He paused and gazed into her eyes. He should say something to get her to stay—to have a late dinner with him. Instead, he heard himself say, "See you then."

Why did it feel like they were turning some sort of corner in their relationship? When they'd been talking with Cord and Alexis, it was like they belonged together. But how could that be?

He wasn't even sure what label to put on this thing between them. Then again, it was probably best not to analyze it too much. It'd only lead him into trouble, and that was something he'd had enough of for one lifetime.

Chapter Ten

PATCH'S INSISTENT BARK ACTED as Ella's fuzzy alarm clock the next morning. She stretched out an arm. Her hand ran over the empty pillow next to her. Her eyes fluttered open, and she was momentarily blinded by the brilliant sunshine streaming through the cabin windows. She blinked. She glanced around the room, finding herself all alone except for Patch. There was no sign of Tony. Then she realized he'd only been a dream—a very vivid dream. A frustrated sigh escaped her lips as she recalled the prior evening.

She could no longer deny it. She wanted to get close to him. After all, he was handsome and kind. And every time she saw him with his nephew, struggling to get the parent thing right, she fell for him a little more.

As a cool breeze rushed through the cracks in the roof, she ran her hands up the uneven skin of her forearms. The scars were a brutal reminder that she had to keep her distance from the sexy cowboy. Once men saw her unblemished face, they expected the rest of her to match. She couldn't stand the thought of Tony turning away from her.

A frustrated groan slipped past her lips. Why did it always come down to her physical imperfections? Was there a man out there willing to see beyond her body and care about who she was on the inside? Could Tony be that man?

These questions tumbled through her mind as she threw back the blanket in order to get on with her morning routine. She couldn't deny that she wanted someone special in her life—someone with whom to do things and share her innermost thoughts. Yet, when she'd thought she'd found Mr. Maybe, he'd turned out to be Mr. Shallow.

Once she'd showered and fed the puppy, who settled on the couch for a mid-morning nap, Ella glanced around the room. It was time to make this place homier.

She retrieved a moving box from the spare bedroom and used a kitchen knife to slice open the top. Opening the flap, she retrieved a tissue-paper-wrapped object from the top. Having no clue what it might be, she pulled back the paper to reveal a silver frame. She found herself staring at a picture of herself at the age of ten, sitting on the monkey bars next to her little brother. She recalled the sunny day with crystal clarity. Her mom had just been hired as a waitress, and they'd celebrated at a local park.

Ella's fingers traced her brother's grinning profile before she hugged the picture to her chest. The piercing sadness and guilt, which at one point had threatened to crush her with its enormity, had faded into a dull ache in her chest. She inhaled a deep breath before placing the frame in the center of the fireplace mantel. After unwrapping a few other pictures, she settled them around the special one of her brother. She made adjustments here and there, until at last they were just as she wanted them.

Ella settled on the couch next to Patch. She stroked her hand over his side, and he exhaled a loud sigh but didn't otherwise move. This place was definitely starting to feel like home. It just needed a little more TLC. A gust of wind rattled the windows, and the loose parts of the roof banged repeatedly.

Patch jumped up, startled.

"It's okay." Ella worked to calm him.

Okay, this place needs a lot of work.

After petting Patch for a couple of minutes, she bent over and placed a kiss atop his head. "Don't worry. I'll keep you safe. I promise."

Just then there was a knock at the door. Not expecting Tony until later, she rushed to the door, curious. A smile tugged at her lips when she spotted Tracey standing on the porch.

Ella swung the door wide open. "Good morning. What are you doing out and about?"

"Enjoying the mountain air and sunshine." Tracey made her way inside and over to one of the stools at the kitchen counter. "And what has you beaming so brightly today?"

"Who? Me?" She was beaming? Really?

"Yes, you. This is the happiest I've seen you since you moved back."

Ella shrugged. "Can't a girl just be in a good mood?"

Tracey sent her a knowing smile, but she let the subject drop. "I was thinking of grilling today. Would you like to come over for the afternoon?"

"I'd love to, but I can't." Ella bit back her next words.

"What are you up to?"

She didn't want Tracey making more of the situation than was necessary. "Getting ready for company. Johnny is coming over to play with Patch."

"Really?" Tracey's tone was definitely one of interest. "So Tony Granger is going to spend the day with you?"

"No, he isn't. He's only stopping by so his nephew can play with Patch." Ella wished her friend wouldn't make a big deal out of Tony's visit.

The Saturday morning rays peeked through the kitchen window and highlighted her friend's animated face. Ella wished she'd never mentioned the visit. Though Tracey had a good heart and meant no harm, Ella wasn't up for being needled about Tony, especially after her dream this morning.

"Are you *sure* that's they only reason he's coming over?"

"Even if I had some crazy fantasy about him, you're the one who told me that he's off-limits. A genuine confirmed bachelor, remember? And before you say anything, I'm not interested in hooking up with anyone, and that includes that sexy cowboy."

"Ah, so you admit it. You are attracted to him." Tracey grinned at her.

Ella busied herself by refilling her coffee mug rather than continuing the ridiculous conversation. "Can I get you something to drink? I'm afraid all I can offer is coffee or water."

"Water's good."

Ella filled a glass and placed it in front of her friend.

Tracey took a sip, then set the glass aside. "You know, you two would be perfect together."

Ella ignored the way her friend's suggestion created a warm spot in her chest. "How do you get that?"

"You have the same goals. Maybe I was wrong to steer you away from him. Perhaps he's exactly what you need to break you out of this shell you're hiding behind." Tracey took another sip of water.

"I'm not hiding."

No one would want her when they found out about her past. Her grandmother had tolerated her because there was no one else to take her in, but the woman never let her forget she was the reason her family was dead. The coffee sloshed in her stomach, making her nauseated. This door into her past had been slammed shut and nailed closed years ago. She wasn't going to open it again for some guy. She wasn't going to explain how she'd become disfigured.

"Tell yourself what you want," Tracey said, "but secluding yourself isn't the right answer for what's bothering you."

"I'm not secluded. I have Patch."

Tracey rolled her eyes. "The puppy's cute, but he's no replacement for a hot, sexy man."

Her friend was right, but Ella refused to encourage her in any way. "Tony and I are never going to happen. He made it crystal clear that he isn't interested in being more than dance partners."

"So you have thought about hooking up with him." Tracey's eyes lit up. "Maybe there's hope for you two after all. But you should know you'll have your work cut out if you want to break through his crusty shell. Ever since Jessie, he hasn't been in a serious relationship. Rumor has it he's waiting for her to come back. I don't know if I believe that, not after the way she walked out on him when he needed her the most."

The thought of Tony pining away for his ex-girlfriend had Ella gripping her coffee cup tighter. "I don't have any intention of threatening his bachelor status."

The phone rang, and she welcomed the interruption. When she heard Tony's tense voice on the other end, she grew concerned as she tried to follow his clipped dialogue.

Before the phone even hit the receiver, Tracey asked, "What's the matter?"

"It was Tony. He and Johnny aren't going to make it today."

"Why not?"

"There's some sort of emergency at the ranch. Someone's hurt."

Worry lines etched Tracey's olive-skinned face. Her arm wrapped protectively around her unborn child. "Did he say who?"

Ella shook her head. She knew Tracey was thinking of her husband, Mike, who was a ranch hand. She wished she could ease her friend's stress. "He didn't give me any details."

The line between Tracey's thin brows deepened. "I better go. I didn't tell Mike I was stopping over here. If he gets home and I'm not there, he'll worry." She got to her feet. "Did I tell you that ever since I told him I was pregnant, he makes a point of coming home for lunch every day?"

"That's so sweet."

"It'd be cute if he didn't coddle me quite so much. He's worse than a mother hen."

Tony's image came to mind. Something told her he wouldn't be a bachelor forever, and when his wife was pregnant that he'd dote on her, too. The thought of him settling down with another woman—with his ex—left a sour taste in her mouth.

Ella followed Tracey to the door. "Don't worry. Everything will be fine."

"I hope so."

Ella stood on the porch and waited until Tracey safely made her way to the road. With a final wave good-bye, Ella stepped inside and closed the door. There was work to be done.

She might as well get busy. There was more unpacking to do. She headed to the spare bedroom and lugged a heavy box to the living room. Patch woke up and barked. He did his best to assist her by trampling all of the discarded newspaper that had been used as packing material. While the puppy amused himself, she uncovered a picture of her grandparents at their fortieth-anniversary dinner. She carried it to the bookshelves and placed it in front of a complete set of Zane Grey novels her grandfather used to read in the evening out on the porch.

She returned to the box and removed a carved jewelry box. Lifting the lid, she stared at her grandmother's diamond engagement ring. When Gran had become bedridden, she'd handed the ring to Ella and insisted she keep the stunning piece of jewelry safe.

Until that point, Ella had never seen the ring before, let alone known her grandmother owned such a fancy piece of jewelry. Ella had grudgingly accepted the ring that had been handed down through the generations. But she didn't like what it represented—her grandmother giving up on her fight to beat cancer. Though she and her grandmother had endured a very rocky relationship, she loved her grandmother and had hated the thought of being all alone in this world.

Ella stared at the sparkling gem, and a crazy idea took shape. Could this be the answer she'd been looking for? Could Gran's ring provide the money she needed to make the necessary repairs to the cabin? But could Ella go back on her word to her grandmother to keep it in the family? Before stressing herself out about parting with the heirloom, she decided to get it appraised. At least then she'd know her options.

After returning the ring to the velvet-lined box, she stashed it at the bottom of her bedroom closet. Even in this safe community, she couldn't afford to take any chances. It was the only thing of value she owned.

A knock sent her rushing back to the living room. Patch barked and raced to the door. Strange. She wasn't expecting company, and her place was too far out of the way for a salesperson.

A glance out the little window didn't reveal anyone. A knock sounded again. Cautiously, she opened the door a crack and spotted Johnny. His dark hair was mussed with a couple of small pieces of straw mixed in. His jeans and T-shirt were rumpled, as though he'd been rolling around in the barn.

"Hi." She yanked the door wide open. "Johnny? Is everything all right?" She craned her neck to search for Tony, who was nowhere in sight.

"I came to play with Patch like we agreed."

She stepped out onto the porch to get a better view of the rutted driveway, but she found only her own little coupe. How in the world had Johnny gotten out here by himself?

Turning around, she noticed the boy had slipped past her and entered the cabin. He plunked down on the floor and started to pet the dog, who in turn climbed into the boy's lap and lathered him with kisses.

Johnny turned a grinning face to her. "He remembers me."

"Sure he does." She recalled her conversation with Tony. She was certain he hadn't said anything about dropping the boy off. "Johnny, where's your uncle?"

The boy didn't move except to continue to scratch under the puppy's chin.

"Johnny, look at me." She waited until he made direct eye contact. "Where's your uncle?"

His gaze slid to the floor as he continued petting the puppy. She'd never gain Johnny's full attention with the dog distracting him. She approached them and scooped Patch into her arms.

"Johnny, where is your uncle? He must be worried about you."

"He was too busy to come."

Johnny's acknowledgment confirmed her suspicion—the boy had run away. Worry, combined with anger, consumed her when she thought of the risks Johnny had taken getting to the mountain. Ella had an urge to make it abundantly clear the risk he'd taken, but at the same time she wanted to gather him in her arms and hug him, relieved that he was safe.

"Who's supposed to be watching you while your uncle is working?" When he didn't answer, she said, "Tell me."

"Doesn't matter." His face scrunched up, and his eyes darkened with anger. "None of them care about me, or they'd let me visit Patch."

Her heart swelled with sympathy for the boy, but that didn't mean he could do as he pleased. And right now she needed to notify someone of the boy's whereabouts.

"How did you get here?"

Johnny reluctantly explained how he'd been at the ranch and had overheard Tracey's husband mention he was going home to check on his wife, so Johnny hid in the back of the man's pickup.

"Do you know how dangerous that was to do?"

"I had to. No one would bring me to see Patch."

Words of warning and a stern lecture teetered on the tip of her tongue, but first she had to reassure Tony that Johnny was safe. He'd already dealt with one emergency. He didn't need to wonder what happened to a little boy on a sprawling ranch with a million different hazards.

"Sit on the couch." She handed over the squirming puppy. "And don't you dare think of leaving. Understand?"

He nodded.

She turned and headed for her bedroom to call Tony. This time, she hoped he would realize the boy needed more discipline than a few stern words.

Chapter Eleven

Fifteen minutes later, Tony's truck skidded to a stop in Ella's graveled driveway. A torrent of relief and anger consumed him as he marched up the worn path. His cowboy boots thudded against the handful of wooden steps leading to the covered wraparound porch. After his brief knock on the door, Ella appeared.

Words of greeting escaped him as he took in her casual appearance. Her face was makeup free. Her bouncy, blond locks were swept back in a ponytail instead of being twisted and pinned up in back. She wore a white long-sleeved T-shirt with a pair of denim shorts that showed off her slender legs. This relaxed, girl-next-door appearance suited her. His hands clenched as he stomped out his current train of thought. He needed to pick up Johnny and leave.

"Hi," she said, pulling the door open wide.

Her smile made his heart palpitate. Concentrate on Johnny, he told himself, dragging his gaze away from her pink lips.

He glanced around, searching for the boy. "Johnny, where are you?"

The boy stood at the other side of the couch holding Patch. "Here."

He immediately approached his nephew and wrapped his arms around the boy, careful not to squash the puppy.

After releasing him, Tony studied the boy. "You okay?"

Johnny nodded.

"Good. Now, I want some explanations. Starting with how did you get here?"

The boy's head hung low. "I hid in the back of Mike's truck."

Tony's chest clenched. Anything could have happened to him. Anxiety over the child's actions bubbled up. This matter couldn't wait until they got home.

"Don't you ever do something so dangerous again!" His words came quickly, and his voice rose as the control over his emotions unraveled. "Do you know what could have happened to you in the bed of the truck with no seat belt? If Mike had hit the brakes too hard, you'd have flown out and been severely injured or worse."

Johnny's face paled. The puppy squirmed out of his arms and escaped to the bedroom.

Tony could see only the ghastly images in his mind of his nephew lying in the roadway. He swallowed hard, fighting back his alarm. "From now on, you'll ask before going anywhere. Do you understand me?"

Johnny's dark head nodded. "I'm sorry."

"This better never happen again." His voice thundered, causing his nephew's eyes to widen. "Are you listening?"

"Ye...es, sir."

Ella cleared her throat. "Can I speak to you outside?" She pushed the screen door open.

Tony glowered at her, not wanting to be bothered until he drove home the severity of Johnny's actions. She didn't take the hint and instead nodded toward the door.

"I'll be right back," he told Johnny. "Go sit on the couch. And don't you dare even think of moving." Once the boy was seated, Tony strode outside to the porch. His gaze met Ella's worried look. "I'm sorry he involved you."

"I'm partly to blame."

"You are?"

She nodded. "I was the one who came up with the playdate idea. I knew how much Johnny wanted to see the puppy. I wanted to help. I never thought it'd lead to this."

"It's not your fault. It's mine."

Approaching the rail, Tony rested his palms against the weathered wood. His gaze moved over the wilderness, but none of it registered. In his mind's eye, he envisioned the fear that had been in Johnny's face when he'd yelled at him. Tony drew in a deep breath and exhaled. He was wrong to let his emotions get the best of him with Johnny, and now he grappled with what to do next. Maybe it wouldn't hurt to talk to Ella.

"I'm losing control of this whole situation," he said more to himself than her. "I'm failing him."

"No, you're not. Granted, you and Johnny still have adjustments to make, but you love him and you are there for him. You take him to his baseball games. You teach him about the animals on the ranch. You are setting a good example for him."

"Then why does it feel like I'm constantly losing ground?"

"Can I ask you something?"

What could it hurt? He nodded.

"How long ago did Johnny's parents die?"

The question made Tony pause. He searched his mind for today's date. He straightened and turned to her. "Last week was the one-year anniversary. In fact, it was on Friday."

Friday. The day he'd had to give up the puppy. Guilt bore down on Tony. How could he have let that monumental day slip by? He'd known the anniversary was coming, but no one in the family wanted to remember the tragic event, so they'd all buried it and not spoken of it, including his mother.

Ella reached out to him. Her hands wrapped over his and squeezed. Heat rushed up his arm and eased the pressure in his chest.

"See? It isn't you," she said soothingly. "Johnny is still grieving the loss of his parents. If you give him lots of love and structure, I'm sure he'll pull out of this. He's a good kid."

"What if the court finds out about this?" Tony blinked repeatedly. "I...I'll lose him."

"No, you won't." She pulled her hand away and moved it to her waist. "You need a game plan to get Johnny back on track. Do you have any idea how to do that?"

He shook his head.

Ella came to stand next to him by the rail. Her hand brushed against his, sparking a wave of awareness. He shoved aside his unwanted attraction. Right now his priority had to be his nephew.

"How did your dad discipline you?"

Tony rubbed the back of his neck as his thoughts spiraled back in time. "Brady and I were always pushing the boundaries and our father's patience.

When Dad caught us up to no good, he made us work on the ranch from morning till night. I still remember dragging myself to bed with aching muscles and painful blisters. I hated every minute of it."

"But you learned your lesson, didn't you?" When he nodded, she added, "Your father sounds like he was a wise man."

"He definitely was."

Memories of his father revived his guilt over his part in his brother and sister-in-law's deaths. His father had raised him to be responsible. Maybe if he'd paid more attention and not been so certain that he knew everything, Johnny's parents would still be alive.

He might not be able to change the past, but he could do his best to keep Johnny from following in his reckless footsteps. He'd teach Johnny to put family first and to see his obligations through no matter what. Tony's fingers started to ache. He glanced down to find he had a white-knuckle grip on the porch rail.

Ella touched his arm. "Tony, are you okay?"

He cleared his throat and pushed the painful memories to the back of his mind. "Uh, yeah. I'm fine." He moved his gaze to what loosely resembled a yard—a safe topic. "This place has seen better days."

"I'm working on it."

Realizing she'd taken his words the wrong way, he struggled to explain. "I just meant that you'll have to be careful, as it poses a fire hazard with all of the dried vegetation. Beneath the pinõn trees, the dried pine needles must be at least a foot or more deep."

Concern flickered in her eyes. "Before my grandmother died, she hadn't visited this place in years. Without my knowledge, Gran let the maintenance man go when money got tight. Yet she couldn't bring herself to sell the place."

Tony gestured at the unruly yard. "So this is the reason you've had blisters on your hands at dance practice?"

She nodded. "I started clearing the brush in the back of the house, but I haven't gotten very far."

He sympathized, but his first concern was protecting her. "You do know that red-flag warnings have already started to go up around the state. We've had a much drier winter than expected, and this year New Mexico is ripe for wildfires."

"Oh. I hadn't heard. I don't have television reception up here." Her face grew pale as she fidgeted with the hem of her T-shirt. "And with having just moved in, I haven't kept up with the news."

"Sorry. Warning people of fire risks is a side effect of being fire chief. In another life, I was a professional firefighter. That was before...before my brother died." He rushed on, not wanting to dwell on that last part. "I also help out at the forest service during wildfire season. It just takes a careless camper, a spark, or a lightning strike to start a blaze in this dry tinder." He glanced over at her, catching the fear in her eyes. He instinctively reached out to run his fingers over her now pale cheek. "I'm sorry. I didn't mean to scare you. I'm just rambling. Anything to keep from thinking about how I'm failing Johnny."

"You're not. He loves you. And I'm here any time you need to talk."

He suddenly didn't feel so alone. Sure, he had his mother to talk to, but with her health problems, he tried not to burden her with his concerns. It was nice to have Ella to talk honestly with. He hadn't realized how much he'd been keeping bottled up inside. There was something special about Ella, something that made him want to believe that happy endings were possible.

Their gazes locked, and the breath caught in his throat. As the tip of her tongue moistened her lips, a desire swelled within him to kiss her. His heart rate accelerated into the triple digits as he continued to stare at her inviting mouth.

The only thought he had at that moment was how much he wanted to press his lips to hers. His thumb moved underneath her chin and tilted her head. Surely her kiss couldn't be as good as he imagined. Nothing could be that good.

Perhaps a brief peck would be enough for him to realize he'd let his imagination exaggerate what her lips would feel like beneath his. One taste, and he'd know there wasn't any chemistry between them.

Anticipation coiled in his gut. He assured himself he was doing it to get her out of his system so that once again he'd be able to think clearly.

His gaze moved to her eyes. She didn't turn away. He lowered his head. His lips tentatively brushed hers. He detected her hesitation and hoped she wouldn't pull away. Not yet. He longed to deepen their kiss, to find the passion she kept under lock and key, hidden behind her conservative clothes.

He reached out to her, his hands naturally landing on her curved hips as he'd done so many times at dance practice. With a gentle pull, he drew her willing body to him. Her chest pressed flush against him. He ached to explore her—all of her.

Her soft, smooth lips moved beneath his, not the least bit resistant. She was like an intoxicating cocktail, and he was instantly addicted to her sweetness. Her touch turned him on more than his wildest fantasy. He longed for more of her.

She snuggled closer. The tip of her tongue slipped between his lips. He eagerly greeted her advance, and soon their tongues moved together in a timeless dance of passion.

Just a little longer, he told himself, and then he'd be able to pull away. Oh, who was he kidding? He never wanted their embrace to end. His desire ran unleashed as she responded to him. Her every touch heated the blood pulsating within him.

The more he tasted her, the more his body thrummed with need. A moan started to form in the back of his throat.

"Uncle Tony."

They jerked apart with the speed of two exploding firecrackers.

"I'm coming." Tony ran the back of his hand over his mouth. *Smooth move*. He glanced back at Ella. "Umm...I'm sorry. I shouldn't have done that."

"You're right, you shouldn't have." The gentleness of her tone belied the sincerity of her words. Her cheeks were a dusty pink and her lips a rosy red—utterly stunning. "We can't do that ever again."

The whole idea of kissing her had backfired. His gaze once more dipped to her lips. He wanted more. He craved more with every fiber of his being.

He gave himself a mental jerk. What was wrong with him? He couldn't follow up that steamy kiss with another one, even if he craved her with every fiber of his being. His jaw tightened. He had to focus on what mattered most, no matter how enticing he found her kisses.

He squared his shoulders. "Don't worry. It won't."

Now, hot and bothered, he walked away. He cleared his throat as he attempted to compose himself. With Johnny in a precarious emotional state, he needed to focus all his attention on his nephew.

Tony entered the cabin, pleased to find the boy hadn't moved. "What's the matter?"

Johnny gave him a sheepish look. "Can I get off the couch now? I want to play with Patch. Pleeease."

His nephew appeared to have recovered from the stern lecture he'd received. Kids were so resilient, especially Johnny. Otherwise, his nephew never would have been able to cope with the loss of his parents so soon in his young life.

"For a little bit. I need to finish speaking with Miss Morgan. I'll be right back." Tony returned to the porch, trying to figure out how to smooth things over with Ella.

"Is everything okay?" she asked.

Tony nodded, then decided to just deal with the situation head on. "I'm sorry about what just happened between us. I hope it won't change your mind about helping Johnny."

Her eyes grew serious when she said, "It won't."

"Thank you." He turned and stared out over the untidy yard. "How about I lend you a hand?"

"You mean with the land?"

He nodded. He'd intended only to pick up Johnny and hightail it home, and yet now he was proposing spending the day here. What was up with him? He had enough to do back at the ranch, but he didn't want to leave her—not yet.

She shook her head. "Thanks, but I don't need any help."

"But you can't do all this work by yourself. You'll need to clear at least a hundred feet of brush to create a safety zone around the cabin to protect it from a brush fire."

Her brow creased. "This is the first home I've ever owned, and I want to do it on my own. And I will."

The more he looked, the more he realized there was too much work here for one person. "I have to pay you back somehow for the tutoring sessions."

"You barely have enough time to run the ranch and be a father to Johnny. You can't take on caring for my place, too. As for paying me back, we already have a deal. You paid my entry fee for the dance contest and the lessons. They couldn't have been cheap."

"But that doesn't feel like enough."

"It's all I'll accept."

Even though he was thoroughly impressed with her independence, he knew she was being foolish. "Are you sure?"

She nodded. "Now we need to discuss another important subject."

He tensed. "What's that?"

"Did you eat lunch yet? I'm starved."

One by one each of his muscles relaxed, and he chuckled at her teasing. The idea of sharing a casual meal with her was a great temptation. Still, he had already been impulsive and kissed her. Common sense said he should decline the offer, but after she'd helped him deal with Johnny, he didn't want to be rude. Besides, she was an ideal tutor, and staying on her good side would definitely help if she bumped into the court investigator.

He could make all of the excuses he wanted, but the truth of the matter was he didn't want to leave.

It had nothing to do with being polite or hoping she'd impress the court. He was drawn to this woman. He wanted to know more about her, and explore some more of those kisses.

"As a matter of fact, I am hungry. Thank you." Needing a few minutes to clarify his thoughts, he added, "Do you mind if I have a quick look around? It's been a while since I've been here on Roca Mountain."

"Suit yourself." She opened the screen door and disappeared inside.

He liked the idea of sharing a casual meal with her. Since their initial encounter, he'd seen her tenacity when tackling their dance lessons and her patience when dealing with his nephew. This woman was full of surprises. He wondered what he'd learn about her next.

Tony strolled around the cabin, surveying the area and making a mental list of all the work that was needed to help protect the place from fire. Although he'd never admit it to Johnny, his stunt had alerted Tony to Ella's predicament.

Tony struggled in places to get through the overgrowth. He was surprised by the level of neglect. Clearing this dried vegetation would take Ella a long time by herself. And no matter what she thought, she'd never be able to get rid of the dead trees on her own. He wished she would let him help, but she was right, he honestly didn't have any spare time.

A few minutes later, he climbed the porch steps. The sound of Johnny chattering with Ella made him pause. It'd been too long since he'd heard his nephew in such a talkative mood. Not wanting to disrupt the growing rapport, Tony peered through the screen.

"Are those your kids?" Johnny asked, pointing to a framed photo in the middle of the mantel.

The long pause piqued Tony's curiosity. Ella had yet to talk much about her past. He moved to the side, out of sight, waiting for her response. He knew so little about her. Did she have a secret life? Children at home with an estranged husband?

"No. This is a picture of me and my little brother many years ago."

Tony expelled a pent-up breath.

"Ah, you're lucky. I always wanted a brother," Johnny said. "Where does he live?"

There was distinct pause. When Ella spoke again, her voice was raspy with emotion. "He died."

Tony leaned against the wall, digesting the information. Why hadn't he guessed she'd experienced a major loss? Thinking back to their first meeting, he realized her reaction had been too strong, too emotional, not to stem from personal experience with a premature death. He recalled the fear that had been reflected in her eyes—the emotion that was evident in her rushed words.

Questions buzzed through his brain. He ached to learn more about this woman with lips as velvety smooth as a rose petal, but he couldn't stroll in now and admit he'd been eavesdropping.

"What's with the dirty bear?" Johnny asked.

Tony moved to peer through the screen door once more. He spotted his nephew reaching for the stuffed animal resting next to the picture.

"Don't touch him!" Ella lunged forward to protect the bear.

The boy jumped. "I didn't."

Ella straightened. Her face paled. "I'm sorry. I…I didn't mean to snap at you. Buddy was my little brother's favorite stuffed animal. The bear and the photograph are all I have left of him."

"Oh." Johnny paused as though computing what she'd told him. "It's okay. I feel the same way about my parents' picture. I keep it next to my bed."

When she turned, Tony again moved off to the side of the door. He assured himself he wasn't spying on her, but that he merely didn't want to interrupt this chance for his nephew to forge a friendship with Ella. Johnny needed someone to confide in when he couldn't turn to him for understanding.

"What happened to your brother?" Johnny's voice drew Tony's attention.

"Would you mind if we don't talk anymore about my brother? It still makes me sad."

"Okay."

"Why don't you help me in the kitchen?" she suggested. "Can you set the table?"

"I don't know how. Never did it."

"You mean you don't have any chores at home?"

"Not many. Usually Uncle Tony does them for me."

There was a pronounced silence. Tony could tell Ella didn't approve of Johnny's lack of responsibilities. Until now, Tony hadn't realized how much he'd spoiled the child in his effort to compensate for the lousy cards life had dealt Johnny. Nothing could make up for the loss of the boy's parents. Spoiling Johnny was only going to hurt him in the end.

Footsteps were followed by the gentle lilt of Ella's voice. "How about I show you where everything goes?"

There was a slight pause. "Okay."

Maybe it was time Tony stopped tiptoeing around Johnny in a feeble attempt to make things normal—whatever that might constitute.

"Am I late for lunch?" Tony pulled open the screen door and stepped into the entryway.

"Not at all." Ella stood to his left in the compact kitchen. "Everything will be ready in a couple of minutes."

He looked over the open floor plan. His gaze roamed around the tidy room, taking in the wildlife paintings on one wall and the built-in bookcases on either side of the gray stone fireplace. Framed pictures of her family, presumably, and the stuffed teddy bear lined the mantel.

This cabin was unlike any of his friends' places, where the guys hung out, played cards, and chugged some beer. This cabin was a home. Ella's home. The last place he should be.

A blue-and-white-block quilt draped over the back of the couch drew his attention. The blanket would be perfect to cuddle under on a cool evening with Ella wrapped in his arms.

"I'm setting the table," Johnny announced, interrupting his errant thoughts.

"That's good, but don't think that gets you out of trouble," Tony warned. "I've decided your punishment. It's about time you start learning about the ranch. So you'll be doing extra chores in the morning and after school."

Johnny's face scrunched up. "Ahh...that's not fair—"

"If you complain, I'll make sure you muck the stalls every morning before school."

The boy's mouth snapped shut. Tony was certain this would teach his nephew a lesson. He wouldn't have to worry about him taking off on his own again.

Tony turned his attention to Ella. "Can I do anything?"

She stood at the stove with a spoon in her hand, looking like a domestic goddess. "Thanks, but Johnny is already setting the table, and the food is almost ready. You don't mind grilled cheese and soup, do you? I also baked some chocolate-chip cookies earlier that we can have for dessert."

"Sounds good."

He noticed how Johnny's eyes lit up with interest as he licked his lips. Tony appreciated the way she made them feel at home, and if he had to hazard a guess, he'd bet she made those cookies just for Johnny. One day soon, she'd definitely make some man a good wife.

Tony stepped further into the common room, consisting of a modest kitchen and living room. There were plenty of ways for a man to fit into this cozy scenario, from replacing the worn carpeting to fixing the leaky kitchen faucet. He looked up at the beam ceiling, finding not one but two new fire alarms on opposite ends of the common room. A splash of red next to the fireplace drew his attention to a fire extinguisher. This woman definitely believed in fire prevention. If he didn't know better, he'd think she was trying to impress him.

Ella should have some guy in her life to look out for her and help her with the yard. So why didn't she have a special someone? Or had she left him back in the city? The thought of her with another man wiped out his appetite.

He reminded himself he had no claims on her, nor did he want any entanglements. He couldn't give the court investigator any more reasons to provide the judge with an unfavorable report. So why get worked up over the inevitable? Ella was a gorgeous woman with a caring heart. Before long, every bachelor in the county would be beating on her door.

Chapter Twelve

Ella stood outside the Golden Nugget Jeweler. Her grandmother's ring was burning a hole in her purse. She had only a few minutes before her Monday dance lesson. Her grip tightened on the purse strap. She considered turning around and leaving.

A little voice inside her screamed that breaking her word to her grandmother was the wrong thing to do, but she couldn't think of another alternative. She wouldn't risk ownership of her beloved cabin on the slim chance she and Tony could do a good enough imitation of Fred and Ginger to impress the dance judges.

She didn't know why she was getting so worked up. Today, her only intention was to have the ring officially appraised—to ascertain her options. There would be plenty of time to figure out her next step later.

Ella pulled open the glass door and stepped inside.

A gentleman peered over his wire-rimmed spectacles. He smiled, and his ruddy cheeks puffed up. "Hello. How can I help you?"

"I was wondering if you could appraise a ring for me?"

"Certainly. Do you have it with you?"

She retrieved the black velvet box from her purse and slid it across the counter.

The man wasted no time retrieving the ring and holding it beneath the jeweler's scope. "This is quite old and almost as beautiful as its owner."

"Thank you." Heat swirled in her chest and rushed to her cheeks. She now understood how this man eked out a living in this desert community. He certainly had a way with putting his female customers at ease.

He glanced up at her. "Is the appraisal for insurance purposes?"

"Um...no." She might as well tell him. He might be able to help her, should she go through with selling it. "I'm considering selling."

The man's gray eyebrows lifted. He didn't say anything, but the questions danced around in his eyes.

"I need the money," she blurted out.

"May I have your hand?" She complied, and he slid the ring on her finger. "Such a pity. It's as though this ring were designed with you in mind. Perhaps you'll reconsider and keep it for when you get married."

Tony's image formed in her mind, kneeling before her with love in his eyes and this ring poised to slip on her finger. Her heart swooned at the thought, knocking the air from her lungs. Realizing how ridiculous the idea was, she banished the image from her mind. She wasn't getting married to Tony—or anyone.

"I don't think so." She slid off the ring. "Could you price it for me? The sooner, the better."

"Normally, I don't handle antique jewelry. I have a friend in Albuquerque who specializes in it. He'd love to see this ring. Would you mind if I let him have a look at it?"

Ella hesitated, debating her decision. She honestly didn't have any other viable options, other than winning the dance contest, to make the necessary repairs to her home before monsoon season or to pay the back taxes. "Go ahead. See what he has to say."

After getting her contact information, the man handed her a receipt. "You're the new teacher in town, aren't you?"

She smiled and nodded. "Let me guess, there isn't much that goes on around this town that all the folks don't know."

He chuckled. "Didn't take you long to get acquainted with Whistle Stop. By the way, I'm Tom Ward."

"It's nice to meet you."

"Well, Ella, I've also heard you're Tony's dance partner. I can see why he changed his mind about entering the contest. If I were a few years younger, he'd have had some competition to be your partner."

At his innocent flirting, her smile broadened. She glanced down at the gold band inlaid with turquoise on his left hand. "And I'm sure your wife wouldn't have had any problems with us dancing together."

A hint of pink tinged his cheeks. "Well, as one of the volunteer firefighters, I'd like to thank you for participating. The community pulling together means a lot. As for this"—he held up the small plastic bag with her grandmother's ring—"I promise to be in touch in the near future."

Back in her car, Ella forced her thoughts to her upcoming lesson and the thought of being held in Tony's capable arms. Anticipation thrummed in her veins. Soon she'd be chest-to-chest with the rugged rancher. Adrenaline started to work its magic on her sluggish body.

She grabbed a tube of cover-up makeup from her purse. She dabbed some on the scar tissue that started at her wrists and trailed up her arms, just like she did before every lesson. She'd do anything to keep her nightmare from coming true.

A few minutes later, she parked across the street from Josie's Dance Studio. She hurried inside, hoping she hadn't kept anyone waiting. Relief swept through her upon finding she was the first to arrive. Before she had a chance to sit down with Josie, the door opened, and Tony strode into the room. A frown marred his face. She wondered if he was still having problems with Johnny.

She approached him. "Sure you're up for this?"

She knew they desperately needed the practice, but the darkness shadowing his eyes concerned her more. Her heart went out to him. She couldn't even imagine the pressure of being an impromptu single parent.

"I'm good. It's just been a long day. Are you ready?"

She nodded.

Midway through their lesson, a dip tweaked a muscle in her back, causing a groan of pain to slip past her lips. She hoped Tony hadn't heard. When Josie suggested they take a short break, Ella headed for the water cooler, and Tony followed.

He shot her a worried look. "I think I'm the one who should be asking you if you're up for dancing today."

"I'm a little sore is all."

"So I've noticed."

"Hey, you aren't exactly Mr. Energy either."

He shrugged. "Been putting in extra hours teaching Johnny the ropes around the ranch."

"Gaining your undivided attention must be helping him."

Tony's eyes lit up. "Johnny is finally speaking to me. Although most of the time, it's to ask when he can see Patch again."

The degree with which she wanted to pounce on the idea startled her, though she didn't say anything. Ever since he'd kissed her, things between them had been different. It was as though an electric current arced between them every time they touched. And all of her thoughts short-circuited, leaving only her need to feel his lips pressed to hers.

She sipped at the cold water, hoping it'd douse her heated thoughts. As much as she wanted to see both Johnny and Tony this weekend, it wasn't advisable. "I...I have plans this weekend. I'll be working in the yard both days."

He grabbed her hand and turned it over, displaying the blisters she'd earned while raking up the dried leaves and twigs. "By the looks of you, I'd say you've done enough. I should have stayed on Saturday and helped."

"I don't need to be taken care of." She stared directly at him, challenging him to push the subject.

He expelled an exasperated sigh and moved to the water cooler for a drink.

"Shall we get back to it?" Josie asked, stepping out of her office.

"Sure." Every muscle in Ella's body protested.

Tony cleared his throat. "I won't be able to practice on Friday. I've got a refresher course with the Forest Service." He turned to Ella. "I hope that isn't a problem."

"Is that part of your fire chief duties?" Ella asked, trying to make casual conversation. He'd been quiet and distant since their lunch on Saturday.

"No." His gaze caught and held hers. "This has to do with fighting wildfires. With me only being a seasonal worker, I go through reviews each year. I hope this doesn't mess up your plans too much."

She shook her head but looked away. "Have a good time."

She told herself she should be happy to spend one less evening in the arms of a man who was totally unsuitable for her. Yet, instead of being pleased with this change of events, disappointment consumed her.

"Ella," Josie said, "if you want, I could arrange for a substitute dance partner for you."

The idea appealed to her. She couldn't help but wonder what it'd be like to dance with someone other than Tony. Would she trip over her own feet? More important, would she experience the same excitement and exhilaration in another man's arms? Was it merely the act of dancing that made her body come alive?

"Sure, I'd like that." Ella noticed the strange expression that crossed Tony's face. Was it jealousy? No, it couldn't be. But the look passed so quickly that Ella was left wondering if she had imagined it. "You don't mind, do you?"

Tony's expression faded to indifference. "Of course not."

"Good." Josie jotted a note on a tablet before turning back to them. "Now, I'd like to go over those last dance steps one more time."

Ella resumed her position, already eager to once again feel Tony's very capable arms around her. She told herself that it was just some crazy crush that she'd get over as soon as this contest concluded. But in the meantime, maybe it wouldn't hurt to savor the moment...just a little.

Time passed quickly, in some ways too quickly. And then the lesson was over. Tony released her, but not before glancing into her eyes and sending her a smile that made her stomach flutter.

Josie strode over to them, breaking the connection. "Ella, I'll give you a call if I have any problems finding a replacement."

"Thanks. I really appreciate everything."

"No problem."

Tony walked away as she made sure Josie had her phone number. Once everything was sorted out, Ella retrieved her purse from the chair. She turned to find him holding the door open for her. "Thanks."

When she headed for her car, he rushed to catch up to her. He reached for her hand. "Ella, wait."

She stopped and faced him. With only a few inches separating them, she craned her neck to look up at him. "What did you need?"

"I wanted to make sure everything is okay between us." Concern filled his brown eyes. "I don't have a choice about going to this review to get recertified."

His fingers were still wrapped around hers, and she had no interest in breaking their contact. "One missed lesson won't ruin our chances in the dance competition."

His thumb stroked the back of her hand, sending a current of excitement throughout her body. "I'm glad you understand." He paused and glanced down at the sidewalk before meeting her gaze again. "Are we okay?"

She knew what he was talking about, and it had nothing to do with dancing. He was talking about the kiss. She withdrew her hand. "Yes, we're fine. Why wouldn't we be?"

"You know, because of the kiss. I don't know what I was thinking. I shouldn't have done it—"

"It's no big deal." *Liar. Liar*. "It's already forgotten." *Not it's not. Far from it*.

His brows lifted. "You're sure?"

"I am. I really need to go check on Patch."

"Oh, sure."

She moved to her car before pausing to watch him walk the short distance to his truck. His tight backside was as hot as his muscled chest and chiseled face. How had she ended up with such a sexy dance partner?

As soon as the thought popped into her mind, she frowned. She didn't need to be drooling over him. She wasn't ready to take a chance on revealing her scars to him—to anyone.

She was still recovering from the last man who'd rejected her. Sure, he'd never stated her scars were the reason he broke up with her, but the timing was too coincidental to be denied. A week after things had heated up and she'd revealed her arms to him, he'd called and said the relationship just wasn't working for him. He hoped they could continue to be friends as well as coworkers. Suppressing her hurt feelings, she'd agreed.

Ella didn't want to relive that experience with Tony. Whistle Stop was too small of a town to avoid him if things went wrong. And she didn't want to start over some other place. This town was growing on her...then again, so was her dance partner.

As Friday's lesson approached, Ella found herself getting nervous about dancing with someone new. She hoped she didn't make any missteps.

After pulling into her usual parking spot across the street from the dance studio, she grabbed her tube of concealer. She dabbed some on the scars just like she did before every lesson. She couldn't be too careful about covering up her past.

The sound of an approaching vehicle had her glancing in the rearview mirror as a pickup pulled up behind her. Cord and Alexis climbed out of the truck. Happy to see someone she knew, she rushed to greet them. "Hi, guys."

"Hi, Ella. Hope you weren't waiting too long." Alexis pointed to Cord. "Some people never leave the house on time."

Ella was confused. "Um...I just got here. Were we supposed to meet today?"

Cord adjusted his tan cowboy hat, shoving it farther up on his forehead. "Josie mentioned that you needed a dance partner since Tony's off doing the refresher course with the Forest Service."

"Oh," Ella said, failing to hide her surprise. "I'm sorry that you guys had to go out of your way to help me out."

"It's no big deal. Right, Cord?" Alexis elbowed him, causing him to grunt in agreement. "We already had a lesson scheduled after yours, so we came a little early."

Ella glanced doubtfully at Cord. "Are you sure you won't mind me stepping on your toes?"

"It'll serve him right," Alexis said, "as he seems to think moving his feet is easier if he's standing on mine."

Both women broke out in laughter.

Cord frowned at Alexis. "We should head inside and get this over with. Unless you two want to continue laughing at my expense."

"Seems my better half is anxious to get in as much practice as possible."

Cord groaned as Alexis led him by the hand across the street and into the studio.

Once Ella started to dance with Cord, it took them quite a while to learn each other's rhythm. Halfway through the lesson, they'd started moving well together, but the shrill whine of the fire whistle brought their dance to a halt. Cord rushed over to where Alexis was sitting.

She held out a buzzing cell phone. "Duty calls."

Cord checked the text message and turned to them. "Gotta go. We've got a brush fire out on Fork Road."

Alexis gave him a brief kiss before tossing him the keys. "Don't worry. I'll just walk over to my father's place. I told him that we'd stop by after practice."

Ella watched the easy interaction between the two. She noticed that Alexis didn't show any signs of concern when she told Cord good-bye. Ella's stomach was twisted in a big knot after hearing the whistle repeat its warning.

"What will they do without Tony?" Ella asked before realizing how Alexis might interpret her interest.

Alexis's eyes lit up. "They'll be fine. Tony has them run drills all of the time. Cord is newer to the crew, but he knows what he's doing."

"That's good." At least for this one fire call, Tony was safe at his refresher course. She wouldn't have to go home worrying about his safety.

Alexis gathered her belongings. "Well, Josie, guess we'll get out of your way since Mr. Twinkle Toes bailed on us."

The petite brunette said, "I'm sorry you didn't get your lesson. Would you be interested in reviewing your techniques?"

The women looked at each other and shook their heads as they smiled.

"Josie, you deserve the rest of the night off," Ella suggested.

"Besides, it's the men who need the practice, not us," Alexis teased and started everyone laughing.

Josie turned off the music. "You can hang out here if you want to talk. Just turn off the lights and lock up on your way out."

"No problem, Josie," Alexis said, not moving from her folding chair. "Good night."

Josie walked toward the office while Ella took a seat next to Alexis. "Does this happen often?"

"What? Oh, you mean Cord getting called away in the middle of things?"

"I bet you get tired of him running out with only a moment's notice." Ella regretted vocalizing her blunt observation with someone she barely knew. "Sorry, that sounded rude, and I didn't mean it to be."

"No offense taken." Alexis shot her a reassuring smile. "He's been a firefighter for most of our relationship. I've gotten used to him being pulled away to do his duty. Oh sure, sometimes I'd prefer if he wasn't always on call, but I know he's out there helping one of our neighbors. So how could I be upset?"

With her curiosity piqued, Ella settled back, eager to get another woman's perspective on being involved with a firefighter—not that she was involved with Tony. She was just curious. "But surely you must be scared to death every time he goes out on a call."

Alexis shook her head. "No."

"Really?" She couldn't fathom Alexis's laidback attitude.

"Cord takes his safety seriously, as do all of the men who have his back. He doesn't take unnecessary risks."

"I don't know. I'd still be scared every time he went out on a call."

Alexis patted her hand. "It all depends on what you consider a risk. A pilot takes his life in his hands each time his plane leaves the tarmac. A bank teller could be held up at gunpoint. And a businessman could get into a car accident on his commute to the office. Life's a risk."

Ella admitted that her new friend had a reasonable argument, but still the thought of loving a man who put his life on the line every day for his job would drive her crazy with worry. "I could never marry a firefighter."

Once the innocent words were vocalized, she saw the curious look Alexis shot her. Ella's cheeks burned. She wanted to deny any ideas about getting married, but she knew there was no way of backing out of this without making it worse.

"You'd be surprised what you can do for love." Alexis picked up her brown leather purse and rose from her chair. "I guess we should get out of here."

After making sure the building was secure, Ella stood next to her car. "It was good talking to you. Would you like to grab some food or coffee? And then I can give you a ride to your father's."

"I don't want to put you out of your way. It isn't far—"

"You won't be. I'd really like the company." She really liked Alexis, and she hoped they'd be good friends. One could never have enough of those.

"Sure. Sounds good."

As Ella drove them the short distance to the Green Chile Cantina, she considered Alexis's observations about being involved with a firefighter. In time, would her heart cease to race when the fire whistles sounded? Could she learn to go about her normal routine while Tony was off facing a life-threatening blaze?

Chapter Thirteen

The Green Chile Cantina appeared to be the hub of activity in Whistle Stop.

Ella gazed around the colorful restaurant. She loved the color scheme, from the red-and-white floor tiles to the cherry red, ladder-back chairs to the white tabletops. It was bright and cheery. The walls were a soft white stucco with red chile ristras interspersed amid colorful Southwestern folk art.

A young waitress in a white T-shirt with the restaurant's logo on it and black jeans hustled through the dining room with a loaded tray of food balanced on her shoulder. Customers laughed, smiled, and sent greetings to each other. The whole place was welcoming. And busy—as in, every table was occupied.

Ella inhaled deeply. Mm…no wonder this place was hopping. Her stomach rumbled its agreement. If the food tasted anywhere near as good as it smelled, she'd be breaking the piggy bank to come back here soon—real soon.

"I don't see any available tables." Ella couldn't help but think it was for the best, considering every penny she had was needed to repair the cabin. Still, the delicious aromas were tempting—very, very tempting.

Ella went to turn toward the door when Alexis called out, "Wait, I see a couple of seats."

"You do?" How had she missed them?

She followed Alexis through the congested room. They stopped next to a table with two young women about their age. They both looked up and smiled.

"Hey, Alexis. Does Cord know you're here?" The one with a long, dark braid grinned, letting them know that she was joking.

"Actually, he doesn't. But he'd probably be happy because then he'd be assured of a good meal instead of one that's a bit on the charcoaled side."

"It's okay." The other woman with short dark hair spoke up. "I count on people like you for job security."

Alexis smiled and shook her head as she took a seat. "Thanks, guys. You sure know how to make me feel better about being a lousy cook."

Everyone started laughing. Ella sat down and smiled, although she didn't have a clue who the other women were, but they sure seemed nice enough.

Then, as though Alexis remembered her, she turned her way. "Oops. Sorry. I meant to introduce you to these two but, well, you saw what happened. They like to pick on me because they're both so talented in the kitchen and I'm lucky if I can cook a frozen dinner."

"I told you we'll give you free lessons on how to use the timer." The young woman with the long braid grinned.

Alexis stuck her tongue out. "But what you're forgetting is that I have a man who's really good in the kitchen. And it doesn't get much sexier than watching him work a spatula."

Everyone at the table nodded in agreement.

"Now if you'll hold the jokes for a moment, I'll introduce the newest member of our group." Alexis turned to Ella. "I guess you could call us the bachelorettes of Whistle Stop."

"Then I guess I'll fit right in." Ella relaxed back in her chair.

Everyone in the small group was quite pretty in their own individual ways. It was so hard to believe they were all single like her. It had started to feel like she was the only one her age not embarking on her very own happily-ever-after.

"Everyone, this is Ella Morgan. She's a schoolteacher, and...she's Tony Granger's dance partner."

The smiles faded from the women's faces as their brows rose in surprise. All three sets of eyes turned her way. Ella forced a smile to her lips as her stomach quivered with nerves. She couldn't tell what they were thinking. Not quite sure what to say, she sat quietly and waited for them to speak.

"Hi, I'm Ana. I own this place." The woman with short dark hair waved her hand around at the establishment. "Any time you don't feel like cooking, I'm here."

"Speaking of which, shouldn't you be working?" Alexis glanced around the bustling room.

Ana smiled broadly. "It's my night off. I just stopped by to drop something off, and I ran into Piper."

"By the way, I'm Piper." The young woman with the long braid leaned forward and smiled. "I own the Poppin' Fresh Bakery in the town square. You definitely need to stop by one of these mornings. If I can't tempt you with a bagel or a muffin, I brew a mean cup of coffee."

"She does have the best coffee." Alexis propped her elbows on the tabletop. "And I'm totally addicted to it."

"I'll make sure to stop by for some coffee on my way to work." Surely she could spare enough in her tight budget for some coffee, especially if it was as good as Alexis claimed.

"And try a muffin. Piper makes the best baked goods in the state." Alexis licked her lips. "By the way, Piper failed to mention that she won't be part of our bachelorette group much longer. She's getting married in the fall. But we decided that she could still be an honorary member." Alexis smiled, but just as quickly the smile faded. "Hey, where's the bling?"

Piper glanced down at her naked ring finger. "I...I gave it back."

"What?" the other two bachelorettes chorused.

The color faded from Piper's face. She shrugged, slouched in her seat, and kept her gaze downcast. "It's over."

The admission was so soft that it almost got lost in the din of conversation buzzing through the crowded dining room. Alexis and Ana sent each other puzzled looks. It seemed that no one knew what happened to the engagement. And Piper obviously wasn't up for talking about it.

Ella's heart went out to Piper. Her one relationship hadn't gotten that serious, so she couldn't imagine what it would be like to find someone you thought you could spend the rest of your life with and then have that dream crumble. No matter what the reason, it had to be difficult. And that's why Ella intended to keep her heart guarded and safe.

The longer the bachelorettes remained silent, the more miserable Piper looked. And it appeared that

Alexis and Ana were so stunned that they didn't know how to react or what to say.

Ella leaned forward and uttered the first thing that came to mind. "So I hear that Tony has some sort of reputation around town." All three women looked at her. Their gazes filled with confusion. Ella swallowed hard. "I...I was just wondering, since we're dance partners, if there was anything I should know."

Alexis was the first to regain her voice. "He's one of Whistle Stop's most eligible bachelors. If I hadn't met Cord first, you might be looking for another dance partner."

"Yeah, right," Ana chimed in. "You and Cord might not be married yet, but everyone in Whistle Stop knows you were made for each other."

Alexis got a dreamy look on her face, and no one had to ask. They just knew she was thinking of her man. "You're right, but that doesn't mean that Ella dancing with Tony won't cause quite a stir around town."

Ana nodded. "You'll be the envy of many women."

"With him as a partner, you'll gain the female judges' votes." Piper spoke softly. Then her gaze shot to Alexis. "Sorry. I know you and Cord will do great in the contest. It's just that, you know, everyone knows that Cord is off the market."

Alexis smiled. "Relax. I know what you mean. And we're really sorry about your engagement."

"Yeah. We're sorry it shocked us." Ana squeezed Piper's arm. "But we're here if you ever want to talk."

"Thanks." Piper sent them a watery smile. "You guys are the best. But I'd rather hear more about the contest."

With the tension broken and the subject of Piper's engagement neatly swept aside for the moment, everyone relaxed. The chatter flowed about the dance contest. Who was entered, who was partnered with whom, who might win. There were shocked gasps, knowing nods, and peals of laughter.

Ella smiled. She really liked the bachelorettes. They were fun, caring, and they made her feel like she was one of them. Whistle Stop was definitely becoming her home.

Who had danced with Ella?

The taunting question wouldn't leave Tony's mind while he was off at his firefighting refresher. And even now that he was back in Whistle Stop, he couldn't stop thinking about her, wondering if she'd found someone more experienced to be her partner.

Whistle Stop had its fair share of young guys who'd jump at the chance to dance with the attractive schoolteacher. The thought sent a strange sensation coursing through him. Could it be—no, he wasn't jealous. *Impossible*. He just had to find out what had happened in his absence—he had to talk to Ella.

"Come on, Johnny. Time to leave," he said, dumping the remainder of the boy's toast and scrambled eggs into the garbage.

"Where are we going?"

Tony wanted it to be a surprise. "You'll find out soon."

"Can't we stay home? I'm tired."

Tony's initial reaction was to give in to his nephew. Then he recalled Johnny stowing away in the bed of Mike's truck to go see Patch and what could have happened. He'd given in to the boy's whining one too many times in the past. "I need your help."

"But it's Sunday, and you said we could do something together."

Tony stopped cleaning the kitchen and shot the boy a serious stare. "We will be together."

"What about my pirate ship? You promised you'd help build it."

He had promised, but he hadn't specified a particular day. Tony exhaled a frustrated sigh. Johnny's newfound independence and outspokenness made Tony uncomfortable. Not so long ago, life had been much easier. Now he understood what people meant when they said that kids grow up fast.

The truth of the matter was, Tony had been putting the boy off about the model kit for one legitimate reason after another, but this wasn't the time to cave in to the boy's wants. He'd witnessed the toll the manual labor had taken on Ella when she'd winced repeatedly during their last few dance lessons. And her hands had been a mess of scrapes and blisters.

Most of all, he wanted to help her restore the yard, to make her home as safe as possible. He hoped to give her a sense of security, a place to set down roots. Then she'd never want to leave, and after the adoption, maybe they could explore this thing between them. The idea filled him with anticipation. Nothing could stop him from going to her.

"We'll work on the pirate ship this evening. Right now, Miss Morgan needs our help."

"Really?" Johnny's face lit up. "You mean we're going to see Patch."

"Not exactly. We're going to help clean up her yard."

"You mean I gotta work?" When Tony nodded, the smile faded from his nephew's face. "You only wanna go 'cause you like her."

Tony finished wiping off the counter and tossed the cloth in the sink. Was it that clear, even to a nine-year-old? Tony inwardly groaned. He didn't want people thinking he had a thing for Ella, especially not his matchmaking mother.

His gut reaction was to order the boy to put on his shoes and hightail it to the truck, but he hesitated. He stared at his nephew, really studying him. Johnny's face had thinned in the past year, losing his baby fat. He was just starting to sprout upward. The boy was no longer a little kid. In a couple of years, he'd be a preteen. Maybe they both had some adjusting to do.

"But that doesn't mean you can't play with the puppy when we take a break."

Johnny sent him a skeptical look. "Can I play with Patch while you work?"

"I didn't say that, but I promise you'll get to spend time with him."

Johnny jumped to his feet. "As long as you promise I can play with Patch, I'll go."

The boy acted like he had a choice in the matter. Tony wasn't in the mood to point this out and start an argument. Besides, it'd just delay them even more. And he had some questions for Ella that he couldn't wait to have answered.

"You can play, but not the whole time. Now let's roll." Tony grabbed his keys from the counter.

"Can't. I lost my hat." Johnny ran out of the room.

The boy was forever losing his baseball cap. He'd wear the hat for a little bit, but then he'd get hot and take it off.

"Did you leave it in the barn?" Tony called out.

Johnny raced into the kitchen. "I'll check."

"Hurry."

"I will." The boy ran outside, letting the screen door bang shut.

Tony shook his head and took the free time to read over the headlines in the local newspaper, a luxury he rarely had time for anymore. He'd just flipped to the sports page when the doorbell rang. He certainly wasn't expecting anyone.

Tony opened the front door and found a familiar brunette standing there—Ms. Sorkin, aka the court snoop. Tony held in an exasperated sigh. These surprise visits were taking their toll on him.

"Hello, Ms. Sorkin," he said, mustering every bit of congeniality he could. "We weren't expecting you on a Sunday. Johnny just ran out to the barn. He'll be right back."

"That's the point of these random visits—to observe you in your natural setting without any pretenses."

She peered around him, and he realized he had no choice but to invite her inside. Getting those answers from Ella would have to wait. Uneasiness churned in his gut as he forced his lips into a smile.

He stepped back. "Please come in. Can I get you something to eat or drink?"

She shook her head. "I stopped at the Green Chile Cantina on my way here, but thank you."

"They do have some of the best food around." He should know, since he ordered takeout from there on a pretty regular basis.

"I overheard some interesting conversations, too." She took a seat on the couch and stared directly at him as he perched on the arm of the chair. "They were talking about you."

His chest tightened to the point he could barely take in a breath. Why in the world would people be discussing him?

Ms. Sorkin continued staring at him, as though waiting to catch an unguarded moment. Well, she'd be waiting a long time. He schooled his features into what he hoped was a neutral expression. If she was waiting for some sort of confession, she'd be waiting a very long time.

"You aren't even going to ask what they were saying?"

"Doesn't much matter. If those busybodies run out of things to say, they invent something. That's why I don't pay them any attention."

Ms. Sorkin's dark brows rose beneath her bangs. "So you're saying you aren't taking part in the dance contest?"

"Oh, that. Yes, I am." The tension in his chest eased. Ms. Sorkin had been pressing him to get involved in the community, so this had to be a plus in his column.

She opened her leather binder and poised her pen over the paper, ready to take notes. "And your dance partner is?"

"A friend." He didn't want Ella involved in this discussion. "I'm helping her out."

"How so?"

He resisted rolling his eyes. No matter what he said, he'd ended up receiving more uncomfortable questions. Seeing no easy way out, he started at the beginning, explaining Ella's need to win the prize money.

"What sort of relationship do you have with this Ella Morgan?"

"We're friends. Nothing more," he said quickly, perhaps too quickly.

"I see." Doubt rang out in the woman's voice as she jotted something on her pad of paper. "Now, as far as Johnny's grades, have they improved?"

He immediately thought of how they'd taken a distinct nose dive since they'd last talked, but that was changing for the better, thanks to Ella.

"His grades are picking up. In no time, they'll be where they should be."

A flicker of surprise, followed by approval, gleamed in the woman's eyes. "That's wonderful. How did you manage this turnaround?"

He swallowed, not wanting to reveal that Ella was the driving force behind the improved grades. "In addition to sitting down with him each evening to go over his classwork, I've hired a tutor."

"Good." She wrote some more in her notebook, and he was dying to read her notes. "And the tutor's name?"

Tony pressed his lips firmly together. He didn't want to say Ella's name. The woman would read too much into Ella's presence in their lives, and now was not the time to analyze the tangled web of emotions he had for Ella.

"Mr. Granger, I need the name for my notes."

"Ella Morgan."

The woman's eyes rounded. She set to work writing note after note. He didn't even want to imagine what she was jotting down. He had to say something to turn this meeting around, to keep them on track for the final adoption proceedings next month.

"She's just a friend—of the whole family. My mother enjoys when she stops over and joins us for lunch."

He stopped. That revelation had Ms. Sorkin scribbling even faster. Why, oh, why did he have to open his mouth and insert his size-twelve boot?

"Uncle Tony, I found my hat," Johnny yelled from the kitchen. "I'm ready to go to Miss Morgan's."

Ms. Sorkin shot him a you-are-so-busted look.

Tony's entire body tensed. He didn't say a word. No matter what he said, it'd just make things worse. All he could do now was appease Ms. Sorkin and hope for the best.

Chapter Fourteen

STEAM ROSE FROM THE dark brew as Ella poured her second mug of coffee that day. She proceeded to drop an ice cube into the mug. Immediately, a pop and a fizzle followed. After a bit of milk and sweetener, she pressed the mug to her lips, taking a long swallow. Mm...

She carried the mug into the cozy living room, wanting to straighten up prior to heading outside to work on the yard. Patch, lying on the end of the couch, lifted his head and eyed her before lowering his chin to the couch cushion.

In between sips of coffee, she grabbed a throw pillow and fluffed it. Next, she aligned two recently purchased gardening magazines on the coffee table. The glossy covers promised landscaping suggestions on a budget. She hoped they'd give her some ideas for what to do with the yard once it was cleared.

One last glance around the room revealed that everything was in order. She grabbed her cell phone from the end table and noticed she had a voice mail. She retrieved it. A male voice came across the line. It was a contractor getting back to her with a quote for the new roof. The price he mentioned was even higher than the ones she'd already gotten. Her stomach churned. What was she going to do if she and Tony didn't win the dance contest?

Return to Albuquerque? But that wouldn't help her in the least. She still wouldn't have anywhere to live.

Ella dropped down on the couch next to Patch. She repeatedly ran her hand over his back, finding that it relaxed her. She leaned back on the couch and let her gaze meander around the room, taking in the changes. For the first time, she felt truly at home here. Could she turn her back on this? Forget all about the amazing friends she'd made? Or walk away from a certain sexy cowboy she couldn't get out of her head?

Besides, there was nothing left for her back in Albuquerque. She could only keep putting one foot in front of the other, and she preferred to do that right here in Whistle Stop.

Anxious to make use of what was left of the morning, she grabbed her newly purchased gloves, hoping to keep the blisters to a minimum. She considered where to start in the yard. Her one major obstacle was finding a way to dispose of the debris. Creating a burn pile would be the most logical solution, but with the drought, fires were strictly forbidden. Besides, a fire was the absolute thing she wanted anywhere near her home—or herself.

She needed someone with a truck to haul everything away. Immediately, Tony's image came to mind. He had offered to help... No, she couldn't impose on him. She'd find another solution.

A knock at the door caused Patch to bark excitedly. Fully expecting it to be Tracey stopping by while out for one of her strolls, Ella rushed to the door. She yanked it open. "Good morning."

"Hi."

Ella's gaze lowered to find Johnny, all by himself. Flashbacks of the boy's antics the prior weekend came rushing back to her. The thud of a closing door had her glancing down the driveway, finding Tony headed in their direction. A sense of relief washed over her.

"Johnny, I wasn't expecting you."

"Uncle Tony said we had to come be neighborly."

"He did, huh?" She arched a brow at Tony, wondering what he was up to. "You're in time for some coffee. I just brewed a pot. Would you care for a cup before we start? And, Johnny, I have some blueberry muffins on the counter."

The boy turned a pleading look to his uncle. "Can I have one? Please?"

"I thought you were full."

Johnny glanced away and shrugged.

"Okay. Go ahead." Tony turned to her. "Thanks, but I'll pass on the coffee."

Ella set the puppy on the kitchen floor before retrieving a muffin. She handed it to Johnny, who sat down on the floor to devour it while Patch danced around him.

Turning her attention back to Tony, she found him as appealing in the morning as he was in the evening at their lessons. His hair appeared to have just been cut, and it was now spiked a little on the top while clipped short on the sides. She wondered if a cowboy like him used styling products. She struggled to hide a smile at the image of him fussing over his hair.

She followed Tony to the porch. She clearly remembered the last time they stood on this porch together. He'd held her in those strong arms he was now using to brace himself against the railing. He leaned forward, looking out over the wooded property. Her heart raced as her gaze moved to his face. Her lips tingled as she recalled the pressure of his mouth touching hers.

She swallowed hard. "So what's this about being neighborly?"

"I thought I'd give you a hand with the yard."

She leveled a hard stare at him. "And if I refuse your help?"

"Why would you? You could hardly move this past week at our dance lessons after you insisted on going it alone. Face it, we all need help from time to time."

She didn't like his implication that she wasn't up to taking care of this place on her own. She knew she was letting her pride stand in her way. And it would be so nice to have someone to shoulder some of the load. To top it off, Tony did have the one thing she really needed—a truck.

"Would you mind hauling some of the debris away?"

"My pickup is at your command. I'll go pull around back."

Not about to let him do the bulk of the work on her property, she said, "I need to put on my shoes, and then I can show you where I want to start."

"Okay." His gaze lingered on her clothes.

"Is something wrong with what I'm wearing?" She tugged at the sleeves of her long-sleeved T-shirt. Sure, she was dressed a little warmer than he was, but she'd be fine.

"Uh, no." He turned to the cabin door.

"I'll be out in a minute."

"No rush."

Certain that she must be a mess, she rushed to the bathroom to run a brush through her hair and redo her ponytail, powder her face, and add some lip gloss.

She knew it was ridiculous, considering she was going to work in the yard, but she couldn't help herself. She wanted to look decent.

Not wanting to appear to be a slacker, she rushed to put on her shoes. By the time she grabbed her gloves, Johnny had finished his muffin. Together, they headed outside to join Tony. Ella rounded the corner of the cabin in time to spot Tony extracting a chain saw from the truck bed.

He turned to Johnny. "I need you to pick up the broken twigs and small limbs over there, away from the tree I'm going to cut down."

"Wait," she said. "I thought we'd start over on the other side."

Tony's brow crinkled. "Why would you want to do that? We'd have to work our way through all of the undergrowth to get over there. We'll start here near the driveway."

"No, we won't." Her hands settled on her hips, meeting his steady gaze. "This is my land, my choice."

She trudged through the mess of weeds, dried vegetation, and fallen limbs. She didn't stop until she reached her bedroom window. "This is where we'll start."

"But why?"

She glanced back at the window. "It's my fire-escape route."

He shook his head. "You're either the most cautious woman I've ever met or you're trying to impress me."

"Impress you?"

"Sure. I'm a firefighter, and you're showing me that you're on top of your fire safety. I've got to admit, no woman's ever taken this approach."

"I…uh…" She thought of correcting his misconception, but feared it'd lead to questions—questions she refused to answer. "What do you want me to do?"

"While I rip out these dead plants, can you and Johnny haul them over to the truck bed?"

She nodded, and they set to work.

"So how'd practice go Friday night?" Tony asked, digging at the roots of a particularly large weed. "Did you get stuck with a real dud?"

She shook her head. "Wait until I tell Cord what you called him."

Tony's eyes lit up at the mention of his buddy from the fire station. "I was wondering who Josie got to dance with you."

"You were curious, huh?"

Color tinged his face. He turned his back to her to continue digging. "Maybe. A little."

She hid a little smile as her stomach fluttered with excitement. This gentle giant had been jealous of her two-stepping with someone else. Her smile widened. Well, he didn't have to worry, because from what she'd witnessed, Cord was very happy with Alexis.

They continued until there was nothing but dirt beneath the window. Her mood lightened because they'd accomplished a very important task.

"Now that we've got that taken care of, I'm going to cut down that tree." Tony pointed to the one directly behind the cabin. "Would you mind raking the dried leaves and pine needles into a heap?"

She retrieved the rake from the porch, glad to have something to do besides appreciate his fine muscles stretching and contracting beneath his navy blue T-shirt. She glanced over her shoulder, catching a glance of his flexed biceps as he started the chain saw. She swallowed hard, turning back to her task.

Sure, he made her heart race every time they danced together, but the pressure to get their footwork just right helped her maintain her composure. But here in the wilderness, it was so much harder to cage her meandering fantasies. She kept wondering if he'd try to kiss her again.

A loud crack caused her to jump. She glanced up as the tree hit the ground. The scent of tangy pine mingled with the fresh mountain air. The chain saw's buzzing ceased, and she turned away. The last thing she needed was to be caught staring.

"Not that way," Tony called out.

Realizing he'd noticed she hadn't been paying attention to what she was doing, she paused and turned. "Excuse me?"

He approached her. Taking the rake from her hands, he asked, "Didn't your parents teach you how to do this?"

His pointed question poked at a tender spot in her heart. She had never known her father, and then her mother had died when she was ten years old. But she didn't want to go down that gloomy path.

And she did know how to rake, but she didn't mention that either. Otherwise, she'd have to explain why she'd been distracted. With Tony and Johnny here, it was so easy to imagine having her very own family. What would it hurt to indulge in the fantasy for a little longer?

A lump clogged her throat. Her one true wish was to someday have a family of her own. She swallowed hard. That wouldn't happen—she didn't deserve a family after what had happened to her mother and brother. All she had were these precious moments with Tony and his nephew. She had to make the most of it.

Tony started raking. "Watch how I do this."

Her attention zeroed in on the sweat glistening on the back of his tanned neck. Her gaze leisurely traveled down over his bulging biceps. Oh yeah, she was watching him. She couldn't think of a thing she'd rather be doing.

"So did you grow up in Albuquerque?" He handed her back the rake.

"I was born in Ohio. My mother followed my father there. He didn't stick around long, and then it was just Mom, Timmy, and me. One summer when I was little, my mother dropped me off to spend the summer with my grandparents here at the cabin, and come August, they drove me back to Ohio."

"Your family must have loved you a lot to make such a long drive."

"I guess they did." The thought had never occurred to her. The knowledge was a balm on her battered and bruised heart.

"Is your mother still in Ohio?"

"No. She died." Dreading where this conversation was headed, she turned her back to him and moved to the other side of the cabin to work.

By the afternoon, she was hot and tired. They'd been working nonstop. You'd think there would be a marked difference in the yard, but as she looked around, she realized there was far more work here than she'd ever imagined. Tony was right. It was more than she could accomplish on her own.

"I'm tired. Can we take a break?"

She turned to Johnny. “Sure. Would you like some ice water?”

The boy nodded.

“Have a seat on the steps, and I’ll get you a glass.”

After getting Johnny situated and leashing Patch to a post on the porch, she joined Tony, who was standing by the wood rail. Enjoying the peaceful silence between them, she sipped at her drink and looked out over the mess that loosely resembled a yard.

“Are you always cold?” For once, Tony’s voice was soft and soothing.

“Cold?” Her body’s reaction to him was flaming hot.

“Every time I see you, you’re wearing long sleeves.”

“Um...I find them comfortable. So how much of this land do you think we’ll be able to clear today?” She hoped to divert the conversation.

“Not much, if I don’t get back to work.”

“I can take your glass for you.” She held out her hand.

“Thanks.” His gaze held hers a few seconds longer than necessary and sent her heart rate soaring before he handed over the glass. “By the way, I know someone who wants to meet you.”

“Me? Who’d want to meet me? And why would they mention it to you?”

His face grew serious. “The thing is, I had a visit today from the court investigator.”

Her stomach plummeted. This was not going to be good.

“She overheard someone at the restaurant talking about how we teamed up for the dance contest. Then when I mentioned you’re tutoring Johnny, she asked to meet you.”

“Didn’t you tell her we’re only friends?”

"Is that what you want me to tell her?"

"Of course. Why would you say anything different?"

He shrugged. "After that kiss last week and the looks you keep sending me, I just wondered..."

"We're friends." Her gaze didn't quite reach his. "It's all we can ever be."

"You mean because of the pending adoption."

"Yes. You don't want to do anything to jeopardize the adoption. Besides, that thing between us was nothing."

A pained expression flitted across Tony's tanned face. She couldn't let it get to her. This was for the best. The thought of getting caught up in an adoption interview made her stomach flip. Sure, she'd passed the background check for her teaching position, but she imagined this persistent investigator would want more of the nitty-gritty details about her life—details best left buried for all of their sakes.

Chapter Fifteen

He'd stepped on her toes—again.

"I'm sorry." Tony swore under his breath the following Friday evening. "I thought after practicing all week I'd have these new steps down pat. Maybe I'm just not cut out to do the Lindy Hop."

In the middle of Josie's Dance Studio, Ella smiled up at him. "Concentrate. You can do this."

In truth, he did have the moves memorized, but every time Ella got close, he forgot what he was doing. Any hopes of being over her and moving past that unforgettable kiss were nothing more than wishful thinking.

When the music stopped, he backed away. He swiped his palms over his dark jeans. Ella tilted her chin upward to peer into his eyes, and his immediate thought was to swoop in and press his lips to hers. Yet, he resisted, remembering Ella's warning that they needed to keep things cool and casual because of the adoption.

She was right. He couldn't give the judge one more reason to delay or suspend the adoption. Tony was certain finalizing the adoption would give Johnny a much-needed sense of security. And Johnny's needs had to come ahead of his own. That's what good parents did—sacrifice for their children.

With the lesson over, Ella moved toward the door without saying a word to him. Something was wrong. The cautious part of him said he should let it go. If she wanted to tell him, she would in her own time. Still, he hated the thought of her walking away, angry with him.

"Hey, wait," he called out.

With her head held high and her shoulders pulled back, she continued down the walk. She either didn't hear him or didn't care.

He picked up his pace. His long strides soon caught up with her. He reached for her arm, pulling her to a stop. "What's up with you?"

"Nothing." She jerked free of his hold.

"Why did you leave the studio in a huff?" Her only response was a shrug. He couldn't leave without an explanation. "Obviously, I did something wrong. So spit it out."

She crossed her arms and raised her chin. "It's you and this contest. You aren't even trying. Most of those dances we did tonight we've gone over numerous times. Yet, you made beginner mistakes."

"I'm sorry. I was distracted. I promise I'll do better next time."

"We're running out of time." She threw up her hands. "Oh, never mind."

When she started to walk away, he moved to block her. "What has you so worked up? And why are you so certain we're going to lose?"

"Remember when you were off getting your firefighting certification?" He nodded. "Cord and Alexis showed me their Lindy Hop. Tony, they're good. Really good."

Cord was a big guy. Tony would never have guessed he was light on his feet. "You think they might win?"

Alarm registered in her eyes. "I do."

Not wild about dancing, he'd been doing everything asked of him to fulfill his obligation to Ella. Now that she mattered more to him than he'd imagined possible, and knowing how much winning meant to her, he wanted to go the extra mile—he wanted to give her a reason to stay here in Whistle Stop.

"What if we practice some more?" he asked.

"But Josie is booked. She doesn't have any more time for us."

"Then let's work on it on our own."

"Shouldn't you be heading home to Johnny?"

"He's helping my mother bake his favorite treat, chocolate-chip cookies. Afterward, he'll settle down to watch a movie. He'll be fine. So what do you say? Shall we practice some more so we can beat those guys?"

"I don't know." She wrung her hands as she turned to watch a passing car. A quiet moment ensued before she softly uttered, "Okay. But where?"

He had her hooked on the idea. Now he needed to reel her in. "I'd offer up my place, but it's nothing more than blueprints and a patch of open land. How about we head to your cabin?"

"There isn't much room."

"We'll move the furniture around. There will be plenty of room."

With her nod of agreement, they climbed into their separate vehicles. Tony let her take the lead. This extra practice would give him a chance to show her that he'd been paying attention at all of the lessons. He wouldn't give her any more reasons to worry about whether they could win.

When he pulled to a stop in Ella's driveway, he promised himself he'd give this practice his full attention. If he wanted to fantasize about her lush lips, rounded hips, and soft hands, he'd wait until they got these dance moves down.

With his game plan firmly in mind, he followed her into the cabin. His first wayward thought was that they were all alone except for one rambunctious puppy. Before his thoughts could go any further, he reined them in. Nothing would happen tonight. They'd practice, then he'd go home. Nothing more.

While Ella fed Patch, Tony called his mother to check on Johnny and let her know he'd be late. Then he made short work of rearranging the living room furniture, creating a makeshift dance floor.

When it finally came time for them to dance, he had his mind set on one thing, making Ella proud of him. He could do this. If Cord could do the Lindy Hop, so could he. And better!

With the puppy safely out of the way in the bedroom, Ella walked him through the series of moves they'd done earlier at the studio. He really focused on the task at hand. He counted out the six beats in his head to keep his rhythm. When he started to get the hang of it, Ella scanned the radio stations until she found an oldies station playing big-band music.

He didn't know how much time had passed when Ella looked at him with one of those smiles that made her eyes sparkle like polished sapphires.

"By George, I think you've got it," she cheered.

Her praise made his chest puff up, and a smile tugged at his lips. He'd wanted nothing more than to please her, and he'd succeeded.

"We did it." He swung her around and set her back down on the floor, but he continued to hold her close.

"Yes, we did." Her face glowed with happiness. "Maybe we'll have a shot at the prize after all."

"There's only one problem."

The smile vanished. "What?"

Tony noticed the tiny crease that formed between Ella's brows. A frown tugged at her very kissable lips. She was so cute that all he wanted to do was pull her even closer and kiss away her worries.

He swallowed down his desires and settled for, "I've worked up a ravenous appetite."

"Oh, you!" She pulled out of his embrace. She swatted his arm, barely touching him. "I thought you were serious."

Without Ella in his arms, he noticed a distinct chill in the air. "I am serious. I'm ravenous."

"How about you put this furniture back while I scrounge through the kitchen and see what I can find that'll feed two?"

While repositioning the couch, his gaze landed on the stone fireplace. The glow and crackle of a burning log would be a nice touch. "Want me to start a fire to take the chill off the evening?"

She kept busy at the stove and called over her shoulder. "No, thanks. Besides, I'll be in bed soon."

Images of them tangled together in sheets, lip to lip, skin to skin... He inwardly groaned, fighting back his yearnings. He refused to let his imagination run unleashed. Ella was his dance partner. Nothing more.

After the furniture was repositioned, he took Patch outside to stretch his legs. When he returned, Ella carried two plates of taquitos and a couple of bowls of white chili into the living room. The spicy scent wafted through the air. His stomach rumbled in anticipation.

"You're in luck," she said. "I had a craving for Mexican food, and there was on sale last week, so I splurged."

"Right about now I'd eat almost anything."

They took a seat on the couch and placed their food on the coffee table.

"How do you like Whistle Stop now that you've been here for a while?" He took a bite of one of the small rolled-up tortillas filled with chicken and cheese.

"The town hasn't changed much since I spent my summers here as a kid. The rustic atmosphere is one of the town's charms."

"Are you saying the slow pace doesn't bother you after growing up in the city?" He wondered if she'd soon grow bored and move on. After getting shuffled around as a child, she'd probably think nothing of picking up and moving on.

"The laidback pace takes some getting used to, but I'm adjusting. I might even swing by the old movie theater one of these days."

"I haven't been there in years." He rewound his memories back to a time when life wasn't so complicated. "I remember when my father would finish up his work around the ranch early on Saturday evenings and round up the family to catch the latest flick."

Her eyes lit up. "That reminds me of how my mother used to take me and my brother to a matinee on Black Fridays. We didn't have money to Christmas shop, but somehow she'd always scrape together just enough for a holiday movie and popcorn."

A smile settled on her lips, but it didn't hide the haunted look in her eyes. There was so much more to this woman than he knew, and he longed to learn every single detail about her. But he didn't want to push her and scare her off.

Ella munched on a taquito. When she licked the sauce from her fingertip, he couldn't turn away, fascinated by her rosy tongue as it swirled around her finger. He mustered all his self-restraint not to help her.

"Mm...delicious," she murmured. "I've always loved these."

Tony's imagination kicked into overdrive, imagining her tongue and fingers on him. The delectable image had him reaching the end of his tether. He tried reminding himself of all the reasons they shouldn't be together, but suddenly those reasons weren't sounding quite so insurmountable.

"Johnny loves them, too." Tony tried to focus on anything but how much he wanted her—all of her.

Ella gave him a thoughtful look, pursed her lips as though to say something, but stopped. Instead, she glanced away. She couldn't leave him wondering if she was having the same sort of thoughts as he was.

"Whatever you're thinking, just spit it out."

"It's none of my business." She gazed warily at him, then said, "I'm just curious. How did you end up being Johnny's guardian?"

The question doused his heated thoughts. He cleared his throat. "Someone had to step up to the plate. Seemed like the thing to do." It was his stock answer whenever poked and prodded, and he felt guilty for not being more open with Ella.

Her gaze lowered to the napkin in her hand. “I’m sorry. I shouldn’t have brought up the subject. I just thought if I understood a little more about Johnny’s background, I might be able to connect with him and be more effective when we’re going over his lessons.”

Tony took a long drink of cold water while wrapping his mind around the fact that Ella was concerned enough about his nephew to risk asking such a sensitive question. She might as well hear the entire truth from him instead of some twisted version from Whistle Stop’s gossip mill.

“A year or so ago, I was living near Santa Fe. My brother had been pestering me to come down to Whistle Stop and see what he’d done with the ranch. It wasn’t his first request, but each time he mentioned me visiting, I found a new excuse. I didn’t want to face the huge responsibility I’d dumped on him, nor hear my mother’s subtle innuendos about how much I was needed at home. I knew my girlfriend, Jessie, wouldn’t go with me. She and my mother didn’t exactly hit it off.”

“It’s hard to imagine Carlota not getting along with someone.”

“Jessie was different. Sort of a wild child, but always lots of fun. I met her at a bar when I was at the firefighting academy. We started dating, and she convinced me to move away. My mother tried to tell me that Jessie was a pack of trouble just waiting to happen, but I thought I knew better.” He paused, waiting for the wave of betrayal to hit him, but for the first time, the anguish had dulled. “I never thought Jessie would hurt me. I guess I was wrong.”

"Maybe she'll come to her senses and come back to you."

He shrugged. "For a long time I thought that—I hoped for that. But it wasn't meant to be. I'm not meant to be happy."

"I don't believe that."

"That's because you…you don't know the whole story."

"If this is too painful, we don't have to talk about it."

He did. For himself. He had to prove he was strong enough to deal with these memories.

"The night before the accident, my brother called. He asked me to drive out to the ranch. He had news to share. Even though I didn't have any plans, I lied and told him I did. I wasn't up for another one of his guilt trips. The next evening, there was a knock at the door. It was my brother and his wife. They wanted me to be the first to know that I was going to be an uncle again. They were hoping it'd convince me to move home and help my brother run the ranch, giving him more time for their growing family."

Tony's throat grew thick. Though a year had passed since the accident, the loss still caused a throbbing ache in his chest. He pushed past the pain, intent on telling the whole, awful tale.

Ella's mouth opened, but before she could utter a syllable, he barreled on. He feared if he stopped now, he wouldn't be able to continue. "I was selfish and could only think about my life and my future. I told them I was happy for them, but I wasn't moving back to Whistle Stop. That was the last time I saw either of them."

He sucked in a ragged breath and blew it out slowly, trying to keep a lid on his emotions. "A drunk driver with a suspended license got on the interstate going the wrong direction... He killed them."

Tony leaned forward, bracing his arms on the table. "When I found out about the accident, I knew instantly what I had to do. My days of acting like a rebellious, self-indulgent jerk were over. I was needed at home to do what I should have done all along—help my family."

The memories came back to him hard and fast. "When I told Jessie I was adopting Johnny and moving back to Whistle Stop, she refused to go. She claimed I didn't owe my family anything. When I disagreed, she packed up and moved out."

"I'm so sorry." Ella's hand covered his and squeezed, easing the tension from his body.

"That's why I'm here, trying to do my best by Johnny. If it wasn't for my own stubbornness, he'd still have his parents and that little brother he always wanted."

"Your stubbornness didn't cause that drunk driver to hit them." Her thumb stroked that back of his hand. "And you've done a great job stepping into what sounds like mighty big shoes. Your brother and sister-in-law would be proud of you."

"From what I've seen, you've done a great job stepping into some mighty big shoes. Your brother and sister-in-law would be proud of you."

With their hands still touching, Tony turned his hand over. He wrapped his fingers around hers. The pad of his thumb stroked her palm. "So tell me about your childhood."

"There isn't much to say." She fidgeted with a spoon. "When I was ten, my mother died, and I moved to Albuquerque. I graduated from UNM and started substitute teaching until my grandmother's cancer progressed to the point of her needing full-time care. Now how about I get these dishes cleaned up?"

Ella jerked away from his touch and practically jumped from the couch like a frightened kitten. She was keeping something about her past from him. And why hadn't she mentioned her little brother? Hadn't they moved to the stage where they trusted each other? Isn't that what he'd proven when he'd opened up to her just now?

Tony helped clean up the kitchen, all the while hoping Ella would share some more of her past with him. Instead, they worked in silence. Had he been wrong to think their relationship had taken a turn?

When they'd finished, he led her outside to the porch. This was where he should say good-bye and head on home. He'd shared more with her during that casual meal than he had on any other date—not that this was a date or anything. Still, he couldn't let go of the thought that things had changed between them.

"Oh, look, the moon is peeking through the tree limbs," she said. "It gives the world a magical glow. Have you ever seen anything so beautiful?"

Tony's gaze remained on Ella. "You're right. The view is stunning."

A light breeze played with the loose wisps of her hair. He ached to run his fingers through her blond strands, to have her gaze up at him with desire. He'd never craved someone like he did her.

Ella turned to him as though his intimate thoughts had summoned her attention. "You aren't even looking at the moon."

"Thanks for dinner." He changed the subject in an attempt to keep things light between them. Oh, who was he kidding? Things had progressed past light and casual a long time ago.

"It wasn't much. I hope you got enough."

"I did."

He stepped closer to her. What would a good-night kiss hurt? His hands slipped around her waist, and he drew her closer. His line of vision drifted back to her supple lips. They taunted him with their fullness. He told himself to stop, to leave, but an overwhelming desire to taste her sweet lips won out.

Just a quick kiss good night, and then he'd be on his way…

He reached behind her, releasing her hair clip. Her blond locks tumbled down over her shoulders. "You're so breathtaking."

She gazed up at him. The moonlight played across her face. But it was her eyes that gave him pause. Was that hesitation he detected in them?

"Do you want me to go?" He would. It'd be tough to turn away from her, but he'd do whatever made her happy.

She shook her head. "I want you to stay."

That was all the invitation he needed.

His head dipped, and he caught a whiff of her citrus-scented shampoo. The invigorating scent ensnared him, drawing him closer. His mouth brushed tentatively against hers. Her lips were smooth and soft, softer than he remembered. Half-expecting her to pull away, he was surprised when she moved closer. His hands gripped her hips tighter, holding on for this exquisite journey.

Any apprehension slipped into the far recesses of his mind. He never wanted to let her go. His fingers ran through her silky hair as her mouth opened to him.

Her tongue stroked his cautiously at first. Teasing. Tempting. Enticing.

She tasted spicy, which fired up his hormones even more. His body pulsed with a need unlike any other he'd known. He stifled a groan of anticipation.

Slow and steady. He repeated the mantra in his head.

He'd never worried so much about pleasing a woman he was kissing. He wanted to sweep her up in this passion and escape to a place where their problems ceased to exist.

Her hands slid up his biceps and across his shoulders, causing a new, stronger wave of desire to wash over him. He lifted her off the ground, bringing her chest-to-chest and hip-to-hip with him. She had to feel his obvious need, his want, and yet she didn't pull away.

When her jean-clad legs wrapped around his waist, his blood pressure shot into triple digits. Their kiss intensified, and all sense of propriety slipped away.

Here, with Ella, he stopped being the man desperately trying to make up for past mistakes. He wasn't a son, uncle, firefighter, or cowboy. He was merely a flawed man falling for the most amazing woman in the world.

"Let's continue this inside," he whispered against her mouth.

He lowered her to her feet. She led him into the cabin, where long shadows danced through the living room. He pulled her to a stop, needing to press his lips to hers once more, needing assurance that this wasn't one of his dreams.

Her eager kisses moved from his mouth, along his jaw, and down his neck. A moan swirled in his chest and rose in intensity. Every place her lips touched felt as if it were on fire.

His hands reached out to her, fumbling with the buttons on her blouse. In his eagerness, a button popped off. Ella grabbed at her shirt and backed away. An inner struggle reflected in her eyes. Her sweet mouth opened, but nothing came out.

"I'm sorry. It was an accident." When she didn't respond, he added, "If you want me to go, I will."

Pink stained her cheeks from his stubble. Her lips were a deep rose and slightly swollen from the intensity of their kisses. But it was the wariness in her eyes and the way she clutched at her blouse that kept him from reaching out to her. His hands dropped to his sides, and he turned to the door.

"Don't go..." She touched his arm. "Please stay...with me."

"Are you sure?"

She nodded before taking him by the hand and leading him to her bedroom. Darkness descended over them. Tony reached for the light switch, wanting to see the passion in her eyes, but Ella's hand covered his.

"Leave it off."

Not about to argue, he instead reached out to her and pulled her close. How had he gotten so lucky to have such an amazing woman with such a big heart wrapped in his arms?

Tonight, all of the rules would change. He didn't know where it'd leave them, but when Ella's lips pressed to his, he realized there would be plenty of time for thinking later—much later.

Chapter Sixteen

ELLA SETTLED BACK ON the bed pillows, breathless from their frantic lovemaking. Every inch of her body tingled. Tony had amazed her with his thoughtfulness in making sure he gave her as much pleasure as he got. He'd been able to maneuver past her reservations and get her to think about only one thing—him.

"You're the most amazing woman," he drawled.

He pulled her closer with one powerful arm. Her head came to rest on his shoulder. For a time, they lay there with their bodies entwined. No matter how much she fought to hold on to the precious moment, the magic faded away and the harsh reality of the situation settled in.

The prickling sensation of panic inched down her spine and spread to every limb. Had Tony detected her scars? Would he turn away in the light of day? A cold wall of protectiveness settled over her.

Flashes of her nightmare came rushing back to her. She couldn't let it come true. She'd made a mistake by letting her guard down with him and getting swept away in a rush of emotions. Though he embodied everything she'd ever wanted in a man, if the scars didn't scare him off, her secret surely would.

How could she let herself be happy when she'd been the one to start the fire that killed her family? She could still hear the echo of her grandmother's bitter accusations reinforcing her guilt.

She had to end things now before either of them got in any deeper. If Tony ever learned what she'd done, he'd know she would only be a hindrance to his life, a stumbling block when it came to him gaining custody of Johnny. She wouldn't let that happen. Tony and Johnny were too important to her to take risks with their future.

Tony's hand caressed her cheek before sliding down her neck and then over her shoulder. With every millimeter his fingers moved, her body tensed and her heart pounded. Had he already noticed her scars? If so, he hadn't said anything. Was it possible that they were more prevalent to her than others?

When his fingers reached the top of her arm, she shoved aside his hand. She wasn't brave enough to find out how he'd react to her disfigurement. "It's late. You should go." She tried to keep her tone neutral. "Johnny will be worried."

She inched away. The parts of her body that had been touching him quickly grew cold. Unshed tears pricked her eyes, forcing her to blink repeatedly.

The moonlight peeking through the window allowed her to spot the frown pulling at his face. She turned her back to him, trying to block out the damage of her words. She hated how her moment of weakness—of giving in to her desires—would now hurt him. She should never have let things get this far.

"Johnny is fine. He's with my mother and long asleep. Now stop worrying and slide back over here."

"Still, it's late. We both have to get up early in the morning."

"Why are you finding every possible excuse to get rid of me? Was it me? Did I push too hard? Too fast—"

"You...you were perfect." She struggled to keep her emotions in check, even though her heart was breaking.

"Then I don't understand. Why are you pushing me away? Don't you know that I care about you?"

She pressed her trembling fingers to her tender lips and blinked repeatedly. She wanted to turn into his arms and burrow her face into his muscled chest. She wanted to feel safe—cared about.

As tempting as the thought was, she couldn't let herself go there. She couldn't make herself any more vulnerable. She remembered too well what happened when she opened up to people—her grandmother, her ex-boyfriend—they pulled away and looked at her differently. They left such a distance that she'd never felt so alone. She couldn't go through that again.

Not even for Tony.

The awkward silence dragged on. What could she say to make this any better for him? A mere "I'm sorry" seemed to lack the depth of her regret at the pain she'd cause him. Her throat tightened as she struggled to hold back her sobs. How could something so wonderful end so badly?

"You're right." He got to his feet. "I shouldn't be here."

The raw emotion in his deep voice broke through her guardedness. She swallowed hard, washing down her unshed tears. She needed to absorb all of the blame. He'd done nothing wrong. He'd been a giving, tender lover.

"It's not you." Her voice wavered. "I'm sorry. I thought I was ready for this, but I'm not."

Tony flicked on the bedside light, and she yanked the sheet up to her chin.

"What's going on, Ella? After all we've shared...after I opened up...revealed my past...my guilt...how can you shut me out?"

An agonizing moment of silence ensued as she tried to find an explanation to make this okay for him. When she finally spoke, her voice was no more than a whisper. "There are things about me you don't know. Things that would make you realize tonight can never happen again."

"Then talk to me. Whatever the problem is, we can work through it."

She shook her head. "No. We can't. You wouldn't understand." Her voice cracked as a tear slipped down her cheek. "And I couldn't bear it if you looked at me with pity in your eyes, or worse..."

"I wouldn't do that. Trust me." He reached out to her, but she backed away, keeping the sheet in place. His hand landed on the mattress with a thud.

Her heart ached, and unshed tears blurred the wounded look on his face. "Maybe someday you'll be able to forgive me. Maybe then we can figure out how to be friends again."

Tony didn't say a word as he grabbed his things. She was asking too much. She knew it, but she couldn't stomach the thought of Tony hating her...forever.

How could something feel so right and end so horribly?

Two days had passed since Tony had experienced, in Ella's bed, the most exquisite lovemaking. Instead of the images fading, they'd continued to taunt him, making him crave her even more.

Ella next to him.

Lip-to-lip.

Skin-to-skin.

The scorching memory heated his blood, making him shift uncomfortably in his seat. He'd sequestered himself in the office to update the ranch's finances, but he lacked the concentration.

He'd tried to contact her, but she hadn't returned his calls. She'd mentioned her past, and his gut told him this had something to do with what he had overheard her telling Johnny about her little brother, but he couldn't complete the connection. Sure, losing a sibling was difficult. He knew that for an unequivocal fact. But why would that make her close herself off from him?

Restless and distracted, he rushed through lunch before saddling up his horse to ride out and check the fence on the southern boundary. He could have sent one of the hands, but he hoped the fresh air and sunshine would clear his mind. However, when he happened upon a neighboring rancher frowning as he surveyed a downed section of fence, Tony knew he'd never make it back in time for their dance lesson.

He told himself that he needed to do this job personally. After all, he'd given his neighbor his word that it'd be taken care of promptly. He refused to accept that he was grasping at any excuse to avoid facing the woman who'd rejected him.

Had she heard rumors about him? Did she think that he was on the hunt for a mother for Johnny?

Because that couldn't be further from the truth. With a frustrated sigh, he gave his head a shake. Wondering about it wasn't going to give him any answers.

Needing tools for the repair job, Tony returned to the barn. He glanced at the clock. Ella would still be teaching. Once he'd left a message explaining the situation at the ranch, he headed out.

On the ride, his thoughts continued to circle around and snag on Ella. Her refusal to open up to him about her sudden change of mind about them still stung. He tried telling himself that pursuing this thing with her could jeopardize the adoption, but he wasn't ready to give up on her. Not yet. Not until he knew what caused her to pull back.

Why had she even bothered to show up?

Ella drove slowly along the quiet Whistle Stop street. A spaghetti dinner at a nearby church had cars lining both sides of the street in front of the dance studio, forcing her to park around the corner. She'd switched out of her work clothes at school, hoping a pair of worn jeans and a comfy long-sleeved T-shirt would help put her at ease. But it hadn't done a thing to loosen the knot in her stomach.

Ella locked up her car out of habit before making her way toward the studio. She knew what was going to happen—Tony was going to call off their agreement. How could he not? She'd made such a mess of things, and just when she and Tony were getting along so well. To top it off, she would lose her chance to win the dance contest, and the money to save her home.

Ella pushed open the door of Josie's dance studio. The thought of facing Tony again made her want to run, but hiding wasn't an option. She was an adult, and she had to face the mess she'd created in both of their lives.

Her mind reeled with regret as she recalled the hurt in his eyes and the plea in his voice when he'd asked her to trust him. He had no idea how much she wanted to do just that, but when she tried to figure out how to phrase it, fear paralyzed her.

Even though Tony's truck hadn't been parked out front, she still found herself scanning the room for him. When she didn't spot him, a mixture of relief and disappointment churned within her. She consoled herself by realizing everyone ran late once in a while. Yeah, right. He wasn't going to show up today or any other day. He wanted nothing to do with her anymore. The thought stabbed at her scarred heart.

"Hello, Ella." Josie stepped out of her office. "Did you not know that Tony canceled?"

"I haven't heard from him. I turned my phone off before work, and I guess I forgot to turn it back on." She couldn't resist reaching for her phone. There was in fact a message from Tony. The knot in her stomach eased a bit. So he was still speaking to her. That had to mean something.

"He said there was a problem at the ranch," Josie added.

Logically, Ella had known he wouldn't show, not after the disastrous way things ended between them. The wounded look in his eyes stood out in her memory. Still, a part of her had been hopeful that they could go back to the way things had been before she'd let her desires run amok.

"Too bad he won't be here tonight. I wanted to go over that new routine we tried on Friday. The chemistry between you two crackles when you're dancing."

Her memory quickly returned to the sizzling kiss that had started this whole mess. Heat warmed Ella's chest, climbed up her neck, and settled in her cheeks. The two of them had crackled on and off the dance floor.

The door opened. Ella glanced up, expecting to find Tony standing in the doorway. Instead, his mother smiled at her.

"Hi. I just dropped Johnny off at Bobby's because I have a surprise." A smile lit up Carlota's face. Then she glanced around. "Where's Tony?"

Ella stepped forward. "He isn't here. There was some sort of problem at the ranch."

Carlota's forehead wrinkled. "Wonder what it is? I haven't been home most of the day."

Ella had assumed this mysterious problem had just been a handy excuse, and Carlota's confusion confirmed it. Not wanting to explain the truth, Ella said, "I'm sure if it was a big deal, someone would have told you."

Carlota shrugged. "I suppose you're right. I'll check on things when I get home." She moved farther into the room. "Am I interrupting anything?"

"Uh...no. I'm just leaving." Ella didn't want to make idle chitchat.

"Since you aren't having practice tonight, let's go see your surprise." Carlota's cheeks puffed as she flashed a broad grin.

Ella turned to Josie. "I'm really sorry about this mix-up."

"No problem. See you Wednesday." Josie smiled. "By the way, tell your partner he isn't allowed to skip class again."

"I…I will." She doubted she'd get the chance. And if Tony wanted to back out of the rest of their lessons, he could explain it to Josie.

Once outside on the sidewalk, Carlota proceeded to walk in the opposite direction of Ella's car.

"Wait." Ella stopped. "My car's around the corner. I can give you a ride."

Carlota continued walking. "You don't need it. We can walk."

Ella rushed to catch up to the woman. "Any chance you'll tell me what the surprise is?"

"Stick with me, and you'll soon find out."

Ella prayed that whatever it was had nothing to do with Tony. The last thing she wanted was to face him in front of his mother. Things between them were such a mess that his mother would surely catch on to the discord and demand an explanation, something Ella was certain neither of them wanted to provide.

Chapter Seventeen

He needed to see Ella.

Even though he'd canceled the lesson, was there a chance she might have missed his message and gone to the dance studio? It was worth a try. The more time that passed, the more urgent his need became to talk with her.

With the setting sun splashing the earth with its last lingering rays, Tony drove through Whistle Stop. Couples strolled along the sidewalks hand-in-hand. Kids rode their bikes. Shopkeepers closed up their stores for the evening. Everything looked normal. But it wasn't—not in his world. In fact, his world was nothing but a jumbled-up mess.

He wasn't sure how to piece things back together with Ella. Was it even possible at this point? He sighed. It'd be so easy to turn around and head back home. But there was something deep inside him, a driving need to put things right with her. He had to at least try.

Tony parked his pickup before rushing across the street to Josie's Dance Studio. He peered inside, but the lights were out. He tried the doorknob just in case they were in the office talking, but it didn't budge. And then he noticed the note taped to the glass: *Be back later.*

Tony swore under his breath. He jumped into his truck. Just in case he'd missed a call from Ella, he pulled out his cell phone. There was no message from Ella, but there was one from his mother. It was a static-filled connection. He could make out only every third or fourth word, leaving him to wonder what she had wanted. He tried calling the house, but there was no answer. Next, he tried his mother's cell phone, but it went directly to voice mail. He'd try again later.

He turned toward the ranch. With Johnny spending part of the evening with Bobby's family, Tony was about to head home to an empty house. The idea of being alone with his troubled thoughts had him easing up on the gas pedal.

If he wanted to be honest with himself, he had to accept that he'd pushed her too hard, too fast. The acknowledgment lodged in his chest, heavy and jagged. He'd been expecting too much from her this early in their relationship. She obviously had trust issues. Why hadn't he taken the time to go slow with her?

He'd never meant to scare her way.

Instead, he wanted to be the person she turned to.

The person she poured her heart out to.

This revelation shook him to the core. For the first time in days, he knew exactly what to do. A hard jerk to the left on the steering wheel had the pickup making a U-turn. He'd find her tonight. She might not speak to him after he'd missed their dance lesson. Still, he had to try to smooth things over.

On the drive to Roca Mountain, he tried to figure out what he'd say to her. His gut knotted up. He'd never been good at apologies, but that didn't mean he wouldn't try. He wanted...he wanted...oh, he didn't know what he wanted, except to figure out this thing with Ella.

When he pulled into her driveway, disappointment coursed through him. The place was dark, and her car wasn't there. Where could she be? With absolutely no idea where else to look for her, he headed back to town. He wasn't ready to go home—not until he got a handle on his thoughts.

The street lamps of Whistle Stop lit up the road. A peacefulness had settled over the town as the shadows of evening grew long. Tony felt anything but peaceful. He slowed when he spotted his mother's car in front of Mrs. Sanchez's house. Her garbled voice mail gnawed at him. What if it had been something important? He pulled over to park. It'd take two minutes to pop in and check with her, then he'd head home.

Ella's mouth gaped open.

This is my surprise?

She stood in the middle of Mrs. Sanchez's kitchen staring at the most gorgeous dress she'd ever seen. The fact that Carlota and her friend had graciously made it for her to wear in the dance competition left her speechless. Tears of joy moistened Ella's eyes as she gazed at the amazing red and white creation. How could she not fall in love with a town filled with such generous souls?

"It's stunning." Ella frantically searched for the appropriate words of gratitude. "You two are wonderful. No one has ever done anything so sweet and thoughtful for me. Ever. I…I don't know how to thank you."

"Oh, don't go getting all mushy," Mrs. Sanchez said. "You'll have my mascara running down my cheeks." She swiped a hand beneath each watery eye.

"Don't pay her any mind." Carlota waved off Mrs. Sanchez. "She gets misty-eyed over everything—"

"Do not." Mrs. Sanchez sniffled.

As though Carlota hadn't heard her friend, she continued, "You really like the dress? I mean, you don't have to. We just thought you might want something special for the occasion."

"I do. I really like it."

Once Ella pulled her emotions under control, she inspected the fancy garment a little closer. Her gaze started with the fire-engine red satin A-line skirt. It was short. She highly doubted it'd reach the tops of her knees. She could easily imagine it fluffing out when she spun in a circle. The skirt was drawn in with a coordinating waistband. A white bodice shimmered with silver embellishments that emphasized a daring neckline. Her breath caught in her throat when she realized the dress had no sleeves.

Hoping they weren't done assembling everything, she asked, "Is…is it finished?"

Mrs. Sanchez beamed. "Yes, it is. We worked on it every evening, except for when Carlota had another date…erm, plans."

Carlota's face filled with color as she cleared her throat, sending Mrs. Sanchez a warning glance. Was it possible that Carlota had a secret boyfriend? Interesting.

Mrs. Sanchez chuckled, before continuing, "I didn't think we'd get done in time, but thankfully I was worried about nothing. Now all we need is for you to try it on so we can mark it for alterations."

Ella kept a smile pinned to her face even though the dress's daring cuts dampened her elation. She normally dressed rather modestly for her age group. It allowed her to fade into the background. There was nothing modest about this outfit. In fact, it was quite the opposite. The dress was glamorous and demanded attention. And without sleeves, how in the world would she keep her scars hidden?

"We should offer her some tea," Carlota said, pulling out a chair at the kitchen table. "Sometimes we get excited and forget out manners. You do drink tea, don't you, dear?"

Ella nodded, and on legs that felt wooden she moved to the designated chair. All the while, she admonished herself for her lack of enthusiasm. After all, she was exceedingly honored these women thought enough of her to take the time to make something for her.

As she sat down at the table, Mrs. Sanchez placed a plate of biscochitos in front of her. Ella didn't have any appetite, but she forced herself to be polite. She couldn't tell these ladies about her reservations. She helped herself to one of the thick sugar cookies. A coating of cinnamon and granulated sugar dusted the top of each one. Ella bit into the delicious treat, tasting a hint of anise.

As they sipped their tea, Mrs. Sanchez filled them in on the latest gossip about the upcoming renovations to the local train depot. She mentioned that plans were to totally modernize it with a bunch of electronic equipment as well as add on an addition for a bus station. Little Whistle Stop was about to have a growth spurt, if all went according to plan.

Ella wasn't sure how she felt about more people moving in. She'd moved away from the city to gain a fresh start in a quiet small town. She hoped Whistle Stop didn't grow too much.

Ella nibbled her way through the cookie. All the while, she thought of every excuse possible to get out of trying on the dress. Carlota raved about how wonderful the dress would look on her. Mrs. Sanchez chimed in about how many years it had been since she had last picked up a sewing needle, but she was pleased with how well the dress turned out.

Ella thought of mentioning her disfigurement, but she hesitated. She knew what would come next—the inevitable questions. Eventually they would lead to the agonizing fact that she had lived while her family had perished. *How could that be?* They'd think it, but they wouldn't say it. And she couldn't blame them. She'd had the exact same thought countless times.

With their snack finished, Carlota guided her to a bedroom. Once the door thudded shut and Ella was alone, she held the dress to her chest. It truly was the most amazing dress she'd ever laid eyes on. She spun around in a circle, letting the material billow out. Feminine and sexy all stitched together. Carlota and Mrs. Sanchez had certainly outdone themselves. No way was she going to hurt the woman who had become so dear to her by telling her she wouldn't wear the handmade dress.

Ella slipped on the dress and turned to the mirror. The beauty of the outfit only partially compensated for the ugliness of her arms. Sure, the scars had faded some, but they were still painfully obvious.

She took a steadying breath as she ran her hands down over the soft material before giving her reflection another glance. The time had come to make a decision. Her stomach grew nauseated as she realized either she insulted those sweet women by refusing to model the dress or she sucked up all of her long-held insecurities and walked out there bare-armed.

Fear cemented her feet to the floor. There had to be a compromise. Some way to keep from hurting their feelings. Some way to cover her scars. A glance around the room revealed a lightweight white sweater hanging on the closet door handle. Surely Mrs. Sanchez wouldn't mind if she borrowed it.

With the little sweater hiding her physical scars, Ella opened the door. A fluttering sensation filled her stomach. She swallowed hard as she forced one foot in front of the other. When she returned to the kitchen, the women were indulging in another cup of tea. Ella plastered what she hoped was a smile on her face as she put her arms behind her back.

Carlota's face creased. "Goodness, girl, are you cold?"

"I can turn up the temperature on the swamp cooler." Mrs. Sanchez got to her feet.

"No. Don't. I'm fine." In actuality, she was quite warm.

Carlota sent her a puzzled look. "You'll have to take off that sweater if I'm going to check the dress."

Ella clenched the tender flesh of her lower lip between her teeth. What choice did she have? Her stomach twisted.

Carlota helped her take off the sweater. The knitted fabric swished the whole way down her arms before she could stop it. Her scars fully revealed, she yanked her arms behind her back. Even if she could speak, she didn't know what she'd say. She clutched her hands, squeezing her fingers to the point they throbbed.

"You were right, Carlota." Mrs. Sanchez circled Ella. "The bodice fits her like a glove. I don't think we'll have to make many adjustments there, but the waist and hem need a bit of work."

Carlota knelt down to pluck a piece of lint from the material. "I told you I have an eye for these things. If I hadn't become a teacher, I'd have been seamstress in Hollywood."

The women laughed. Ella stood there, eyeing up the hallway. If only her legs would cooperate, she could make an excuse and slip away. Once she was back in her long-sleeved T-shirt, her heart would quit pounding and the heat would leave her face.

Carlota straightened. "Relax your arms."

Ella hesitated. Then, sucking in a deep breath, she let her arms hang limp at her sides, revealing her scars.

The women's intent gazes swept over her from head to toe. Ella was unable to tell if it was her scars or the dress they were studying so intently. Feeling subconscious, she once again put her arms behind her back.

Carlota patted her shoulder. "Relax, child, I've got worse scars after having two kids than you do. You really shouldn't hide beneath those long sleeves."

Stunned that Carlota truly didn't think much of her arms, she stood there, dumbfounded. How could this be? The kids in school had taunted her, saying she had cooties. Her own grandmother insisted she keep her scars covered, as though they were too awful to stomach. And her last boyfriend—a man she foolishly thought she could trust—had turned away.

How could Carlota be so different? So understanding? Of course, it'd all change if Carlota found out the whole story. Of that, Ella was certain. She wanted to believe the woman, but she knew her scars were big and ugly. Though their redness had faded years ago, they were still as evident as the outline of the Rocky Mountains on the horizon.

Mrs. Sanchez sent her a reassuring smile. "You have nothing to be ashamed of. You're very pretty."

Ella's eyes misted over. When she spoke, her voice was rough with emotion. "No one's ever said that to me before."

Carlota's caring gaze met hers. "Well, they should and often. Now I need to make a few adjustments."

"I'll go grab my sewing box and a stool." Mrs. Sanchez shuffled out of the kitchen.

"Relax." Carlota sent her a reassuring smile. "You and my son will make a great couple—for the dance, that is."

Ella didn't know what to say to that, so she said nothing. Thankfully, Mrs. Sanchez returned and placed a wooden stool in the middle of the floor.

They had her stand on it while they adjusted the lustrous material and pinned it. The women chatted as they worked, but Ella soon learned that when their mouths moved, their fingers stopped. The adjustments took much, much longer than she'd ever imagined.

When they finally finished, Carlota said, "Come on. Give us the complete view."

Ella stepped off the stool. She twirled around the kitchen floor, letting the skirt puff out.

"Perfect," the women announced in unison. They clapped their hands in excitement.

"Wait," Carlota said, rushing up beside her. "Let's try this."

She reached up to release Ella's hair from the barrette and used her fingers to gently comb it into submission.

Stepping back, the older woman said, "The dress may be beautiful, but it can't compare with your own natural beauty."

Her scars were never mentioned again. For a moment, Ella wasn't quite so self-conscious. Maybe it was being near these amazingly kind women, or maybe it was this fancy dress, but for the first time in her life, she actually felt beautiful—inside and out.

Tony, still holding the doorknob, watched from the doorway. He couldn't believe his eyes. Ella looked like—he struggled for the right word—an angel. No, an angel wouldn't cause the excitement coursing through his body. His gaze took in the waves of golden hair flowing over her shoulders.

"You look stunning," he uttered. It wasn't until her compelling, blue eyes met his that he realized he'd spoken out loud.

His gaze moved from her long, slender neck to her lush bosom, which threatened to spill over the restraints of the tight material. He'd already known she was hot, but seeing her in this low-cut dress was more tempting than any of his fantasies. He ached to take her into his arms and kiss her passionately.

"I agree, Tony," Mrs. Sanchez said. "You'll be the most stunning couple in the competition. All the available men will be jealous."

"You better be careful, son." Carlota arched a brow at Tony. "Or someone might just steal your dance partner."

Ella looked away as her fingers twisted together, making him realize he was still openly ogling her. A glance at his mother's amused grin only increased his discomfort.

Carlota offered Ella a necklace. "Let's try this on with the dress."

Ella hesitated before reaching for the strand of sparkly beads. Her lips lowered into a frown. He wondered what was troubling her, but then he noticed the webbed scars on her forearms. He'd seen too many fire victims not to recognize them instantly as burn scars. This newfound knowledge hit him like a sucker punch.

At last, he knew her secret.

The picture of her little brother and the teddy bear on her mantel flashed through his mind. He remembered the tremble in her voice as she told Johnny her brother was dead. The pain from her scars ran much deeper than her skin. In that moment, he was truly seeing her for the first time, and he understood her in ways he had never imagined.

This was why she'd insisted on the thorough fire-safety precautions at the cabin. And why she insisted he clear the brush from outside her bedroom window. Most of all, this was the reason for her insistence on the darkness when they made love, why she'd jerked away from him in bed when he'd tried to comfort her. The pieces all started falling into place.

Sure, her past had been painful, but why had she decided to reveal her scars to his mother and not him? The jagged thought poked at his chest. He'd opened up to her about his deepest, darkest moment, and it hadn't meant a thing to her. He didn't know what else he could have done to gain her trust. He'd obviously been wrong about her—about them.

Not about to have this conversation in front of witnesses, he turned and walked away.

Chapter Eighteen

Ella watched in horror as Tony made a hasty exit. Just as she'd feared, he was walking away from her after seeing her scars. But, no, she refused to let another man reject her because of something as superficial as scars. She rushed out the back door after him.

"Wait," she called out to him. "You can't just walk away."

His shoulders straightened, and he turned. "Your mother and brother died in a fire, didn't they?"

She swallowed, determined to face him and finally tell the truth. She could do this. "Yes, when I was a child."

"I'm sorry. I can't imagine how devastating that was." His voice grew rough with emotion. "Why didn't you tell me, especially after I opened up to you about my own brother's death?"

Deep down, she wanted to share her awful secret with him. Maybe he'd understand. As she considered where to begin, an overwhelming fear consumed her that she hadn't experienced since she was a child. For a second, she was that little girl again in the hospital after the fire, with her distraught grandmother, the one who heaped all of the blame on her. It was her grandfather who'd been understanding. Her grandmother had never understood. How would Tony react?

Fright twisted and mangled Ella's thoughts. She was wrong. She couldn't do this. "It's too difficult to talk about. I…I can't. Not yet."

Hurt shadowed his eyes. "This is why you pushed me away the other night, isn't it? You didn't want me to see your scars."

She couldn't let on there was more to her secret than her disfigurement. "Have you ever thought about the difficult position it would put me in to have a romantic relationship with the parent of a boy I'm tutoring? How it might look to the school board, especially while they're considering me for a permanent position?"

"No one would care. Don't try to make up excuses." Tony's gaze narrowed as he stared at her as though trying to read her thoughts. "You've been avoiding talking about your past all along. What else don't I know?"

Scared of him digging too deep, she threw out a question of her own. "Why is my past so important to you? Or are you mad because you unknowingly became involved with someone who is disfigured?"

"You can't be serious. You're the most beautiful woman in the world." The anger brewing in his eyes stole the joy of his compliment. "Do I come across as someone who's so superficial that I can't see past a couple of scars?"

She didn't think that of him. He was the greatest guy she'd ever known, which made this discussion all that much harder. Somehow she had to make it clear this was her burden to carry alone. "My past is something I won't share with anyone—not even you."

He raked his fingers through his hair, scattering it into a mass of tiny spikes. "I thought over these past few weeks we'd been growing closer, learning to trust each other. But I guess I was wrong to let down my guard and let you in."

"No, I was wrong...to assume I could move to this small town and expect some privacy."

"Don't worry. You'll be getting all the privacy you want. I'll make sure not to bother you again."

His enraged words hit her glass heart like hurled rocks, shattering it into jagged pieces. Her chest ached, and her vision blurred.

Letting her pain rule her mouth, she choked out, "Moving here was a mistake."

A moment passed, and his frown deepened. Then his gaze narrowed. "You're right."

He turned and strode away without a backward glance.

Chapter Nineteen

Would the pain and loneliness ever ease up?

After school the following day, Ella let out a string of yawns as she drove home. Thoughts of her argument with Tony lurked around the edges of her mind, keeping her awake most of the night.

The thought of revealing her secret—the one she'd kept locked up for years—frightened her more than anything. She honestly didn't know if she had the strength to peel back the layers of guilt and remorse in order to confess. Though, for the first time, she wanted to open up. She wanted to share everything with Tony. She was torn by her conflicting emotions, and her head began to throb.

Once she reached the cabin, she tended to Patch. Then, she pulled out some leftover chicken noodle soup for herself, but just as quickly she returned it to the fridge. She'd agonized over her problems with Tony to the point of making herself sick.

She needed a distraction and moved to the built-in bookcases that lined each side of the stone fireplace. Her fingers ran along the smooth wood shelves her grandfather had lovingly crafted. His love for the cabin was evident in everything he'd touched. She took comfort in having all of these family heirlooms surrounding her and being able to call this place home.

Ella selected a romance novel she'd bought before leaving Albuquerque. It'd be nice to escape, to read about someone having a happily-ever-after, since she wouldn't be having one of her own.

She curled up on the couch next to the puppy, opened the cover and forced her attention on the words. Every time she came to a detailed description of the sexy hero, her thoughts turned to Tony. By the time she reached the bottom of that page, she couldn't remember what she'd read. Starting at the beginning again, she soon lost her train of thought as her mind filled with images of the hurt in Tony's eyes.

With a frustrated sigh, she set aside the book and decided to call it a night. In the bedroom, she slipped on an old T-shirt and crawled beneath the covers. The wind howled as a draft moved through the room, forcing her deeper under the blankets.

Patch pawed at her closet door, anxious to get into his favorite hiding spot. She sighed and crawled out of her snuggly cocoon of blankets in order to open the door for him.

The air whistled through the tiny crevices around the old window and sent Ella scurrying back into bed. She closed her eyes, envisioning Tony next to her, sharing his body heat. Oh, how she longed to snuggle with him.

Sometime during the night, she at last dozed off, only to be abruptly awakened by a loud bang. The powerful winds had thrown something against the side of the cabin. Startled and nervous, she slipped out of bed and padded over to the window. In the dark, she wasn't able to see much. After checking the rest of the cabin, she slid back under the covers, but sleep evaded her.

When her alarm went off, she grudgingly climbed out of bed. The first thing she did was take Patch outside. Dark clouds scudded across the early morning sky, and trees bent to and fro as lightning lit up the sky. The gloomy weather seemed to fit her mood.

The blustering wind frightened the pup to the point where he would barely move from the steps to do his business. When she picked him up, he buried his head in the crook of her arm, hiding from the flashes of lightning. She set him down inside, and Patch immediately ran for the bedroom, undoubtedly returning to the closet to snuggle on a fleece shirt that had fallen from a hanger.

Once dressed for work, she set out Patch's food and called him, but he didn't budge. He seemed calm in his hideaway. She didn't have the heart to force him into his crate. She'd call her neighbor, Tracey, and ask her to check on him later.

She hated to leave the little guy, but it was only a little wind. Everything would be fine, she told herself. Right now she had her job to do.

By the time she reached school, the winds hadn't let up. In fact, they might have been even stronger. She parked and rushed toward the building. The fierce winds whipped sand and dirt in her face. She pressed her lips tightly together to keep the grit out of her mouth. Once inside, she ran her hand over her hair, smoothing the loose strands. This was going to be a challenging day, of that she had no doubt.

A half hour later, a gust of wind rattled her classroom windows. Lightning lit up the sky, followed by the echoing boom of thunder. A chill of apprehension ran up her spine.

She wondered if Tony was keeping an eye on the sky, too. Since he was a volunteer firefighter, she imagined he'd be on standby. The thought of him protecting the community gave her a sense of security, knowing he would respond should this electrical storm create havoc in their normally peaceful corner of the world.

A knock at the door drew her attention. She turned and found Melissa standing in the opening. Children skirted around the woman and filed into the room. "Hi. Do you have a second?"

"Sure." Ella joined her in the hallway.

"I thought you'd want to know the radio announced that the authorities raised a red-flag warning. They say this storm has cloud-to-ground lightning strikes."

The fine hairs on her arms rose. Patch! He was all alone. Thoughts of the dry tinder around her cabin and the way the winds would fan flames made her shudder. "Thanks for the update. Let me know if you hear anything else."

"Try not to worry too much." Melissa's words were meant to comfort, but her drawn mouth and the lines creasing her brow underscored the dire circumstances. "I need to get back to the office. I'll be in touch."

Ella returned to her desk and grabbed her cell phone. Maybe Tracey could collect Patch and keep him safe. But when the phone switched to Tracey's voicemail, Ella could do no more than leave a message.

She inhaled a deep breath, reminding herself to stay calm. Everything would be all right. She turned to the class and asked them to open their math books. The children, feeling the undercurrent of energy in the air, grew restless. She continued with the planned lesson, hoping if she acted normal, the students would be able to ignore the cracks of thunder, the brilliant flashes of lightning, and the flickering of the classroom lights.

Everything will be all right.

She had to believe that. She didn't want to give the children any further reason to be concerned.

Sirens blew off and on throughout the day, each time causing her thoughts to stray to Tony. She mentally chastised herself for dwelling on him and his safety when she had a class to teach. He would be safe. He was a professional. He knew what he was doing.

After the final school bell, Melissa once again stopped by her classroom. She had her son, Bobby, and Johnny in tow. "Wait here," she said, leaving the boys in the doorway.

"Has something happened?"

Her friend's brow wrinkled as concern filled her eyes. "There's a fire on Roca Mountain."

"No." Ella's veins ran ice cold with fear.

"Don't panic." Melissa put a comforting arm around her shoulders. "The reports indicate the fire's not near your cabin."

Roca Mountain was vast, but that didn't mean the blaze wouldn't spread. Her home was in danger—again. Her hands balled into fists. Wasn't it enough that a fire had stolen her family? Would she have to endure losing her home again, too?

"I don't know what to do," Ella said, her voice rising. "My cabin. My puppy. I need to get Patch before the fire..."

Tears sprang to her eyes as her words faded away. This couldn't be happening. Her breath came short and fast. She had to save her home—and her sweet, furry baby.

"Calm down. It'll be okay." Melissa turned to the boys. "Why don't you guys go shoot hoops in the gym? I'll stop by as soon as I grab my things from the office."

Johnny looked at Ella with worry in his eyes. "Is Patch going to be okay?"

Ella snapped out of her panic in order to comfort Johnny. "Of course he'll be okay. The fire's not in the same area, so don't worry. Go ahead with Bobby."

Melissa's cell phone rang as Ella rushed to clear off her desk. She overheard half of the conversation, but she was unable to tell who was on the other end of the call. She caught a glimpse of Johnny still lingering in the doorway and started toward him when Melissa held up her hand, stopping her.

"You know that my husband, Moe, is Whistle Stop's assistant fire chief, right?" When Ella nodded, she continued, "He said they've evacuated the whole mountain and closed the road."

Ella grabbed her cell phone and selected Tracey's mobile number. *Please let her have Patch.* The phone rang once, twice, three times. Ella's grip tightened on the phone. *Answer the phone.*

"Ella?" Tracey's faint voice came across the line. "Ella, where are you?" The line crackled with static.

"At school. Do you have Patch?"

"No. I was forced to leave before I could—" The line went dead.

Ella tried calling back, but all she got was a strange beeping sound.

She swiped at the dampness on her cheeks. "I have to save Patch."

Melissa hugged her. "I'll call Moe back and let him know. I'm sure he'll get some firefighters to get Patch. Everything will be okay."

Ella prayed her friend's words would come true. But she knew how unpredictable life could be, how everything could change in a heartbeat. One second you were part of a loving family, and the next you're alone and you don't fit in anywhere.

Seconds dragged by as Melissa talked to Moe. At last, she turned a somber face her way. "Moe will do what he can to get someone up to your cabin as soon as possible. But right now they're shorthanded, and no one can be spared. I'm so sorry."

"Thanks for trying. You...you don't need to stick around. You should take the boys home."

"Come with us."

Ella didn't miss her friend's unspoken words. She might as well go home with them since she couldn't get to her own home. Her chest tightened. Would it survive the wildfire?

When Ella didn't answer, Melissa persisted, "Come on. Moe will be gone all evening. So it'll just be me and the boys. I could use the company. I have a couple of things to do in the office before I leave. I'll stop back when I'm done. I'm going to put together some water bottles and food for the firefighters, do you want to help?"

"Umm...sure. Just give me a couple of minutes to grab my stuff."

When she was alone in the classroom, frantic thoughts crowded into Ella's mind. Frustration balled up in her chest. There had to be something she could do. Unable to sit still, she rushed through her daily routine of straightening up the classroom before leaving.

Flashbacks of her childhood crowded her mind. Memories plagued her of helplessly watching as her home went up in flames with her mother and brother trapped inside. She hugged herself as the unleashed tears ran down her cheeks. She couldn't bear to lose Patch in the same horrific way. She'd promised Johnny she would keep the puppy safe.

With the classroom in order and a chance to think through the situation, she grabbed her car keys and purse. She resolved that there was nothing she could do about Patch. The realization stabbed at her, but she can't do anything foolish and make matters worse.

Ella stepped into the hallway when Melissa came rushing toward her. "Have you seen Johnny? I can't find him anywhere."

"No. Not since..." He had been standing in the doorway when Melissa told her about the wildfire. A sense of dread coursed through her. Did he get it into his head to save Patch?

"Since when?"

"I haven't seen him since you sent both boys to the gym."

"Bobby says Johnny went to the boys' room a while ago. I was hoping maybe he forgot something and stopped by his classroom."

The women split up and explored each classroom. No sign of Johnny. Ella's thoughts relentlessly returned to her concern that the boy had run off to try to save the puppy. She prayed she was wrong.

"You'd better call Tony," Ella said. "I'll drive around town and see if I can spot him."

Once in her car, she set off searching the streets for any sign of the boy. Following a hunch that he might be at the baseball park, she drove through the parking lot, but she didn't spot him on the playground equipment.

What she wouldn't do now for a brave, strong cowboy like...Tony. Disregarding the awkwardness between her and him, she stopped by the fire station where two of the three bays were empty. She jumped out of her car. Without bothering to close the door, she rushed over to the station house.

A young firefighter paused from checking some equipment on the back of the remaining fire truck. "Can I help you?"

"Is Tony Granger here?"

"No. He's been on Roca Mountain most of the day. You're the second person looking for him."

"The second?"

"Yeah, his nephew came by a bit ago."

"Do you remember when?"

The guy ran a hand over his scruffy beard. "The same time some trucks stopped here before heading up to the fire. I'd say fifteen, twenty minutes ago."

His words triggered her memory of how Johnny had stowed away in the back of her neighbor's truck to get to her cabin. Had he sneaked aboard a fire engine? Or hidden in someone's personal vehicle?

"This is really important. Do you remember seeing him after the trucks pulled out?"

"Nah. He must have gotten bored and headed home."

"So you didn't actually see him walk away?"

The fireman shook his head.

"I need you to radio those trucks and ask them to check if he's onboard."

The blond guy gave her a frustrated look. "They aren't going to take a kid on a joyride when they're on a call."

"Is there a place on a fire truck for a small boy to hide?"

He shrugged. "No one's ever tried before. Do you really think he'd do something like that?"

That little voice inside her was screaming at her that Johnny was in very serious trouble. Though she hoped that she was wrong, she couldn't afford to take any chances.

The thought of Johnny putting his own life in danger to save the puppy sent a chill of apprehension rushing down her spine. "Yes. I think he's capable of stowing away. He's done it before. Please hurry and check."

"Okay. Okay. I'll go radio them." The man rushed into the office.

Ella paced in the empty bay, more certain with each passing second that Johnny was headed for Patch. She hoped and prayed that they'd catch him before he reached the mountain.

A couple of long minutes later, the firefighter returned, shaking his head. "They're already at the scene. Someone checked the trucks, but they didn't see any sign of the boy."

She clasped her hands to keep them from shaking. This didn't mean Johnny hadn't been onboard and slipped away before they checked.

"Thanks."

After she climbed into her car, she grabbed her phone. When she spotted a new voice mail, hope filled her chest. *Let it be good news about Johnny.* Her shaky finger swiped over the touch screen.

An unfamiliar voice came over the line. "Ms. Morgan this is the Golden Nugget. I have that appraisal on your ring. I think you'll be very pleased with the amount—"

Ella jabbed her finger at the touch screen, ending the message. She didn't have time for that right now. She had much more important matters to deal with.

She immediately called Melissa. Johnny still hadn't been located, and Melissa hadn't been able to reach Tony. Ella finally vocalized her suspicion that Johnny had gone to Roca Mountain. Melissa promised she'd drive over to Carlota's place and tell her in person what had happened. They both worried about the older woman's health and that the news could have an adverse effect on her. This way, someone would be with her just in case…

Ella dialed Tony's cell phone. It went directly to voice mail.

"Tony, I need you. Johnny has gone missing, and I'm afraid—" Her voice crackled with emotion. "I think he's planning to try to rescue Patch from the wildfire. Oh, what if—please God, not again." She tossed the phone into the passenger seat.

Dread filled her heart as she raced toward the mountain. What was she going to do once she got to the road block? She could tell the firefighters about Johnny, but would they let her through? Even if they didn't, she'd find a way to save Johnny and Patch. She wouldn't let the past repeat itself.

Chapter Twenty

SHE COULDN'T BE TOO late.

Not again.

After pushing the speed limit the whole way, Ella braked for the turnoff to Mountain Road. Wooden barricades blocked the roadway, and flares lined the edges. She slowed to a stop behind six cars waiting in line. The officer standing in front of the blockade leaned in and talked to each driver before waving for them to turn around.

Her gaze kept shifting between the clock on the dashboard and the idling cars. Good grief. How long did it take to say the road was closed?

She didn't have time for this—Johnny and Patch didn't have time. Wheeling her car into the other lane, she drove forward. The uniformed officer stepped in front of her vehicle and glared at her.

He approached her window. "Where do you think you're going?"

She ignored his gruff tone. "I need to get through. My home is on the mountain."

The state trooper leaned farther down to the open window. "The road is closed to everyone but the firefighters. You need to turn around."

"Do you know Fire Chief Tony Granger?"

The man shook his head. "No, ma'am. I'm not from around these parts."

Not wasting any more time, she said, "Who's in charge? The Whistle Stop Fire Department?"

"No. This is out of their jurisdiction. The Forest Service is running things."

Ella frowned. She didn't know anyone in authority. "I need to get through. This is a matter of life and death. I live on Roca Mountain, and I think a young boy is on the mountain trying to make it to my cabin to rescue my dog."

A look of concern flickered through the man's eyes. He paused as though considering the validity of her statement. "Okay, pull off to the side of the road. You'll have to walk up to the command post."

"Thank you." Once he stepped back from the car, she parked.

Glad she'd decided to wear khakis and comfortable shoes that day, she ran past fire equipment, pickups, and cars littering both sides of the asphalt like one big parking lot.

"Hey, you can't be here." A firefighter held up his hands, blocking her.

"I—" She had trouble catching her breath. "I have to get to my home."

He shook his head. "No way. The area is closed off."

"You don't understand—"

"The winds have picked up, and the blaze is out of control. We can't even get planes in the air. I'm sorry, but you need to go to the shelter."

"You aren't listening to me. A little boy is up there."

The man removed his black helmet and ran a sooty hand over his damp forehead. "Are you sure about this?"

"No. But I've got good reason to believe the boy's trying to save a puppy in my cabin."

"Let me check something." The man turned and walked between the parked vehicles.

She followed, not about to let him out of sight until she was certain someone had been sent to rescue Johnny. When the firefighter came to an abrupt stop, she bumped into him. He turned and looked at her as though he was surprised to find her dogging his steps.

"Wait here," he ordered.

She'd stay put as long as he remained in her line of vision.

Ella glanced up at the ominous gray cloud of smoke hiding the sun. The wind pulled strands of her hair loose from her French twist. She brushed them out of her eyes. She didn't need anyone to tell her the wind was the accelerant turning this wildfire into a huge, horrendous monster. Time was most definitely not on Johnny's or Patch's side.

While waiting for the man to return, she overheard a couple of the firefighters trying to assess the situation on the mountain. She took a couple of steps closer, hoping to make out more of what they were saying.

"We've got close to a thousand hot acres up there," a man with grunge and sweat on his face said to another firefighter. "With the wind kicking up, it won't be long before the fire doubles in size."

The other firefighter with his back to her said, "These gusting winds are making everything difficult, especially since all of the planes are grounded. This thing has the potential to evolve into a badass blaze."

The increasing blare of a siren drowned out the rest of the men's conversation. She glanced over her shoulder to find men headed for the approaching fire truck.

She wrung her hands while searching out the man who had gone to get help. He was talking to another man, hopefully about Johnny and Patch. While she waited, she glanced around for Tony, praying he'd appear. He would see that action was taken, that everyone was rescued. If only he was here.

The fireman returned. "All of the residences have been thoroughly searched, and the evacuees were relocated to the gym at Whistle Stop High School. You should check there."

Johnny wouldn't have arrived at the cabin by the time the firefighters ushered the people down the mountain. She shook her head vehemently. "You don't understand. I can give you—"

He held out a hand, halting her flow of words. "I know you're upset, but I'm sure he's safe in the shelter. I don't have the school's number on me, but I'm sure information can give it to you."

The firefighter had disappeared into the crowd, and she was left on her own. She grabbed her phone, looked up the phone number for the school and called. It took a bit but eventually she spoke with a person with a comprehensive list of evacuees and Johnny's didn't appear on it. No way was she heading back to town, not with her gut screaming out that Johnny was in trouble.

"Excuse me," she said to another firefighter.

"The chow line is that way," he said as he kept walking.

He thought she was there to make food? Oh, what was the use in wasting any more time?

For an instant, she was swept back in time, once more a scared child trying to save her mother and little brother. Regret clawed at her. She'd been too young to save them, but she was a grown woman now. If no one would help her, she'd rescue Johnny herself.

If I'm wrong, and he's not up there, that'd be a relief. But I can't stand here and do nothing if that little boy needs me.

She walked to the edge of the bustling group, and quietly slipped into the trees. She paused. Her fingers trembled as she reached for her cell phone. Not knowing what she might face on the mountain, she wanted to get word to Tony of what she'd discovered. But when she dialed his number, nothing happened. She held the phone in front of her and found she had no signal. A frustrated groan rose in her throat.

Her gaze rose above the distant tree line. The smell of smoke hung heavy in the air as it marred the blue sky. Her heart pumped faster. She had to keep moving. Johnny needed help.

She switched between running, stumbling, and slowing down to navigate over rocks and fallen tree limbs. She wanted to run up the road, but she'd be stopped by firefighters being transported to and from the fire. She knew if they spotted her, they'd demand she be taken to the evacuation center. Dread clawed her chest as she headed farther up the mountain, but a deeper, more primitive protectiveness drove her onward. She wouldn't let the past repeat itself. She refused to lose another loved one.

The toe of her shoe struck a rock, which sent her stumbling forward. Her leg caught on a fallen limb.

Tears stung her eyes, and she blinked them away. There wasn't time for a pity party. She sucked up the pain and stood. A glance down at her legs revealed a cut in her pants. Blood stained the material. Nothing major. She continued onward—toward Johnny and Patch.

A low-hanging branch caught her hair and pulled it loose from its pins. She ran her hand over her head, pushing the annoying strands away from her face.

Smoke stung her eyes as she swiped the back of her hand over her sweaty brow. Her mouth was dry, and grimy dirt already caked her lips.

The rising temperature made her feel as though she were in a sauna. Shoving up the long sleeves of her T-shirt, she forced one foot in front of the other. Johnny and Patch were counting on her.

Tony had just returned to base camp. He moved away from the crowd in order to touch base with Melissa and check on Johnny. He checked his cell phone and found nineteen missed calls. Nineteen? A chill of apprehension inched its icy fingers down his spine. For a man who didn't spend much time on the phone, this was a record number of calls.

Something is wrong. Something is very wrong.

Ella's voice caught his immediate attention. Panic laced her words. "Tony, I need you." He grew heartsick at the realization that she'd reached out to him and he hadn't been there for her.

When she mentioned Johnny, Patch, and the wildfire all in one breath, his chest tightened with alarm.

Johnny had run off again. What would make the boy think he was any match for this roaring inferno?

He tried to call her back, but the call went to voice mail. After a brief conversation with Melissa, he learned that his troubles had doubled. Ella, believing Johnny was headed for the cabin, had chased after him. Hopefully she got help from his fellow firefighters instead of charging up the mountain to go after him on her own.

Tony hustled over to the large map attached to a dry-erase board. He refused to give in to the fear clawing at the back of his throat. He swallowed hard. He had to remain clear-minded if he was to mount a successful rescue.

"Planes are grounded until the winds die down," Charlie Lucas, head of the Forest Service, was saying to a group of firefighters. "So we'll be working this fire from the ground."

"Listen up, people," someone bellowed from up front by the map.

Tony waited and listened. He needed more details about this monstrous blaze before venturing back into it to save the people who meant the world to him.

"The latest report states the fire jumped our break on the north ridge." Charlie pointed to a spot on the map. "It's headed straight for quadrant C3, which is over here, and has a number of homes in the area." Someone approached the man and whispered something in his ear. The color drained from his face. "A crew is trapped. Two merging fire lines have them pinned down."

Tony's chest constricted as though a vise grip had just been ratcheted tighter. Not only were his nephew and Ella in the middle of this disaster, but now his buddies, the same guys who had covered his back numerous times, were facing the most harrowing moments of their lives.

"This is going to be dicey," Charlie continued. "With the planes grounded, we need every available man—"

Tony had heard everything he needed to know. Ella's cabin sat in quadrant C3, and he didn't have time to waste.

He hitched a ride with the next ground crew headed up the mountain. Without help from the sky, the inferno would be nearly impossible to contain. It'd take every bit of manpower to free the trapped men.

"Let me off here," he called out.

"Why here?" the driver asked.

"I've got a report of some lost hikers in the area. I'm going to check into it."

"We can go with you," one of his fellow firefighters from Whistle Stop volunteered.

"Thanks, but I've got this. The fire hasn't reached this far. Take care of the guys who are trapped. They've got families waiting for them."

After the men headed farther up the mountain, Tony called into home base to let them know his location before he set off to face the unknown. The one thing on his side was the fact the wildfire was still at a higher elevation. Since fire traveled slower going downhill, that would hopefully give him the time he needed.

Dried twigs and leaves crunched beneath his boots as he rushed toward the cabin, trying to avoid sticks and rocks. The stench of smoke hung thick in the air as he bounded over downed trees and scaled boulders. He refused to be deterred or slowed down. The temperature soared as ash rained down from the darkening sky. His pulse raced, both from the physical exertion and his fear about Johnny's and Ella's safety.

He envisioned sweeping Ella and Johnny into his arms and getting them to safety. He ached to tell Ella how sorry he was for being so short with her, but he feared those words would never have the chance to cross his lips.

When her cabin finally came into view, Tony breathed a sigh of relief that it was unharmed. He sprinted the rest of the way.

"Ella! Johnny!"

He took the steps two at a time and burst through the unlocked door. He scanned the room and found Johnny, who sat in the far corner, crying.

Tony rushed to the boy and held out his arms. "Hey, little man, everything's going to be okay. I'm here now."

Johnny hurled his body into him and burrowed his head in Tony's neck. The boy clung to him as though afraid to let go.

After a few seconds, Tony held the boy at arm's length to get his attention. "Are Ella and Patch here?"

"I couldn't find Patch. Then I got scared with all the smoke outside." He paused and took a deep breath. "I didn't know what to do."

"Maybe Ella took the puppy into town."

Johnny vehemently shook his head. "I heard her. She didn't."

Why had the cabin been empty when Johnny got there? It didn't make any sense. Tony recalled his conversation with Melissa. She was certain Ella had gone after Johnny. So where was she? Surely she wasn't lost on the mountain—the same mountain about to be taken over by a blazing inferno.

"Johnny," came a shout from outside. "Johnny, are you here?"

They ran to the porch and spotted Ella trudging up the driveway. Tony's pent-up anxiety escaped in a relieved sigh. He observed her messed-up blond hair as well as the soot and dirt smeared over her pert nose and cheeks. But it was her slight limp and the bloodstain on her knee that gave him pause. The mountain had gotten the best of her, but she still held her shoulders in a rigid line, as though ready to conquer the world.

"Miss Morgan, are you here for Patch?"

She rushed over to the boy. "I'm here for you."

Johnny's brown eyes opened wide. "Really?"

Her head bobbed up and down.

Johnny wrapped his arms around her.

"Thank God, you're safe," she said between deep breaths. "I was so scared."

Unable to hold back the rush of relief, Tony strode over and pulled her against him. He kissed the top of her head before resting his cheek on her silky hair. Her body slumped into him, and he welcomed her weight. He would be her support, and she would be his.

"I don't know what I would have done if something had happened to you," he murmured.

Ella pulled back and looked around. "Where's Patch?"

"I couldn't find him." Johnny's worried gaze moved from Ella to Tony.

"He has to be here." Ella's voice held a note of certainty. "He's probably scared and hiding."

A loud cracking sound in the woods caused her to jump. He looked into her fear-filled eyes.

"It's coming!" she shrieked. "It won't win this time."

She pulled away from his embrace and ran to the side of the cabin. What was she doing? They needed to evacuate. Instead, she was fidgeting with something at the cabin's foundation.

"Help me!" Desperation rang out in her voice.

Help her do what? When she grabbed a hose, he knew her intent—to make a last-ditch effort to save the cabin.

"Hurry!" She sprayed the wall with water. "If you use the hose, I can fill up a bucket inside."

The panic edging her voice had him running to her side. When she gazed up at him, he saw the glassy look in her eyes. Hysteria had a firm grip on her. He took the hose from her. Before she could escape his grip, he wrapped his arms securely around her.

"Ella, this won't work. We have to take Johnny and get to safety—"

"No! No! No!" Her voice reached a fever pitch. "I'm not leaving. The fire can't have this home, too."

Tears welled up in her eyes. They splashed onto her cheeks, streaking through the muck. His chest ached for her.

He'd do anything for her, anything at all. But this fire was too powerful, too big. Without some help from Mother Nature, nothing was going to stop it.

Ella braced her hands on his chest and pushed. He tightened his hold. All the while his heart was breaking for her. He couldn't let go, not until she listened to reason.

"Let. Me. Go."

"Ella, I can't."

She struggled, fighting his embrace. "I have to try." Her breath came in short gasps. Her hands balled up and pounded his chest. "Don't you understand? I can't give up. This is my home."

"I know, baby. I know." He pulled her tightly against him.

"Please. Help me."

"I am," he murmured.

She dissolved into a string of soulful moans. Her raw anguish tore at him as her cries reverberated through his body. He blinked repeatedly against his own tears.

With Johnny standing close by, Tony held her until her sobs lessened to soft, mournful whimpers. The last thing he wanted to do was pull away from her, but they had to get to safety.

The wildfire that was blowing its hot, sticky breath down their necks wouldn't wait for anyone.

Chapter Twenty-One

TIME WAS RUNNING OUT.

The fiery monster was hot on their trail.

"We have to go." Tony held Ella at arm's length and looked into her watery eyes. "The fire isn't far behind us."

With his thumbs, he attempted to swipe away the tears from her cheeks. He longed to soothe her misery, but right now he had to concentrate on getting them to safety.

"Where's Patch?" Johnny choked out as a hot gust of wind blew smoke in their direction.

"He's in the cabin," Ella said in a defeated tone. When Johnny shook his head, she added, "Did you check the closet in the bedroom? It's where he hides when he's scared."

"I'll get him." Johnny ran toward the cabin.

Tony chased after the boy, catching him on the bottom step.

"I'm not leaving without Patch," Johnny sobbed, wiggling to get free. "He's just a baby. We gotta save him."

"I'll get him. You go wait with Ella."

Once Johnny headed back to Ella, Tony bounded up the steps. He reached for the doorknob, but the door wouldn't budge. Someone must have bumped the lock on the way out. In the background, sap from the trees crackled and popped before exploding from the heat. He didn't have much time. He had to get Johnny and Ella to safety.

He dropped his gear on the porch and grabbed his trusty Pulaski. With the kitchen window in front of him, he turned his face and blindly swung the single-bladed ax, which easily shattered the windowpane. He ran the metal head around the windowsill to clear the shards of glass.

"What are you doing?" Ella screamed.

He didn't have time to explain or apologize. Not that him breaking one window mattered now that the fire held the cabin in its cross hairs. He had no doubt the place would soon be reduced to cinders.

He used his sleeve to brush aside the remaining broken glass before climbing through the window and landing in the kitchen sink. Once he made it to the floor, he strode toward Ella's bedroom.

Hovering at the doorway, he called out, "Patch! Here, boy."

He approached the closet, pulling the sliding door wide open. He knelt down and started to search. The pup whimpered from his place on a gray fleece top. Tony scooped up the squirming dog. It quickly became apparent that trying to carry Patch off this mountain like this wasn't going to work. He wiggled way too much. Tony needed something to put the dog in so they could make a quick escape from the inferno. A loud crack echoed through the room, followed by the sound of a tree falling, confirming the need to make a hasty exit.

Scanning the closet, he spotted a medium-sized wicker basket with a lid. With the whining pup under one arm, he yanked the woven bin out. He flipped the lid open and tossed out the various linens and spools of thread. In an effort to make the trip more comfortable for the dog, he grabbed the fleece shirt from the floor of the closet. He stuffed the garment in the bottom and set the yipping pup on the soft material. Once the lid was shut, he latched it, ignoring the barking.

On the way out of the cabin, light reflected off something on the mantel. The picture of Ella and her brother sat next to the stuffed teddy bear. His heart clenched at the thought of her losing not only her home, but also all of her belongings. He rushed over to the fireplace and grabbed the two precious mementos. Next to them sat Patch's red leash. He took the coiled-up strap, too. Careful not to let Patch out of the wicker basket, he placed the items beneath the fleece shirt and closed the lid.

Outside, he noticed the wind had lessened, but the temperature was still on the rise. Once he retrieved his firefighting gear, he headed over to Ella and Johnny. He turned to check the fire's progress and caught sight of a wall of flames bearing down on them.

Using his radio, he called in to the command center. "This is Tony Granger. I've got two civilians with me. The fire is about to overtake us. We need to be evacuated ASAP."

"Negative, Granger. All planes are grounded. What's your location?"

He gave the coordinates and walked a short distance away, lowering the volume on his radio. Ella and Johnny didn't need to hear any bad news.

"Granger, get out of there. You're standing in the line of fire."

"We can't outrun it. Not with a child and puppy."

"The map shows a small body of water to your east. Use it to gain some cover."

"I'm on it."

He glanced back up at the fire. If the wind picked up again, it wouldn't take much more than a few healthy gusts to overtake them. He hoped—no, he *prayed* the command center would be able to put some planes in the air soon.

"Uncle Tony, what're we gonna do?" In that moment, Johnny looked about three years old and scared to death. The boy started coughing.

"Pull the collar of your T-shirt up over your mouth and nose." He removed his helmet and placed it on Johnny. It was big for the boy, but it'd help protect him. "Keep that on. It'll help keep you safe." Tony turned to Ella. "You need to cover your nose and mouth too."

Tony removed his red bandanna from his neck. Adjusting the material so it covered the lower part of his face, he tied it behind his head. "Ella, do you know your way to the pond?"

She pointed over her right shoulder. "It's about a hundred yards that way."

"Uncle Tony, what'll happen if the fire catches us?"

Tony didn't want to contemplate the thought. He had his fire tent with him, but he doubted all three of them would fit inside. Their first priority was getting to safety.

He ruffled the boy's hair. "Don't worry, Johnny. We'll be fine."

Tony wished he felt as confident as he sounded.

They set off at a brisk pace toward the pond. Tony elected to take up the rear in case Ella or Johnny tripped over roots or tree limbs. He glanced back often, making sure the monster wasn't licking at their heels. For once, Lady Luck was on his side, keeping the flames at bay.

He started to think about his plan, which at this point wasn't really much of a plan at all. In his rush to find the safest scenario, he hadn't stopped to consider the pond might be as dried up as the creek bed they were following. Then again, Ella would have said so if that was the case.

"There's a clearing just ahead," Ella called.

He didn't breathe easily until he spotted the body of water. Due to the drought, the water level was down, but it was still plenty deep for them to swim out to the middle and wait out the firestorm.

"Johnny, do you remember your swim lessons?" When the boy nodded, he continued, "Good. I'm going to need you to paddle out into the middle."

"All the way out there?"

Tony rested his hand on the boy's shoulder. "I'll be right beside you."

"I can try. What about Miss Morgan? Can she swim?"

Tony turned his attention to Ella, but he found she'd walked away. Now wasn't the time to be running off. They needed to stick together so he had a better chance of protecting them.

"Ella," he called out.

She motioned for him to follow, and then he spotted her destination—an old rowboat. He ran ahead to drag the boat into the pond, inwardly cheering when he found the thing water worthy. Once he helped them into it, he hopped in and started to row.

Trees exploded as the fire jumped from one to the next. He gauged the height of the cottonwoods circling them to be about seventy feet. The water's circumference should be large enough to keep them safe should the timbers start to fall.

He looked up at the mountain as the fiery monster hissed and gurgled. The wildfire teased him with its strength. Tony wanted to be out there fighting the blaze, but for the moment he had to protect the people he loved from being swept up in the firestorm's clutches.

He refused to let the fire win.

Ella wrapped her arms over Johnny's shoulders, longing to give him a sense of security while Tony worked the single oar to guide them to the center of the pond. His biceps contracted and expanded with each stroke of the oar. She couldn't help herself. She needed to concentrate on anything but the flames, which now danced along one side of the pond.

The air thickened with heavy smoke, and Johnny began to choke.

"Dampen the cloth you've got over your faces," Tony instructed. "It'll help filter the air."

"What about Patch?" She hadn't heard him bark in a while, and her body grew tense. Could the smoke be too much for him?

"I'll check on him," Johnny volunteered.

"No, you won't," Tony said. "You dampen your T-shirt, and I'll take care of the puppy."

Ella helped Johnny dip the cloth into the water so he wouldn't fall overboard. All the while, she kept glancing over at Tony and the wicker basket, praying her little buddy survived.

"He's okay." Tony's steady gaze held hers.

She could do this. They'd get out of this mess—somehow.

Ella scooped up water and dampened her own top, while Tony unbuttoned his long-sleeved yellow shirt and then yanked off a black undershirt. His abs rippled with muscles as he leaned over to dampen the undershirt in the pond. Then he opened it up and forced the garment down over the basket.

"This should help the little fella breathe easier." He slipped back on the yellow shirt. "If the winds get worse, we'll have to get in the water. Even if we're safe from the actual fire and falling trees, we'll have to keep an eye out for blowing debris. The water will lessen our exposure."

Ella's line of vision moved to the ridgeline as the flames roared and lashed out at anything in their path. Had it been like this for her mother and brother? Had they known the fiery monster was coming to get them and that there was nothing they could do to stop it? She shuddered, imagining their final moments.

"Ella," Tony called out to her, jarring her back to their present situation. "Can you put the basket between your feet?"

She glanced at Tony, seeing nothing but strength and determination in his eyes. His calmness gave her comfort. "Yes."

"Good. I'll work on keeping the boat positioned."

The ever-increasing heat had her clothes drenched in perspiration. She ran the sleeve of her shirt over her damp forehead.

As heavier debris started blowing around the perimeter of the pond, Johnny asked in an unsteady voice, "What's happening, Uncle Tony?"

Tony remained quiet as he gazed off in the distance. Ella followed his line of vision, catching sight of the fire that now surrounded them, held back only by the water lapping the shore. They were trapped. The breath caught in her throat. This couldn't be happening. Terror clutched her heart.

"Uncle Tony, the fire's gonna get us," Johnny wailed before seeking comfort in Ella's embrace.

Ella's eyes burned from the smoke, making them water. With Tony seemingly lost in his thoughts, she patted Johnny's back. "I'm sure your uncle has a plan for how to get us out of here. Right, Tony?"

"Of course. We'll be down the mountain in no time." Tony smiled, but the optimism didn't reach his eyes.

Minutes dragged on as the flames lunged at the water's edge. She struggled not to give in to the sobs that clawed at the back of her throat. She kept herself focused on Johnny by saying any words she could think of to try to make him feel safe.

"Granger, this is command center. Do you read me?" squawked a voice over the radio.

"I read you. Go ahead."

"We have a break in the wind. We're sending up a couple choppers. I'll have one clear a path for you. What's your location?"

"We're trapped in the middle of a pond in quadrant C3."

There was a long pause.

The voice on the radio came back. "Get ready. They'll be there soon. Hopefully, it'll give us a big enough break to get you out of there."

Ella's gaze rose skyward every few seconds. The black smoke grew denser, blocking out most of the daylight. She kept her shirt pulled over her nose. She shifted anxiously on the seat, straining to detect any sign of help.

A whirling sound grew increasingly louder, drowning out the hiss of the wildfire. The air rushed and swirled around them. Ella glanced upward. Squinting, she tried to locate the source of the noise, but she couldn't see through the grayness.

"Cover your heads and hunch down," Tony shouted, shielding Johnny with his own body.

Ella obeyed, but couldn't help peeking up at the sky. A helicopter was transporting a huge bucket suspended by cables. Water spilled over the side. As the chopper moved closer to the shore, the water doused a portion of the fire, giving them an escape route.

Once the chopper departed, Tony worked double-time rowing them to shore. She eyed the smoldering gap in the ring of fire, and as they drew nearer, her body grew rigid with paralyzing fear.

Tony raised his voice over the crackle of burning timbers and the swoosh of the oar. "The fastest way out is to skirt the outside of the wildfire until we reach the main road. Are you up for this?"

The thought of walking through the fire made the hairs on her arms stand on end. In her mind's eye, she was back in her childhood home, fighting her way to the bedrooms, intent on saving her family. Her breathing grew rapid as she relived the moment when the ceiling started to disintegrate and began to fall onto her outstretched arms. She rubbed the scars. Her respiration accelerated until she became dizzy.

"Ella, are you listening to me?" Tony grabbed her upper arms and stared into her eyes. "I need you to keep it together. Okay?"

In the middle of the disaster, he still radiated a calm strength and determination. Her breathing slowed to a normal pace.

Continuing to stare into his dark pools of reassurance, she gathered her thoughts. "Yes. I'm fine."

All four of us will live through this disaster.

With Tony by her side, she could do this.

Tony glanced at his nephew. "How about you? Think you're up for hiking out of here?"

Tilting up the helmet, Johnny stared up at him. "Yeah. Remember, I'm your little man."

"You certainly are. Now we need to get moving before those winds pick up again."

Tony took the lead and marched them toward the road. She kept a vigilant eye on Johnny, afraid he wouldn't be able to keep up with the rapid pace. The rough terrain lacked any sort of path. Periodically, Tony would pause to help them over the large rocks and roots jutting out of the earth. Their progress was slower than she would have liked. She kept glancing over her shoulder, making sure the fire wasn't hot on their heels. The terrain was scorched with puffs of smoke here and there.

Her breath came out in small huffs as she was not used to this much physical exertion. Still, the threat of the fierce fire had her putting one foot in front of the other. Her eyes burned and watered from the smoke.

A quick glance at Johnny's exhausted face told her she wasn't the only one wearing out. Still, she kept moving, regardless of her exhaustion or her scratchy throat. Step after step, they marched along. Vigilantly, she looked over her shoulder to reassure herself the fire wasn't catching up to them.

Tony paused and turned, still holding the basket with Patch. The man's face was etched with exhaustion as he checked on Johnny. "You doing okay?"

Johnny nodded.

"Can I carry the puppy?" she offered, hoping to lighten Tony's load as he still had his backpack strapped to him.

"How about we take a breather first?"

Her feet ached and her lungs burned. "Do you think it's safe?"

"We're far enough down the mountain to rest for a couple of minutes."

They stopped next to a small boulder. She settled herself on the edge of the rock, relieved to get off of her feet. All around them was undisturbed vegetation. The fire hadn't made it this far yet. With the wind blowing the other direction, the smoke has lessened.

Tony alerted command central that they were safe before easing off his backpack. He withdrew a bottle of water and handed it to Johnny. "Here. It's all I have so we'll have to share."

She'd never seen anything that looked so good in her life, and she anxiously awaited her turn. When the bottle made it to her, she was tempted to chug the wet, refreshing liquid, but she refrained.

After she handed the bottle to Tony, she asked, "You wouldn't happen to have a sandwich or two in that backpack, would you?"

He smiled. "Afraid not. But I did grab the dog leash." Tony rested the basket on the ground. "Johnny, use the helmet as a water bowl for Patch. And then you can take him for a little walk. But make sure you stay within sight."

Tony helped Johnny get out the excited puppy and hook up the leash. Ella sat quietly, observing the father-son relationship and yearning to be an official part of their family. Yet, she knew as long as she carried her secret, she could never have her greatest desire—a family of her own.

"Penny for your thoughts." Tony took a seat next to her.

"With inflation, I don't think you'll get much for a penny these days."

"You have a point. But seeing as I don't have any cash on me, all I can offer you is a shoulder to lean on and a willing ear to listen."

She glanced over at him. His intent stare pierced her with its depth. This was her chance to let him inside. She took a steadying breath. After today, she decided, she was strong enough to face just about anything.

"I was thinking about the past."

He nodded in understanding. "I can't even imagine what you must be feeling."

Johnny knelt down to pet Patch. He was close enough to keep an eye on, but far enough away not to overhear their conversation.

Her insides quivered with nerves as she contemplated her next words. She swallowed hard, clearing the lump clogging her throat.

She had to do this.
She had to take a chance on Tony.

Chapter Twenty-Two

Where did she start?

"It was winter in Ohio." Ella's thoughts drifted back to the most horrific period of her life. "I was just a kid."

She laced her fingers together and squeezed them tight, mustering the courage to continue with her story. She could feel Tony's gaze on her, but she couldn't face him—not yet. Instead, she stared straight ahead at Johnny and the dog.

"The night was cold. Ice cold." She hesitated. "I'm sure you don't want to hear this. You have enough on your mind."

"I want to hear whatever you have to say. That is, if you're willing to trust me enough to tell me."

She nodded. "We...we were very poor. They'd shut off our power that week. My mother had set up an old kerosene heater in the bedroom I shared with Timmy." Ella sucked in a ragged breath. "My mother and I had a fight that night. She ordered me to bed. She told me not to get out of it. Only, I had a nightmare and, forgetting about the lack of power, I climbed out of bed, planning to go curl up on the couch to watch television until I fell back to sleep."

The events stood out clearly in her mind. She wrung her hands, twisting her fingers so tight they hurt, but not as much as the memories. Anguish stiffened her muscles as she began to relive the nightmare that had held her prisoner for far too many years. Tony's hand settled over hers. She took comfort in his sure, steady touch.

"I grabbed the blankets from my bed and dragged them along behind me. I tripped over something, and I heard some stuff fall." Her voice wobbled as two teardrops rolled down her cheeks. "I couldn't see anything in the pitch black, so I kept going. I...I thought it was some of my brother's toys."

"I was wrong. We should talk about this later." Tony reached out and swiped away the tears with his thumb. "You shouldn't have to relive this now. Not after what you've just been through—"

"Yes, I do. If I don't, I might never have the courage." She leaned out of his reach. She had to do this on her own. "Before the fire, during the fight with my mother, I told her I hated her."

A small cry escaped her lips. She pushed a shaky hand to her mouth. Why had she said such a nasty, hurtful thing?

"I didn't mean it. I was just angry and lashing out. I...I never got a chance to tell her I was sorry. That...that I didn't mean any of it. Those awful words were the last ones I ever spoke to her." She held a sob captive in her throat as tears dropped to her cheeks.

"You were only a child. I'm sure your mother knew you loved her."

She swallowed down her pain. "No. Don't. I don't deserve your sympathy. This guilt is my punishment...my burden."

"But why?" Tony got to his feet and knelt down in front of her. "Because you lived and they didn't?"

All she could muster was a nod. If she didn't finish this now, she never would. At last finding her voice again, she continued. "The fire inspector said the blaze was caused by an overturned kerosene heater. If only I had listened to my mother, I wouldn't have knocked it over... I started the fire."

A sob tore from her throat. She pressed a hand to her mouth, holding back the rush of emotions. She'd thought all of these memories had been buried so deep that they couldn't pierce her heart, but perhaps keeping it all bottled up for so long hadn't helped at all.

She lowered her hand and inhaled an unsteady breath. "I tried to reach them...a wall of smoke rolled over me. The burning embers started to fall onto my arms... A neighbor found me choking and carried me outside." She swiped at her damp cheeks. "I begged the firefighters to save them...but...but it was too late."

Her shoulders drooped beneath the weight of her guilt. Tony reached out and pulled her to him. She let herself be drawn to him. She pressed her face into his shoulder, smothering her sobs.

"It was an accident," he murmured, running a hand over her back.

"Don't you get it? The fire was my fault."

"How can you be sure you started the fire?"

She straightened. Hadn't he been listening? What didn't he understand?

"I told you. I tripped on my way out of the room. I knocked something into the heater."

Tony shook his head. "You only think you did. Didn't you say you couldn't see in the darkness?"

She jumped to her feet. Her hands rested on her rounded hips. "Don't play games with me. There's no other way for the fire to have started—"

"Yes, there is. I'm a firefighter, remember? Accidents happen all of the time. Maybe your brother got out of bed to go to the bathroom or to grab his blankets from the floor and knocked something into the heater." Not giving her a chance to argue, Tony continued, "I'm guessing your mother also had a kerosene heater in the bedroom next to yours."

Ella nodded.

"Then she might have been the one to accidentally start the fire. Don't you understand? It was a horrible accident, but blaming yourself won't bring them back. You need to make peace with what happened and move on."

"You're just trying to make me feel better."

"Look at me." He gripped her shoulders. "This isn't about me. This is about you and the guilt that keeps you from living a full life. Is this self-recrimination what your mother and brother would have wanted for you? Is this the legacy your mother would have wanted to hand down to you?"

Ella thought about it for a moment. "No, but my grandmother blamed me—"

"I'm sorry that your grandmother was so mean. She must have been caught up in her own grief, and who knows what else, that she couldn't see you were an innocent kid who deserved love, not blame."

His words struck a chord in her memory. "My grandfather used to come to my defense, but my grandmother didn't want to hear any of it."

"He was right." Tony took her hand in his. "It's time you let go of the past, of the horrible things your grandmother said, and move on. You can't change the past. But you can change how you see yourself and your future."

She wanted to believe him. Oh, how she wanted to escape this suffocating blanket of guilt. She knew she'd never be able to totally let it go, but if he could still care about her after seeing her scars and hearing about what she was certain she'd done, maybe they had a chance for a future. The crazy notion was a much-needed soothing balm on her aching heart.

There was no more time to talk as the winds picked up, pushing the heat and traces of smoke in their faces. She followed Tony and Johnny as they led the way to the access road.

All the while, her mind replayed Tony's words. He had a point. She'd never know the exact cause of the fire. She was struck by his initial instinct to defend her and not blame her—unlike her grandmother—who'd gone to her grave believing the worst of her granddaughter. All Ella had ever wanted was her grandmother's forgiveness and understanding, but instead, Ella had come to believe that she didn't deserve either.

She glanced at Tony, catching his gaze. The warmth in his eyes soothed her nerves. She'd known all along Tony was a great man, but his insistence that she let go of the past made her realize how much she wanted to hold on to him.

At last, the road came into sight, but she was too physically and emotionally exhausted to celebrate. They climbed up a small rise to the side of the asphalt road. They took a breather before starting the rest of the way down the mountain.

Their steps were slow and labored. She had no idea how much time had passed before some trucks came into sight. But they were all heading in the wrong direction, uphill into the inferno. After stopping to check on them, the rescuers steered the trucks onward, toward the fire. Ella shuddered, thinking of all those people risking their lives. They were the unsung heroes—men and women facing a fiery monster to spare lives and homes.

Long minutes later, a truck headed downhill picked them up. Once seated, she opened the basket to find Patch lying down. His little tail swished when he spotted her, and she paused to run her hand over his soft fur.

"I can hook up his leash, if you want to get him out," Tony offered.

"Not yet." She closed and secured the lid. "Wait until we reach the bottom of the mountain."

"You won't have to wait long." Tony's voice was reassuring.

She struggled to find the appropriate words to thank him for all he had done. After all, how do you thank a man who has just saved your life? And your dog's? And a little boy's? Tears welled up in her eyes as she reached out for Tony, but Johnny's voice made her pause.

The boy launched into an endless string of questions about the wildfire. Her thank-you would have to wait until later. In the meantime, she thought over what she and Tony had gone through that day by saving Johnny and Patch. History hadn't repeated itself. This time, fire hadn't been able to snuff out the lives of those she loved.

When they pulled to a stop at the command post, Tony lifted Johnny from the back of the truck. Then he held out his hands to her. He firmly grasped her waist, and she willingly followed his lead.

Her gaze met his, and the air trapped in her lungs. She'd already told him her deepest, darkest secret, so why did the thought of telling him how much she cared about him make her stomach quiver?

Before she could utter a word, Carlota and Melissa rushed over to greet them. Ella watched Tony retrieve the puppy from the bed of the truck. She moved off to the side, letting Tony's mother hug him. Johnny joined them and wrapped his arms around both his grandmother and uncle.

Moe, Melissa's husband, appeared out of nowhere. He hugged Tony and patted him on the back. Then he chewed him out for pulling such a foolish stunt by rushing up the mountain alone. After getting it all out of his system, Moe's voice lowered. "You did a good job. Next time, take backup. Better yet, make sure there is no next time."

Moe's gaze landed squarely on Johnny. The boy fidgeted. "There won't be." Johnny's finger crossed his heart. "I promise."

There were hugs, kisses, and tears of joy to go around. Once they'd been processed through triage and checked for smoke inhalation, Doc Willard declared them healthy, aside from a few scratches and bruises. Mrs. Willard handed them each a bottle of cold water and sent them on their way.

The women escorted an exhausted Johnny to their car. Tony, still holding the basket, walked Ella to her car. He placed the container in the passenger seat, hooked the leash to Patch's collar, and lifted him out.

He set the puppy on the ground, where the little guy could use the length of the leash to explore his surroundings.

Ella dropped the water bottle on the front seat. She turned back to Tony, and their gazes locked. With a new lease on life, she no longer wanted to hide how she'd grown to care for Tony. Life was far too short to put off the important bits. She took a step forward and wrapped her arms around his neck. Ignoring the flash of surprise in his eyes, she lifted up on her tiptoes and pressed her mouth to his for a quick kiss.

He cleared his throat. "What was that for?"

"I thought that would be obvious. Maybe I should try again."

With her arms still clasped around him, she moved closer, letting her lips brush his. She heard his swift intake of air. His mouth pressed to hers with a fiery intensity. His fingers combed through her hair, holding her mouth against his.

She immediately opened to him, letting him lead the way. Her heart hammered against her ribs. This was where she wanted to be, where she wanted to stay.

His hands wrapped around her waist and pulled her to him. His fingers slid beneath her shirt and moved rhythmically against the small of her back. A moan formed deep in her throat as she leaned fully into him. Shivers of excitement and anticipation raced up her spine, leaving goose bumps on her arms.

"I love you," she said in a breathy tone.

His tender kisses stopped as he drew back, leaving behind a cold, empty spot. He wrenched himself free of her embrace and stepped back. "Don't say those words."

"Why not?"

"Don't say them because you don't mean them."

"I do mean them." She needed him to believe her. "My feelings for you are real."

He shoved his fingers through his messy hair. "No. You don't know what you're saying. You're high on adrenaline. When you calm down, you'll realize I'm not what you want, what you need."

"You're my hero."

"I'm not your hero. I'm not anybody's hero." His head hung low as he uttered the denial. "If I was, you and Johnny wouldn't have ended up in the middle of a wildfire."

She rested her hands on her hips. "You can't read the mind of a nine-year-old boy. No one can."

"You obviously did."

She shrugged. "I happened to be in the right place at the right time to figure out his next move."

"That's what I'm saying. I should've known he would try to save the puppy."

"You've got to believe me. You're a hero to me and to your nephew." She took a step toward him and leaned forward to repeat their kiss, but he grabbed her arms.

"Stop." His harsh tone was at odds with the desperation in his eyes. "This is a mistake."

"Don't you understand?" she asked, searching his dark eyes for comprehension. "Nothing you say is going to change the fact that I love you."

His face became void of expression. Why was he so distant all of the sudden? What happened to his joyous reaction at finding her at the cabin? He had been so warm and comforting then. Why was he acting so cold now?

"No, you don't." He turned to her car, pressing his palms against the trunk. With his back to her, he said,

"You're just worked up after the fire. In the morning, you'll realize what you're feeling is gratitude for being alive. Not love."

"I was sure of my feelings before the fire, and I'm sure of them now. They'll be the same tomorrow and all of the days that follow—"

"Stop." He turned to her. His eyes were filled with remorse. "You have to realize you've been through a trauma. You're reacting to the moment. This wasn't the first time you were caught in a fire, and I'm so sorry you had to go through this horrible experience again. With the cabin gone, you have nothing tying you to Whistle Stop. You can chase your dreams wherever they lead you."

Was this his way of saying he didn't love her? Or did he believe she'd walk out on him like his ex had? "My life is here with you and Johnny—"

"I can't do this now." He stared straight ahead, refusing to look in her direction. "Not while a wildfire's breathing down on Whistle Stop."

A wave of frustration hid her wounded ego. "Go. Do your job."

"I'm sorry." He turned and walked away without a backward glance.

Ella's heart ached as she picked up the puppy and stroked his silky fur. Sucking up her crumbling emotions, she climbed into the car. She turned the ignition and was about to put the car in gear when she realized she'd lost everything—all of her worldly possessions. She didn't even have a fresh set of clothes to change into. Worst of all, she was homeless.

As hard as all of that was to swallow, there was an even bigger loss she had to contend with—Tony. Heat scorched her cheeks as she recalled uttering her love to him with the expectation that he'd return her feelings. She'd never ever thought he would tell her that she was imagining her love for him. Did he have any idea what it had cost her to put her heart on the line?

Memories of the horrific day tumbled through her mind—from the fear for Johnny's safety to the flashbacks of the night she'd lost her own family, and finally to Tony's rejection. Tears welled up in her eyes. She didn't care if that made her wimpy. So be it. Her feelings gushed forth until her nose was stuffed up and her eyes were sore from rubbing them. Her life had come full circle, and even though none of them had perished in the fire, she still felt as though life would never be the same.

The puppy whimpered and crawled into her lap. She scooped up Patch and hugged him. A tap on the door had her swallowing her sobs. She sucked in an unsteady breath as she swiped away the tears. Trying to get her emotions under control, she rolled down the window.

"Sorry to startle you." Carlota sent her a worried look. "I wanted to make sure you're okay."

"I'm fine." She attempted a smile, but her lips wouldn't cooperate. "You don't have to worry."

The concerned expression on Carlota's face said that she didn't believe her. "You're staying with me for as long as you need."

It wasn't a question. It was an order, the kind mothers handed out when they were worried and not in the mood for an argument.

"But—"

"No buts." Carlota's voice took on a you-will-lose-this-argument tone. "It's not like Tony will be there. You can stay in his room. I'm sure he won't mind. He's got this fire to deal with right now, so it'll be a long time before he's home again."

Ella's stomach knotted. She wanted to say no, but she really didn't have any other options. And at the moment, she was bone-tired. "If you're sure—"

"I am. I'll ride back with Melissa and Johnny. We'll meet you there." Without another word, Carlota turned and moved away with an uneven gate.

Ella groaned, causing Patch to bark and look at her warily.

"It's okay, boy." She ran her hand over his downy soft fur. "You're safe now."

Hesitant to make herself an unwanted guest, she tried to come up with alternative lodgings. She drove into Whistle Stop and found a No Vacancy sign at the only motel in town. She considered asking Melissa if she could stay with her, but she realized imposing on her unsuspecting friend when Carlota had already offered her a room would be childish—even if it was Tony's bed.

Chapter Twenty-Three

The next day Ella awoke with a start. Even as she opened her eyes, the nightmare of flames seemed to chase her into the daylight. Her breath was unsteady as she shot up in bed. It took a few seconds for her to realize it'd all been a nasty dream. No, more like flashbacks to yesterday and their narrow escape.

When she leaned back against the pillow, Tony's spicy scent wrapped around her, and she remembered spending the night in his bed—alone. This time when she closed her eyes, she envisioned his tanned face with its strong jaw and chin and soft, kissable lips.

She wished he'd returned home during the night, safe and sound, but she knew that wouldn't be possible with the raging wildfire. Determined not to dwell on something she couldn't control, she rolled out of bed, shocked to find it was close to lunchtime. She really had been physically and emotionally exhausted.

Even though she'd showered the night before, she needed the warm spray of water to help wake her up. As the sleepiness wore away, the reality of yesterday's events settled in. The cabin by now was a complete loss. She no longer had a place to call home. Thank goodness Carlota had welcomed her with open arms.

Still, her mind circled back to the homeless part.

Tears pricked her eyes. Everything she'd ever owned had been reduced to cinders. Her chest throbbed as she grieved for all the possessions she'd lost. Now, with Tony rejecting her love, she needed to reconsider her plans. Once she completed her temporary teaching position, perhaps she should leave Whistle Stop.

She emerged from the bathroom to find new clothes waiting for her and a brief note from Carlota telling her to choose what she wanted and that she and Johnny would be home later. This time, Ella's eyes misted over with happy tears. Carlota was the sweetest lady. Tony was so lucky to be able to call her mom.

Dressed in pink, drawstring jogging pants and a white long-sleeved T-shirt, Ella meandered into the kitchen. There was something Ella needed to do, and it couldn't wait. She grabbed the phone and dialed Tracey's cell phone. Instead of her friend answering, it was her husband. Tracey was in the hospital with complications related to her pregnancy. Her husband promised to call as soon as Tracey was up for visitors.

With a heavy heart, Ella grabbed a cup of coffee and sat down at the kitchen table. The newspaper was laid out. The headline read: *Roca Mountain Ablaze*.

Ella didn't have the heart to read the article. She opened the paper and flipped through the pages until she got to the classified section. She needed a place to live until she decided whether to rebuild the cabin, not that it'd ever be the same, or whether she needed to move on to a different town, a different state.

After scanning the page, she picked up the phone, calling the first listing for an apartment that she could reasonably afford. She stuttered in surprise when she found herself talking with Mrs. Sanchez. It appeared the woman had a little efficiency apartment above her place. The kind woman promised to hold it for her, if Ella could look at it that afternoon. Ella quickly agreed.

A knock at the door interrupted Ella's continued perusal of the classifieds. She folded the paper and got to her feet. She felt weird about answering Carlota's door, but she supposed it was only polite to take a message.

An attractive female stood at the door. "Hi. Is Tony home?"

Ella didn't recognize the young woman. "No. He isn't."

"How about Carlota or Johnny?"

Who was this woman? She appeared to be no older than Tony. In fact, she might be a bit younger.

Ella eyed the woman closely, taking in her tailored slacks and colorful summer top. Her made-up face and bobbed dark hair only enhanced her natural beauty.

"They aren't home either." Who was this woman? She'd never seen her around Whistle Stop. "Can I give them a message?"

"That's too bad. I was hoping to catch Tony. I need to talk to him. It's personal. He isn't out at the barn is he?"

"No, he's not. And your name would be?"

"Too bad I missed him," the woman said, not acknowledging Ella's question.

Obviously, the woman wasn't a local or she would know that every trained firefighter was on Roca Mountain, protecting the community.

"I need to go. I have an appointment." She hoped the woman would get the hint and leave.

"Are you staying here?"

Ella moved so her body filled the gap between the door and wall. She refused to invite this pushy woman inside. Then an awful thought occurred to her. Could this woman be Jessie? Tony hadn't described her, but it'd certainly explain how she knew the whole family. Ella's gaze narrowed. Had she finally figured out she'd made a mistake and come here to make things right with Tony?

The thought made Ella sick to her stomach. She swallowed hard. That couldn't happen. This thing between her and Tony wasn't over. He said they'd talk later. So if this woman had any ideas of getting her claws into him, she'd have to get past her first.

"Yes. Tony invited me to stay here."

The woman's eyes lit up. "Really? Are you his girlfriend?"

Refusing to give the woman a direct answer, she said, "You might say that. We've grown close during our practice for the upcoming dance contest."

"Oh, you must be Ella."

She knew her name? "I'm sorry. Do we know each other?"

"I'm Mary Sorkin, the court liaison working on Johnny's adoption, and you have presented me with an interesting wrinkle. I think you and I have a lot to discuss."

This was the court investigator? For some reason, Ella had imagined a more mature woman with graying hair and glasses, not a beautiful young woman. This would teach her for assuming things.

Ella's heart sank as she caught sight of the woman's expectant look. What had she just done?

Chapter Twenty-Four

Everything was out of sync.

It'd been a few days since her talk with Ms. Sorkin. The woman had gone over a long list of questions with Ella, but the Q&A had gone only one way. Ella's questions had been deflected or outright ignored. By the end of the meeting, Ella hadn't known where things stood. And when Tony finally got home, she had the distinct impression he wouldn't be happy about the development, not happy at all.

With a sigh, Ella stepped out of her newly rented apartment over Mrs. Sanchez's home. Who'd have thought the town busybody would become her landlord? But Ella had come to have a soft spot in her heart for the woman who had taken time out of her busy life to help stitch her an elegant dress for the dance contest.

With the fire on Roca Mountain still raging, the school was serving as a temporary shelter. Classes had been canceled for the week. Ella used the free time to visit Tracey in the hospital. She'd delivered her baby a little early due to complications exacerbated by the stress of losing her home to the wildfire. The baby, though a little on the small side, was a healthy boy named Zackery.

Now, as evening settled over the town, Ella couldn't stand to be cooped up in the tiny apartment. She needed to be doing something, anything. With Patch fed and settled in his brand new crate, she started down the steps.

She had some really big decisions to make—decisions that she'd been putting off for one excuse or another.

The stark truth was, with her cabin nothing more than a pile of ash and still no word on the permanent teaching position at the school, she didn't really have anything tying her to Whistle Stop—especially after Tony had rejected her love. Her heart ached as she recalled how he'd dismissed her feelings before he turned and walked away. She gave herself a mental jerk, chasing away the disturbing thoughts.

Having no appetite, she hoped a walk around town would settle her mind. She couldn't avoid a decision about her future indefinitely, but for one evening she wanted to think of anything but her troubles. They'd been all she'd thought of recently.

She stepped onto the sidewalk and noticed lots of people. They were everywhere. She paused, taking in the scene. They were all walking in the same direction. What in the world?

"There you are."

The familiar voice came from behind her. She turned to find Mrs. Sanchez stepping onto her porch. "Where's everyone going?"

Ella moved to the front of Mrs. Sanchez's house. The covered porch had a swing where the woman spent many evenings sipping sweet tea. Ella knew this because she'd joined her a time or two.

For Ella, taking up residence in Whistle Stop sure wasn't like living on the mountain, but Mrs. Sanchez made an allowance for Patch, and there were benefits to living in the heart of town. Everything was within walking distance, even the school. There was no chance of growing lonely. All you had to do was step outside to find a friendly face. And there was no need for an alarm clock, as the train whistle blew repeatedly at six a.m. No one could sleep through that blaring sound.

Mrs. Sanchez joined Ella on the sidewalk. The older woman hooked her arm through hers. "Didn't you hear? There's an emergency town meeting."

"A town meeting? About what?"

Mrs. Sanchez arched a brow. "Where have you been, girl? There's a wildfire. We need to do everything we can to help the victims who lost their homes on Roca Mountain—people like you." She paused and lifted her gaze to the sky that held the haze of smoke. "I just hope it doesn't head in our direction."

The thought of facing the fire again sent goose bumps cascading down her arms. Mrs. Sanchez gave a tug on Ella's hand, not giving her much time to consider such a devastating event. "Come on, girl. We don't want to be late."

"I...I don't know. I'm not really a resident of Whistle Stop—"

"Sure you are." Mrs. Sanchez stopped walking and faced her. "You do want to help, don't you?"

"Of course. I'll do whatever I can." The residents of Whistle Stop had welcomed her with open arms.

Whether she stayed or left, she wanted to do whatever she could to help.

Mrs. Sanchez smiled. "Good. I knew we could count on you. Now let's get moving before all of the seats are taken."

They joined the crowd of people hustling across the small town. Mrs. Sanchez appeared to know them all on a first-name basis. She introduced Ella to many of them, but there were so many faces—so many names—that Ella couldn't keep all of them straight. She smiled and nodded, letting Mrs. Sanchez do the bulk of the talking.

In no time, they arrived at the oblong community center with a bright red tile roof and cream-colored adobe walls. So many people had turned out for the meeting that there was a line up the walk as people waited to get inside. This was Ella's first town meeting, so she wasn't sure what to expect.

They'd just stepped inside when Mrs. Sanchez clasped her hands together. "Look! There are still a few seats up front."

Wanting to fade into the crowd, Ella said, "Go ahead. I'll just hang out back here."

"Nonsense." Mrs. Sanchez grabbed her hand, and Ella, not wanting to be rude and cause a scene, followed the woman.

Ella glanced around the crowded room, looking for familiar faces. Alexis caught sight of her and waved, but she was already seated in the middle of a row, so there was no chance for them to speak. Ella kept moving forward, and then she spotted Melissa standing with the mayor, deep in conversation.

No sooner had Ella and Mrs. Sanchez asked people to move down so there could be two seats together than there was the bang of a gavel calling the meeting to order. Silence settled over the spacious room. Mayor Ortiz, dressed in a dark suit and a gray dress shirt that was unbuttoned at the collar, stood at the podium. His dark hair was speckled with threads of silver. His clean-shaven face wore a serious expression as his eyes scanned the crowded room.

"Thank you all for coming. I know that everyone is busy and has their hands full, especially with the schools closed until this emergency is under control. At this point, we still need the school for temporary shelter for evacuees. We are working diligently to find them more permanent housing."

"Any word if the fire has been contained?" a man called out from the back of the room.

"I was updated about an hour ago. The good news is, other than the smoke and haze, Whistle Stop is safe." A round of chatter filled the room. Mayor Ortiz banged his gavel again. "The bad news is, without some help from Mother Nature, the fire continues to ravage the mountainside. Every available firefighter is doing their best under very tough circumstances."

"My boy is a firefighter on that mountain," hollered out a woman. "Is there any word when they're coming home?"

Ella waited anxiously for the answer. She wanted to know the same thing about Tony. She was worried about him. When she'd spoken to Carlota that morning, there hadn't been any word from him. Ella prayed that he was safe.

The mayor shook his head. "I'm sorry. There's no way of knowing when the fire will be contained. They're waiting for the wind to die down."

The questions kept up, one after another. The mayor didn't seem to know any more than Mrs. Sanchez, whom Ella had kindly dubbed Whistle Stop's queen of gossip. The woman was like a sponge. She soaked up information, and it didn't take much to squeeze it out of her.

"You don't seem to know much," a man grouched. "Why'd you call us here?"

"Because we need to pull together and help those of us who have been displaced by the fire. There are a number of families that live on Roca Mountain. Most won't have a home to return to."

The crowd erupted in a murmur of voices. Ella squeezed her hands together and sucked down the rush of emotions at the thought of her cabin being nothing more than a pile of smoldering ash. But thanks to Tony, she hadn't lost everything. Her most cherished positions had been saved—the picture of her family and her brother's teddy bear. When she'd found them at the bottom of the basket, tears had welled up in her eyes. When she saw him again, she owed him a big thank you.

The mayor banged his gavel to silence the uproar of chatter. "Ladies and gentlemen, I know we all have opinions about how to help these unfortunate people, but we can't all speak at once. Now raise your hands, and I'll call on you one at a time."

And so the process began. Resident after resident threw out their ideas of how to help.

"A rummage sale."

"A bake sale."

"A bachelor auction."

Mrs. Sanchez shifted in her seat as she held up her hand each time and yet the mayor passed over her.

Ella had a pretty good idea that the mayor was worried Mrs. Sanchez would commandeer the meeting, but Ella had been around the woman long enough to realize that Mrs. Sanchez had a knack for coming up with some very helpful ideas. And she for one wanted to hear what the woman had to say. So Ella put up her hand.

A few minutes later, the mayor hesitantly called on Ella. "Yes, young lady. What's your idea?"

Ella, not used to being in the spotlight, didn't get to her feet. Instead, she remained seated and raised her voice. "I suggest we listen to Mrs. Sanchez."

The older woman glanced her way, smiled, and squeezed her hand. Not waiting for the mayor to respond, Mrs. Sanchez got to her feet. Without saying a word to the mayor, she turned to the people. "You all have fabulous ideas. And if we had more time, we could implement a number of them. But let's face it, these people need help now, not a month or two down the road—"

"What are you suggesting?" The mayor had a pained look on his face, as though he were preparing for an unpopular answer.

Mrs. Sanchez glanced his way. "I'm getting to it."

The mayor made a point of checking his watch. Ella couldn't blame him. Mrs. Sanchez was well known for being long-winded. But something told Ella that it'd be worth the wait—at least, she hoped so. People like Tracey and her husband, not to mention that precious little baby, needed all of the help they could get. The sooner, the better.

Mrs. Sanchez turned back toward the people. "I want to petition the community to take the money we raise from the dance contest and—"

Voices loud and soft rumbled through the hall. Mrs. Sanchez's words got lost in the cacophony opinions. Ella liked the idea. Her thoughts turned back to her friend.

Tracey had a new baby and no home to take him to. She'd lost everything, from the baby booties that Ella had splurged on to the heirloom cradle that her husband had lovingly restored. But even with insurance money, they would still need some assistance to get situated in a new home.

Mrs. Sanchez sat down with a thump and shook her head. "Unbelievable."

Ella glanced over at her friend. She looked a bit on the pale side. Mrs. Sanchez had been on the go helping families since the fire started. She'd probably worn herself out.

Ella couldn't just sit by and let this meeting run amok. Mrs. Sanchez may not be up for a fight, but Ella was. Images of Tracey and her newborn baby flashed in her mind. She had to do what she could to help them.

The mayor banged his gavel repeatedly until silence fell over the room. Ella immediately jumped to her feet. She caught the mayor's surprised look, but she ignored it as she turned to the citizens of Whistle Stop.

"My name is Ella Morgan. I'm new to your town, but I would like to say that I have good friends who've lost everything they own. It's all gone—everything they bought for their newborn. All of it has been decimated by the wildfire. Can you imagine having a brand new baby and having no place to take him when you leave the hospital? They aren't the only ones who have been deeply hurt by the blaze. I know that many of you were counting on the fundraiser to fix up the town, but isn't it more important to help your neighbors, your relatives, your friends?"

Complete silence fell over the crowd. Some people nodded in agreement. Others lowered their heads. And some pressed their lips together, holding their tongues.

Satisfied that she'd made her point, Ella sat back down.

The mayor appeared a bit flustered as he moved the gavel aimlessly through the air. Then, as though realizing that it was not necessary to bang it, he set it aside. He cleared his throat. "Thank you, Ms. Morgan." His gaze met hers, and he smiled. Then he turned to the crowd. "Could I have a vote on reallocating the funds from the dance contest to a fund for the fire victims?"

Ella raised her hand. Mrs. Sanchez raised hers. The mayor raised his. Then Ella turned to a sea of raised arms.

This time, she was the one to lean over and squeeze Mrs. Sanchez's arm. "You did it."

"No, dear. We did it."

But there was still something nagging at Ella. Everybody else was donating their time and cash. She not only needed to talk the talk but also walk the walk. She needed to donate her share.

With the meeting wrapped up, she slowly made her way to the door. Somehow, she'd lost sight of Mrs. Sanchez in the crowd. All the while, Ella pondered the best way to help Whistle Stop. It was in that moment that she realized this place was now her home in every way that counted. And she wouldn't let what happened with Tony run her off. They were both adults. They'd learn to deal with each other.

This still left her with the problem of what she could donate to help the town. She didn't have much. And then a thought came to her. She had one valuable possession that hadn't been destroyed in the fire.

Her grandmother's engagement ring.

It was still at the jeweler. She had yet to pick it up, because she hadn't known whether to sell it or keep it. But with this revelation came her original dilemma—could she break her word to her grandmother and sell the ring? She wrestled with the decision, torn between her grandmother's wish and her own longing to make a home for herself.

Tony's words came back to her: *It's time you let go of the past, of the horrible things your grandmother said, and move on. You can't change the past. But you can change how you see yourself and your future*.

He was right. First thing in the morning, she'd head to the Golden Nugget Jeweler. A portion of the money would go to the victims' fund. She hadn't decided what exactly to do with the rest, but it'd have something to do with her settling in Whistle Stop—for good.

Now if only her problems with Tony could be rectified this easily. But the truth was, he didn't feel the same way as she did. He couldn't have made that any clearer when they were up on the mountain. She had to accept that and move on.

If only her heart would listen to her mind...

Chapter Twenty-Five

HOMEWARD BOUND...AT LAST.

Friday morning, Tony stared out the windshield of his pickup as he pulled up to his mother's house. The sun shone brightly in the clear blue sky. The dousing rains over the last couple of days had aided in controlling the fire. The change in the weather was exactly what they'd needed so they could bring in some tankers to douse recurring hot spots.

All morning, the only thing he'd been able to think about was getting home. He wasn't in the mood to see or talk with anyone but his family—and Ella. He regretted how he'd turned her away at the command center. She had no idea how hard it'd been for him not to pull her into his arms and return her words of love.

Yet, he couldn't forget the night he'd seen her trying on her sexy dress for the contest and how she'd admitted that moving to Whistle Stop had been a mistake. Now with her home reduced to mere cinders and no permanent job, he didn't want to tie her down to this quiet little town. Eventually, she'd come to resent him for holding her back. And that was something he couldn't bear.

He stepped out of the pickup and rushed to the house. "Hey, Mom," Tony said, stepping inside the kitchen door. "I'm back and all in one piece."

"Thank goodness." She rushed over, ignoring his filthy state, and gave him a tight hug.

"Sorry about the dirt and grime. I haven't seen a shower in quite a while."

"I'm just glad you're home." She returned to the counter, where started filling the coffeemaker with fresh coffee. "We need to talk, but it can wait until you get cleaned up."

His mother wasn't the person he needed to talk to—it was Ella who filled his mind. But the problem was, he still didn't know what to say to her, other than he was sorry for being so abrupt. He hadn't been expecting her to blurt out that she loved him. He'd handled the whole situation shabbily. But he'd known she was worked up after the fire. He couldn't—wouldn't—take advantage of her emotional state. By now reality must have set it.

Wanting to ask where Ella was staying, he rolled the words around in his mind. It didn't matter how he phrased the question, his mother would read more into his curiosity than he wanted. Instead, he kept his thoughts to himself.

"I'll be back. Would you mind throwing together some food? It doesn't matter what. I'm so hungry."

Tony, deciding a cool shower was a definite necessity, headed down the hall to the bathroom. After a brief shower, he toweled off and yawned. Maybe he'd lie down for a couple of minutes until the food was ready. After he ate, he'd seek out Ella. Then a worrisome thought struck him—was she even still in Whistle Stop? Had he chased her away for good?

He dressed and stretched out on his bed. The scent of Ella wrapped around him. It was so real that he opened his eyes and glanced around the room, certain she must be there, but he was all alone—alone with his thoughts.

She wouldn't have left already, would she?

His eyes grew heavy and drifted shut as Ella's image danced in his mind...

An entire day slipped by before Tony meandered back to the kitchen. He found his mother standing at the stove. "Sorry about falling asleep and missing all of yesterday. I didn't get much sleep while I was on the mountain."

"I understand. You had to be exhausted. I made sure Johnny left you alone, but he's anxious to see you. He stayed overnight at Bobby's. Melissa should be dropping him off any time now." She moved to the fridge and grabbed a carton of eggs. "I should tell you that I gave Ella permission to stay in your room while you were away."

The memory of her scent surrounding him in bed came rushing back. So it hadn't been his imagination. She'd been sleeping in his bed. The thought warmed a spot in his chest.

His mother added a couple of eggs to the sizzling-hot skillet and then popped some bread into the toaster. "I hope you don't mind."

"No. Not at all." He fidgeted with a cow-shaped saltshaker. "But where did she stay last night?"

"She was able to rent Mrs. Sanchez's apartment." His mother returned the carton of eggs to the fridge. "I've got a couple of things for her if you're planning to head over to see her this morning."

"I'm not." His hasty reply had his mother arching a brow at him. "I mean, I wasn't planning to go into town. I need to check on the ranch and then the fire station." After some much-needed sleep, he was having second thoughts about seeing Ella. What would he say? Besides, she would most likely slam the door in his face after the way he'd acted on the mountain.

Carlota set down the spatula and turned. "Ella hinted that there was something wrong between you two. She doesn't think you still want to be her dance partner. I hope that isn't the case. The competition is this evening. You should know we had a town meeting. The money raised is now going to the victims of the fire."

"That's sounds like a really good idea. About the fund, that is. I know those people will need help getting relocated."

"Does that mean you'll still participate in the dance?"

Tony shrugged. "To tell you the truth, I hadn't given the dance too much thought."

Carlota gave him another puzzled stare. "You aren't trying to avoid Ella, are you?"

He didn't want to get into this. "Why does it matter? I don't have time for a relationship."

Carlota removed the skillet from the burner, slid the eggs onto a waiting plate, added toast, and placed it all in front of him. She pulled out the kitchen chair directly across from him. "I should have had this conversation with you a long time ago, but the time never seemed right with you always rushing here and there."

He lifted a piece of toast and was about to take a bite when her words sank into his exhausted brain. She was about to unearth the past. The memories he'd tried so hard to bury were about to see the light of day. He dropped the toast on the plate and clenched his hands. "We don't need to ever have this conversation."

"Yes, we do." Her voice was rigid. "You need to move on with your life. The deaths of your brother and his wife were not your fault." When he didn't say anything, she continued, "This is important. You've been carrying around this unfounded guilt for far too long. Do you hear me?"

He nodded.

"No. I want you to say the words, and then maybe they'll start to sink in."

"In my mind, I know it wasn't my fault. But then I'm haunted by the thought of what if—"

"No. Don't go there. You can't. I did the same thing at first. If only I'd done this or that, they wouldn't have been on the road at that particular moment. But they were, and we aren't to blame. You've got to believe that."

He'd never known his mother had similar thoughts. Somehow, he no longer felt alone. "I know. I do."

Why did this conversation sound so eerily similar to the one he'd had with Ella? If he expected her to take his advice and let go of the past—of the guilt—he should try to do the same thing. Funny thing was, it was so much easier to dole out the advice than to take it.

Carlota sent him a sidelong glance. "There's something else you should know. I'm planning to move on with my life. You and I have been stuck in the past for too long now." She reached into her pocket and pulled out a diamond ring. Her ring. "Here. I want you to take this."

His mother's engagement ring dropped into his palm. Stunned, he stared at her. "Why? Why would you give me this?"

"You need to settle down with a family of your own."

"I can't take this." He tried to give the ring back to her, but she shook her head and scooted back in her seat. "Life is too short to keep looking back."

"But—"

"A life without love isn't much of a life at all. I have someone new in my life—Mr. Wilson."

"You mean the guy who owns the hardware store?"

She nodded. "You'll meet him tonight at the dance competition. He's my escort."

"Are you serious?" Tony knew how that sounded, but this was all news to him and a bit of a shock, to say the least.

"Of course I'm serious. I'm getting on with life. Now it's time you did the same. It's time you quit closing yourself off from life and love."

Stunned, Tony gazed at the ring as the light danced upon the diamond. It'd be perfect on Ella's finger.

Was it possible he and Ella could have a future? He shook his head. He was daydreaming. By now she would have had time to calm down and realize she'd blurted out her love for him during a moment of excitement—that she hadn't meant any of what she'd said.

Or had she?

Nah. No man was that lucky.

"Now, I have a thousand errands to run before the dance contest this evening. I have your outfit pressed. It's hanging on the closet door."

"I won't be needing it." There was no way Ella would dance with him now.

His mother frowned. "Everyone is expecting you."

The back door squeaked open, and Johnny bounded into the room. "Uncle Tony!" The boy launched himself into Tony's outstretched arms. After a tight hug, Johnny pulled back. "Stay here. I have something to show you."

Johnny tore off down the hall, leaving Tony to wonder what had his nephew so excited. "Do you know what this surprise is?"

His mother shook her head, but a knowing smile tugged at her lips.

Johnny ran back into the room holding a small manila envelope. "I got my report card. I only got one A, in art, but I didn't get any bad grades."

Tony looked over the encouraging note from Johnny's teacher and the much-improved grades. He smiled broadly. Thanks to Ella's influence, Johnny's grades were headed in a positive direction. And remembering how Johnny's parents had rewarded him, Tony reached for his wallet. "Looks like this deserves a reward."

"Gee, thanks. I'm going to put this in my bank. I'm saving up for a rocket." Johnny's whole face lit up as he accepted the money and ran from the room.

Carlota waited until Johnny's bedroom door slammed shut before speaking. "Are you sure giving him money for good grades is a good idea?"

"No. I'm not. But I'm still figuring this parenting stuff out. It's what Johnny's mother did, so it's what he's used to. I don't know what I'll do in the future. I have a lot to figure out."

"Okay, well, you need to get moving. Johnny will expect you to be there to watch him perform tonight before the contest."

"I won't miss it."

"And Ella will be expecting you to dance tonight."

He sighed. "After everything, I doubt she'll still want to dance with me."

"Guess you'll have to go and find out. And make sure you wear that outfit. I went to a lot of trouble making the vest and doing alterations." Without giving him a chance to argue, she grabbed her purse and went in search of Johnny to take him with her.

Tony went through the motions of working the ranch, but his heart wasn't in it. His thoughts centered on Ella. Had she calmed down and realized that she didn't love him?

The not knowing was driving him nuts. He needed to talk to her. If her feelings for him had changed, he'd learn, in time, to live with the gaping hole in his heart. But if she stood by her words, he wanted a chance to beg her forgiveness and to tell her that he loved her, too.

Chapter Twenty-Six

Ella paced back and forth. She tugged at the shirttails of the sheer white blouse she wore over the dress and tied just beneath her chest. Her gaze kept returning to the doors of the community center every time they opened. Would Tony skip out on her tonight?

She glanced up as Carlota came through the doorway on the arm of a distinguished older man. Carlota was positively glowing. Ella couldn't help but wonder if Tony was pleased with his mother's new romance. Then again, Ella wondered if he even knew, as Carlota had been quite tightlipped about it until tonight.

As the gentleman handed over their tickets, Carlota spotted her and made her way over. "You're gorgeous. Although you'd be so much prettier if you'd quit hiding behind that blouse. I realize you're self-conscious about your scars, but I think you should know they aren't nearly as noticeable as you think they are."

Ella fingered the edge of the sleeves. She'd toyed with the idea of going bare-armed, but at the last minute she'd grabbed something to cover herself. "I don't know."

"Trust me, dear. You can't hide who you are forever. If people care about someone, they need to accept and love them, flaws and all. And I happen to think you are beautiful inside and out."

Ella's gaze met Carlota's. Her friend was right. The time had come for her to make peace with her body. She pulled at the knot in the blouse.

Carlota held out her hand. "I can take it over to the table for you."

"I'll go with you."

"No. You wait here. Your dance partner should be here shortly. I'm afraid I tied up the bathroom getting ready, so he's running behind." Carlota's hand remained outstretched, waiting for her to hand over the blouse.

Taking a deep breath, Ella slid off the top and relinquished it.

Carlota positively beamed when her date joined them. "Ella, I'd like you to meet George Wilson. He owns Wilson's Hardware here in town." She lowered her voice as though sharing a secret. "He…he's my boyfriend."

"It's so nice to meet you, Ella." The silver-haired fox held out his hand and gave her an easy smile. His handshake was firm but gentle. "Carlota says you and Tony are the couple to keep an eye on tonight."

Ella worried her bottom lip and glanced toward the door. "I'm not so sure Tony's going to make it."

"He will, dear. Have faith." Carlota gave her a brief hug before slipping her hand through her date's arm. "We'll be rooting for the two of you."

Ella just hoped there was something for them to root for. Where was Tony? Surely he wouldn't skip out on the contest just because he didn't feel the same way she did. Would he?

He was late.

Tony rushed into the dimly lit community center. He'd had second and third thoughts about showing up—about what he should say to Ella. In the end, he decided that he had everything to gain if he took a chance on being honest with her.

He glanced around at the crowd, not finding Ella among the familiar faces. This section of the room was lined with dining tables. At the far end stood the stage, which currently had bleachers full of youngsters dressed in red, white, and blue.

"Everyone, take your seats." Mayor Ortiz stood in front of the kids. "It's time for some of Whistle Stop's youngest talents to open tonight's festivities with a couple of songs. While the children are singing, volunteers will be making the rounds with tickets for the 50/50 raffle. Remember, tonight's event will now be benefiting the victims of the wildfire. So please dig deep and give with a generous heart."

Tony scanned the group as they belted out *America the Beautiful*. He spotted Johnny in the back row. Tony eased his way closer to the stage, wanting Johnny to know he was there for him. He waved, doubting Johnny could make him out in the dark, but the boy's face lit up, and he waved back.

When the children concluded their singing, Tony made a beeline for his mother, who was serving punch. "Mom, I need to talk to you."

Carlota ladled more red fruity drink into a clear glass and handed it off to a young boy. "Is something wrong?"

With his patience unfurling, Tony got straight to the point. "I can't find Ella. Have you seen her?"

"Of course. She's right over there." His mother pointed to a group of tables in the far corner. "She's been waiting for you. She already has you both signed in for the competition."

Through the throng of people, he spotted Ella. She looked gorgeous in the red and white dress that his mother and Mrs. Sanchez had made for her. And he noticed that her arms were bare. A smile tugged at his lips. Ella was no longer letting her past dictate her life.

He strode over to her. "You look absolutely gorgeous."

Ella crossed her arms as though self-conscious about her scars. "I'd feel more comfortable with a shirt or something on."

"Trust me when I say that no one's going to be looking at your arms. There's so much more to you to appreciate. Especially that amazing smile of yours."

Color filled her cheeks. "You really think so?"

"I do." He held out his hand. "Are we still friends?"

Her hesitant gaze moved to his outstretched hand. Seconds passed. Then she unfolded her arms and placed her hand in his. "Yes. We're still friends."

He gave her hand a squeeze before reluctantly letting her go. "I need to go congratulate Johnny on the show. Don't disappear." He knew he'd only end up tracking her down, unable to resist following wherever she led. "We have a few things to discuss."

She'd wait for him as long as it took.

Ella's insides quivered. What did he want to talk about? Had he changed his mind about them? Or had he talked to the court investigator and found out how she'd messed up everything?

She turned toward the dance floor as Alexis and Cord performed their version of the Texas two-step. Their movements were fluid and flawless. It was as though they could read each other's thoughts. They were definitely tough competition.

Ella glanced around the room, searching for Tony. Her gaze stumbled across a trophy consisting of a piece of white marble with a gold replica of a hat resting on a pair of cowboy boots. It sat front and center on the judges' table. Not so long ago, winning that trophy and the prize money had meant the world to her, but now her focus was on Johnny and Tony.

First, she had to confess to Tony what had gone down between her and Ms. Sorkin. Her stomach sloshed. He wasn't going to like what she had to say. Not at all.

"Now it's time to talk." Tony moved to stand in front of her. "I owe you a big apology for what I said at base camp. I shouldn't have been so rude."

"I understand. Wrong time, wrong place. Right now I have to tell you something important." She considered blurting out what she'd done, but yelling above the music from the competition wasn't the right way. "Can we go outside, away from the noise?"

"First"—he took her hand in his—"I need you to forgive me, truly forgive me."

Their gazes met, and her heart skipped a beat. "Your apology is accepted."

"I was so worried that you might have left town after I blew it so badly when we last spoke."

"I rented a place in town."

He took a step back and smiled at her. "So you aren't planning to leave?"

"Why would I?"

"Never mind," he said. "But there is something I have to know. Did you mean what you said up on the mountain? Do you love me?"

She couldn't answer his question, not yet. First, she had to get this burdensome confession out in the open.

Before she uttered a single syllable, a voice on the loudspeaker interrupted. "Could the next couple step onto the dance floor?"

"That's us," she said, holding out his numbered tag.

Disappointment dimmed his eyes. "I guess you better put that sticker on my back."

She moved to stand behind him. Her fingers refused to cooperate. She couldn't decide if it was nervousness over the competition or their impending conversation that had her hands trembling.

"Let me." Melissa appeared at her side and moved in to make quick work of pinning the tag to Tony's back.

"Thank you." Ella smiled at her friend, even though her insides quivered like gelatin.

"Relax, girl. Have fun out there." Melissa sent her an encouraging smile.

Ella nodded. She turned to Tony and held her hand out to him. "May I have this dance?"

He looked her directly in the eyes, making her pulse race. "I'd love to dance with you."

"Let's go show these people what we've learned."

Once they assumed their proper positions, Tony's hand slid down her bare arm to entwine his fingers with hers. She froze, wondering if he had changed his mind about her revealing her scars.

"Relax. You're the most beautiful woman in the room," he murmured, bolstering her courage. With his free hand, he grabbed her waist and pulled her to him. "In the whole world."

Overcome with emotion, she missed the first two beats of the music, but she quickly recovered and forced herself to concentrate as a wonderful euphoria kicked in.

They moved across the floor in perfect time. His gaze held hers with an intensity she'd never experienced before. When he drew her to him, he held her closer than had at any of their lessons. Her body hummed with excitement as they brushed against each other. Their bodies flowed together in harmony.

When the music faded away, they remained center stage while the judges critiqued their performance and presented the scores. Two nines and one ten. She stifled a squeal of excitement as she realized the results had them in the hunt for the trophy. Maybe she had more of a competitive streak than she'd thought.

She led him off the floor amidst an explosion of clapping. "Let's step outside where it's quieter."

Once the door clicked shut behind them and they'd moved off to the side, Tony spoke first. "Did you—I mean, do you still feel the same way about me?"

"Yes, I do," she said without any hesitation. "But there's something you need to know."

"Whatever it is, we'll deal with it. Together."

She sure hoped he felt the same way after she finished her confession.

"It happened while I was staying at your mother's. This woman showed up at the door looking for you." Ella explained how she'd mistaken the woman for Jessie.

His smile faded. "Jessie was there?"

"Worse."

His dark brows arched. "How so?"

"The woman was Mary Sorkin."

The color leached from his face. "What did she say?"

Ella's gaze dropped to the ground. "Thinking she was Jessie, I implied you and I were involved."

"How did she take this news?"

"She said I created a wrinkle in the adoption."

Tony combed his fingers through his hair. "Having you in Johnny's life will never be a bad thing, and the court will see that. We'll deal with this together. After all, you're good for Johnny. You're good for me."

"I am?"

A smile lifted his lips. "Yes, you are. Don't ever doubt it."

Ella sucked in a deep breath, trying to stem her rising emotions. "Once I knew who she was, I answered all of her questions."

She'd even mentioned her past. Ms. Sorkin had made a few notations but hadn't made a big deal about the fire. Was Tony right? Had she assumed the worst when everyone else was willing to accept it was an accident, no matter how it started?

"Did she seem satisfied with your answers? Did she say how this would impact the adoption?"

"I couldn't tell. She was full of questions and wrote a ton of notes. She didn't disclose anything. I'm truly sorry. I…I never meant to do anything to hurt you or Johnny."

Ella started to turn away, but his fingers wrapped around her hand, stopping her.

"Don't go." His gaze met and held hers.

"But I messed everything up."

"No, you just moved the process along faster than I anticipated."

"What process?"

He drew her into his arms. "The one where I tell the court that I love you."

Her heart thumped hard and fast. "Are you sure about this?"

His unwavering gaze held the certainty she needed. "Definitely, absolutely, one hundred percent positive."

"I love you, too." Her soft words winged through the air, bringing a smile to his face.

He leaned down and kissed her. His touch was gentle. Her mouth opened, and the tip of her tongue traced the outline of his lips and slipped inside to taste the subtle hint of mint. It was as though they were exploring each other for the first time.

A moan escaped her as she let down all of her defenses and let his love flow into her heart, filling in the cracks. At last she was where she truly belonged—in his arms. Wherever life led them, her home would be comprised of deep and abiding love.

Her hands slid up his muscled arms and wrapped around his neck. She inhaled a fresh soapy scent combined with his own rugged male scent. It was utterly intoxicating. Her fingers toyed with the short strands of hair along his neckline.

His tongue moved in and out of her mouth as though their tongues did an intimate dance of their own. Everywhere he touched her, an electrical charge zapped through her needy body. If this was a dream, she never ever wanted to wake up. This was everything that she'd ever hoped for and yet so much more. Her heart swelled with love for Tony.

A tap on her back caused a groan of disappointment to rise in her throat. She pulled back from Tony. She swung around to find Johnny standing there. She swallowed down her frustration as she ran a shaky hand over her tender lips.

"You and Uncle Tony dance good together." The boy grinned at them. "You should have had all tens."

"Thank you, Johnny," she said, trying to hide her embarrassment.

Carlota came up behind her grandson. "I agree."

Just then the president of the school board walked past them. He quickly retraced his steps. "Ella, I'm so glad I ran into you. I've been meaning to call you, but with school being canceled all week because of the fire, I'm behind with everything. Anyway, I wanted to give you the good news. You've got the job."

Ella grinned. She had to be dreaming. At last, the pieces of her life were falling into place. "Thank you so much."

"I'll get back to you next week so we can iron out the details. I better go before my wife hunts me down. Good luck tonight."

"Thanks again," she called after him.

"Congratulations," Tony said, bending over to give her a big hug. "Things are going our way."

"Almost," she whispered in his ear. "There's still the adoption."

"I told you we'd deal with it together. I promise everything will work out."

"Just think, when they get married," Johnny interrupted, "Ella will be my aunt and Patch will be my puppy again."

They pulled apart in time to see his huge grin.

"Slow down," Carlota said. "We don't want to rush them. Although I'd love a chance to help plan a wedding." She sent them a wistful look. "Come on, Johnny. Let's check out the competition."

Ella hoped the thought of wedding bells and making everything official didn't have Tony rethinking his proclamation of love. After all, she didn't expect him to drop down on one knee, although the notion made her heart swoon. It was enough that he loved her.

"We should head inside," she suggested.

On the way to the table, Tony excused himself. Thinking he'd headed to the men's room, Ella was surprised when she spotted him conversing with the judges. Her chest tightened. What was he up to?

He soon returned to her side, just in time for their next performance. Tony held out his arm to escort her. Out on the dance floor, she turned to him to assume their positions, but he stepped away. Tony pulled a microphone out of his back pocket. This wasn't part of their performance.

Chapter Twenty-Seven

ALL EYES WERE ON them.

Heat rushed to Ella's cheeks as she stood there in the spotlight. She still hadn't figured out what Tony had in mind. A hush fell over the audience. The breath caught in Ella's throat as she waited for him to speak.

"I've never been a man of many words."

Tony knelt down on one knee, making her stomach twist in a nervous, excited knot. "Tony, get up," she whispered. "What are you doing? This isn't what we rehearsed."

He pulled a ring from his shirt pocket. It wasn't her grandmother's heirloom ring, but that was okay. The one thing she'd learned up on the mountain was not to cling tightly to material possessions because there were other more important things in life.

Ella's eyes misted over with tears of joy as Tony took her hand in his. "Ella, I haven't always been easy to put up with, but you've never given up on me. You've changed my life and taught me to trust again. I love you, and I'd be honored if you'd agree to be my wife. Will you marry me?"

"And me," Johnny piped in as he rushed to his uncle's side.

Realizing she was holding her breath, she exhaled the words, "Yes! Oh, yes. Yes. Yes."

"I love you." Tony stood up.

"I love—" His lips pressed to hers, smothering her words.

His tender kiss caused her heart to swell with love. Her arms slipped around his neck, pulling him closer. Their kiss deepened, cementing their lifetime commitment to each other.

The host cleared his throat, and they parted. "Everybody, please give them a round of applause." Once the place quieted down, the announcer continued, "Now, I know all of you spectators are dying to kick up your heels after the competition, so we'll get this contest moving."

"First, I need to do this." Tony held out the ring and slipped it on her finger. "Perfect. Just like you."

They both knew that wasn't quite true. But if he wanted to send compliments her way, she wasn't about to argue. Not a chance. He was pretty perfect himself.

Ella struggled to remember her proper starting position.

"I love you," Tony mouthed.

Her face was frozen in a permanent grin. Concentrating on her footwork became increasingly difficult. All she wanted to do was stare into Tony's eyes and ask him to repeat those three magical words. She'd never tire of hearing them.

When the dance finished, he escorted her to their seats.

"You've earned my vote," came a female voice from behind them.

They both turned to find Ms. Sorkin.

"I didn't know you were coming," Tony said.

"Your future wife invited me. After speaking with her at the house, I couldn't resist a chance to observe you two together."

"About that," he said. "I meant to tell you. It just happened so quickly."

Ms. Sorkin's face remained expressionless. "I've also talked to Johnny. He had a lot to tell me."

Ella held her breath, waiting and wondering what the woman made of all of this information. "I really care about Johnny. He's such a sweet and intelligent boy."

"There's also the matter of him rushing into a wildfire to save a puppy." Ms. Sorkin's brow arched as she eyed both of them, making Ella want to squirm in discomfort. "He assured me that he learned his lesson. I'm hoping you two as his parents will put tighter reins on him."

"We will." Tony's tone was solemn as his fingers tightened around Ella's hand. "I'll never let anything happen to him."

"Johnny did mention how both of you chased after him and worked together as a family to get to safety. I think that speaks a lot about the both of you. I just thought you'd want to know my report to the judge will recommend that you both will make good parents for Johnny."

A huge grin pulled at Ella's lips as the grip around her lungs loosened. If all went well, Johnny would soon be theirs in every way. They thanked the woman and shook her hand before she disappeared into the crowd.

Tony leaned over, and with his lips teasingly close to Ella's ear, he said, "I told you it'd work out. And I always keep my word."

When the smile slipped from his lips, she asked, "What's wrong?"

"I was thinking about where we'll live. Due to some unexpected expenses on the ranch, I don't have quite enough money to break ground on a new house until fall at the earliest."

"Don't worry," she said, thinking of the money from the sale of her grandmother's ring and the insurance money from the cabin. "I have an idea or two."

Nearly every person in the room came by their table to congratulate them. Carlota beamed with pride and gave Ella a welcoming hug.

While they prepared to announce the winners of the dance competition, Ella longed to go home and celebrate with Tony, alone. She leaned over to him and whispered a plea to leave.

He smiled and squeezed her hand. "We will. First, let's hear who the winners are. We don't want to come across as bad sports."

Ella applauded for the third-place couple, Melissa and Moe, but the light dancing off her engagement ring kept distracting Ella. She continued to smile as her gaze moved to her brand new fiancé, and she thought of the incredible husband he'd make. She was the luckiest woman in the universe. She could only hope to make him just as happy.

Tony took her hand. "Come on."

She grabbed her purse from the table and hurried behind him. Finally, they could go home and celebrate in private.

Realizing he'd led her onto the dance floor, she stopped. "What are we doing out here?"

He glanced over at her and chuckled. "Too busy daydreaming about our private celebration?"

"Sort of," she said sheepishly.

The host handed her an engraved plaque. "Ladies and gentlemen, please give a round of applause to our runners-up, Tony Granger and his future wife, Ella Morgan."

When Cord and Alexis accepted the first-place trophy, Ella vigorously applauded. She was thrilled for her new friends. Everyone was walking away a winner this evening.

Tony whispered, "Now we can go home and celebrate."

Ella looked up as he leaned down and planted a kiss on her eager lips. They might not have received the beautiful trophy, but she'd already gained the most important thing of all—Tony's love.

Return to Whistle Stop with **A Moment on the Lips** as baker Piper Noble runs the Poppin' Fresh Bakery and barista Joe Montoya moves in next door—right in the place Piper had been planning to expand her business. You can learn more here:

https://www.jenniferfaye.com/books/a-moment-on-the-lips/

Afterword

Thanks so much for reading Ella and Tony's story. I hope their journey made your heart smile. If you did enjoy the book, please consider...

- Help spreading the word about A Moment to Dance by writing a review.
- Subscribe to my newsletter in order to receive information about my next release as well as find out about giveaways and special sales.
- You can like my author page on Facebook or follow me on Twitter.

I hope you'll come back to Whistle Stop and read the continuing adventures of its residents. Coming next is Piper and Joe's story in A Moment on the Lips.

Thanks again for your support! It is HUGELY appreciated.

Happy reading,

Jennifer

Also By

Other titles available by Jennifer Faye include:

THE BELL FAMILY OF BLUESTAR ISLAND:

Love Blooms

Harvest Dance

A Lighthouse Café Christmas

Rising Star

Summer by the Beach
Brass Anchor Inn

SEABREEZE WEDDING CHAPEL:

The Bride's Dream Wedding

The Bride's Pink Shoes
The Bride's Christmas Dress

WHISTLE STOP ROMANCE SERIES:

A Moment to Love

A Moment to Dance

A Moment on the Lips

A Moment to Cherish

A Moment at Christmas

TANGLED CHARMS:

Sprinkled with Love

A Mistletoe Kiss

GREEK PARADISE ESCAPE:

Greek Heir to Claim Her Heart

It Started with a Royal Kiss

Second Chance with the Bridesmaid

WEDDING BELLS IN LAKE COMO:

Bound by a Ring & a Secret

Falling for Her Convenient Groom

ONCE UPON A FAIRYTALE:

Beauty & Her Boss

Miss White & the Seventh Heir

Fairytale Christmas with the Millionaire

THE BARTOLINI LEGACY:

The Prince and the Wedding Planner

The CEO, the Puppy & Me

The Italian's Unexpected Heir

GREEK ISLAND BRIDES:

Carrying the Greek Tycoon's Baby

Claiming the Drakos Heir

Wearing the Greek Millionaire's Ring

Click here to find all of Jennifer's titles and buy links.

About Author

Award-winning author, Jennifer Faye pens fun, heartwarming contemporary romances with rugged cowboys, sexy billionaires and enchanting royalty. With more than a million books sold, she is internationally published with books translated into more than a dozen languages. She is a two-time winner of the RT Book Reviews Reviewers' Choice Award, the CataRomance Reviewers' Choice Award, named a TOP PICK author, and been nominated for numerous other awards.

Now living her dream, she resides with her very patient husband and two spoiled cats. When she's not plotting out her next romance, you can find her curled up with a mug of tea and a book. You can learn more about Jennifer at www.JenniferFaye.com

Subscribe to Jennifer's newsletter for news about upcoming releases, bonus content and other special offers.

You can also join her on Twitter, Facebook, or Goodreads.

Made in United States
Troutdale, OR
03/16/2024

18518926R00176